THE EEL AND THE ANGEL

RODGER CARLYLE

Published in the United States by Verity Books,
an imprint of Comsult, LLC.

First published in 2021.

ISBN 978-1-7360074-2-6 (e-book)
ISBN 978-1-7360074-3-3 (paperback)
ISBN 978-1-7360074-4-0 (hardcover)

Editing: Inventing Reality Editing Service

Cover design and formatting: Damonza

www.rodgercarlyle.com

CHAPTER 1

ANDERSON AIR FORCE BASE, GUAM

JUAN PEDRO PARKED his patrol car on the tiny dirt track off from the main patrol road, leaving the engine running as he made his way toward the ocean at the end of the runway. Somewhere in his brain he thought that he had seen a flicker of a red light through the trees above the rocky bluff that protected the end of the runway from the occasional violent Pacific storm. He didn't bother to call in the siting, deciding to wait until he knew for sure what had attracted his attention.

Besides, there were no flight operations that moonlit April night and a need to stretch his legs in the moonlight might, just might, be what had triggered his response. He left the road, moving to the crude trail along the edge of the bluff, a place where the only sounds were from the surf below. Every night he seemed to find some excuse for a stroll along the ocean, usually about halfway through his 10 p.m. to six in the morning shift.

Juan had come to the tiny Pacific Island as an Air Force policeman more than twenty years earlier and fallen in love with the lazy island life. He'd finished his twenty-year enlistment struggling to figure out what came after the military life.

Returning to Guam, the one duty station where he was truly happy, he had used his former service to land a job with a civilian security-contracting firm and less than a year later Juan had married an island girl half his age and started a new family.

He strained his eyes, looking for the faint glimpse of red light that his brain told him was out there, seeing nothing. His relaxed stroll reflected the complete lack of security threat. The last time anything remotely dangerous had happened was back in August 2019 when some idiot, being chased by local police, had crashed the main gate of the base and disappeared into the jungle. The nutcase was discovered hiding the next day, and rather than just surrender, he attacked one of the guards and was shot dead by an Air Force cop.

Juan stopped at the edge of the bluff, staring off into space, as he often did on these clear nights, still in wonder at a sky that had never been part of his childhood in the bright lights and polluted skies of southern California. Below and to his right, a faint sound lowered his gaze. It sounded like someone clipping a wire with a pair of cutters.

There was something moving only ten feet away. As he reached for the tiny penlight on his belt, he felt a slight prick on his left thigh, followed by what must have been a lightning strike. The most excruciating pain he had ever felt dropped him onto his stomach, writhing in agony. He couldn't take a breath to scream. His eyes fluttered at light speed, as they and every other part of his body tried to come to grips with a wave of burning that seemed to start in the center of his body, radiating out so that even his fingernails seemed on fire. His arms and legs pounded again and again into the ground as his torso contorted. The pain intensified as waves of electric fire swept his body. He prayed for the pain to stop, but it just grew worse.

Through his tears, a person dressed in a black suit knelt beside him and leaned down whispering. Through his tortured ears he thought he heard, "I sorry, you were supposed to pass out." It was hard to tell, the words spoken were delivered with an accent that even in normal times he would have misunderstood. Perhaps his hearing was failing. Juan's shoulder was pulled down as whoever was next to him, knelt on his arm to stop its movement.

He never felt the needle as a full syringe of air was injected into a vein in his wrist. He never felt the edge of a sharp rock as it tore across the wrist, destroying any indication of an injection. A moment later another man grabbed his other arm and the two men together dragged Juan into the jungle holding him until his body stopped moving.

The men went back to the job they had come to do, finishing only minutes later. One of the men tugged Juan's boots from his feet and slipped them onto his own. He handed his soft rubber shoes to his partner as he hoisted Juan onto a shoulder, then followed his partner down a steep trail to the water below. Carefully lacing Juan's boots onto the dead guard's feet, he slid his body into the water. He and his buddy retrieved their air tanks and fins from the brush and slid into the turbulent water, pushing silent winged electric underwater scooters in front of them. They pulled Juan's body out to sea as they headed into the endless ocean.

A couple of hundred meters offshore, they released the body and dove, navigating to their ride home using a tiny display strapped to their arms.

Five hours later and thousands of miles away, a technician sitting in front of a computer console read the signal from the acoustic listening device now operating at the end of the runway at the American Air Force base on Guam. He called up another screen, copying the signal onto a second page where he compared it to a library of acoustic sounds gathered over years by dozens of operatives from around American Air Force facilities. He called to a tall thin junior officer.

"Sir," he offered, pointing at the display, "you can inform the general that an American KC-46 Pegasus tanker has just departed Guam. We are operational."

"That is good to hear," replied the officer. "It is one more move in our ability to track the American military and gives our country another data source to offer our allies. The more they keep the Americans off guard using what we sell them, the lower the chance that China will end up confronting American military power."

At almost the exact same moment, a small boat from the American naval base reached the dock with the body of a security guard who had been missing for hours. The Navy doctor who helped lift the body from the boat stepped onto the dock, shaking his head.

"Any idea what happened, Commander?" asked an Air Force colonel staring down at the body.

"No, sir. Other than a small abrasion on his wrist, I see no obvious wound. Maybe an allergic reaction to a bug bite or a heart attack." The doctor leaned over the body, pulling at a khaki pants leg. There's a small puncture through the fabric on the front of his left thigh, and there appears to be a small swelling below it. God only knows what might have caused it. There are a lot of animals whose sting or bite that can quickly kill you once you end up in the Pacific." The doctor watched as two medics lifted the body onto a stretcher. "Maybe he just went for a walk and fell. The shore below the runway is really rugged."

CHAPTER 2
VIRGINIA

MATHEW CHANG, DIRECTOR of the CIA had called the meeting against his own better judgment. He'd always managed to avoid conspiracy theories that weren't vetted by his own agency. A young naval lieutenant from the Farragut Technical Analysis Center, the technical analysis group for Naval Intelligence had forwarded a report up the chain of command that created a minor furor in his own office. Some Whiz Kid, as two deputy directors referred to him, managed to patch together half a dozen unrelated stories and deduced a new threat that no other source was reporting. Chang read the synopsis and personally called several counterparts to find confirmation. Hell, no other source even considered the report credible; just two of his own deputies.

Right on time his phone rang, the reminder of a meeting that he just didn't have time for. The Director picked up his briefing folder and coffee cup, slipped through the side door of his office and into his small private conference room. Deputy Director of Science and Technology, Pete Wilson squeezed the shoulder of the spit and polish young officer, busily taping on the laptop at one end of a small rectangular table. "Lieutenant Gritt, this is Director Chang."

Chang could tell that the young man was trying to figure out whether to salute or shake hands, so he extended his hand. He had always believed the best way to get rid of a pest was to kill it with kindness before sending it on its way with an assignment that would take the rest of the pest's life to accomplish. "Okay Lieutenant, show me what you came up with. I've only got about fifteen minutes."

"Yes sir," offered the young man, tapping on the laptop, as Wilson, Chang and the fourth party at the meeting, Jana Taylor, the recently appointed CIA director of Operations slid into their chairs.

Chang was impressed as the young man immediately launched his presentation, wasting no time on introducing himself or background. The brevity was unusual and refreshing.

"My first slide is a photograph taken nineteen months ago on the coast of Washington State. It shows two FBI agents with a box that was found at an unmanned control station and hub for a major cross-Pacific fiber optic cable. The box was inside the small facility, actually sitting in one of the equipment racks along with equipment that was supposed to be there. The technician who discovered it has no idea how long it has been installed. He was trouble shooting a problem and noted that the box did not appear on any of his 'as built' drawings. It was plugged in and had patch cords connecting it to the cable frame used by our military to communicate with facilities in Hawaii and Alaska."

The young lieutenant tapped another key, and a new photo popped up on the screen.

"This is a collage of pictures that one of our assets in Taiwan forwarded to us. He did not divulge where he got it. The Chinese have infiltrated the military in Taiwan over the last several years, but the other side of that is the Taiwanese also have a solid intelligence network on the mainland. You will note that they are all of the flight tests of the new F-35C that were being conducted at the Whidbey Island Naval Air Station in Washington state fourteen months ago. The last one, lower right, shows two Navy technicians holding a box that is substantially different from the one collected in slide one. This one was found in the tiny hut where radio and telemetry data for the test is converted from radio to terrestrial signals. The box had no purpose in the facility."

The lieutenant tapped another key, bringing up another frame. The picture looked like the kind of incidental trash you might find along any highway. "This, sir, was picked up by some facility maintenance people at the Newport News Shipyard. The location where it was found offers a view of the final assembly area for our Ford class nuclear carriers. The trash isn't as important as the fiber optic cable that security found coiled just under the surface of the bay. There was nothing connected to the cable. They traced it and found that it ran more than a mile out into the Atlantic where they found the other end resting on a large cement block." The man tapped another key, bringing up a split photo. "The one on the right is the end on the land, and the other is the abandoned end on the block. You will note that the block has bolts that would allow a box, approximately three feet by four feet to be anchored, although there was nothing on the block when it was found."

"Lieutenant," said Chang, "would you scroll back one photo."

The picture of trash came up.

"Can you blow that picture up? I'd like a better view, a close-up."

The lieutenant spent a few seconds on the computer before enlarging the image and then enlarging it again. "I'm told that you grew up reading and speaking Mandarin, sir," offered Gritt. "We believe that what you have on the screen are wrappers and plastic pouches of the same rations that the Chinese issue to their Marines. They had been buried, but some dog at the Newport facility dug them up, or we would have never found any of this."

"The Lieutenant has three more similar photos," offered Wilson. "The boxes you have seen, and the photo of trash all seem to be of Chinese manufacture. The Navy's analysis of the Newport News materials may indicate that while the *Gerald Ford* was being constructed, someone had a camera recording the whole process, sending the recordings to some type of capture device offshore. We're guessing that both the camera and capture device were pulled after construction, and that whoever planted the camera got what they needed and aren't interested in detail on the new ship, the *Doris Miller*."

"Mat," offered director Taylor, rising from her chair and standing next to the young officer, "these incidents all indicate a very sophisticated ability to penetrate our best security. The areas where these intrusions happened are all blanketed with acoustic and magnetic sensors. If the Navy is right, then somehow the Chinese got close enough to send in divers and plant recording devices and even put men ashore to take pictures in spite of our millions spent to keep them out."

"Didn't we tap the underground cable that allowed the Russians to communicate along their bases from Vladivostok to north of Kamchatka? We pulled that off decades ago," replied Chang.

"True," replied Taylor, "but we did it by infiltrating Russian territorial waters where there were virtually no defenses. Unless one of their destroyers had passed directly over the submarine we used while operating their underwater sensors, there was no way for them to detect the intrusion. This is different. We had our best defense up."

Mat Chang smiled as he read from the screen. "Energy bars with raisins and hydration drinks with salt and sugar," he offered. "The people who buried this crap were on land long enough to require a drink and food." He sighed, realizing that this wild goose chase had just become a goose hunt.

"Lieutenant Gritt, what is the Navy's opinion of how this could be accomplished?"

"Sir, a decade ago, your folks sent us some sketchy intel about the Chinese working on a completely stealthy submarine. We looked at the data and came to the conclusion that no submarine that was a threat, meaning attack or boomer, could possibly be built using the concept in that intel. Maybe we weren't broad enough in our threat evaluation. The Chinese have perfected a small undetectable submarine and are using it to pick our pockets."

"Lieutenant, we need a few minutes to digest all this," said Chang. "Make sure that Dr. Wilson knows where to find you."

"Pete, if you will show Lieutenant Gritt out to his escort, I'll cancel my lunch with Senator Wurtz and get Maggie on some sandwiches. We will reconvene in ten minutes.

❧

"Okay, Jana, you called this meeting. Beyond the obvious, what is the threat here?

Jana Taylor had started her government career as one of the first women to complete the hell that was Navy Seal training. With few missions available to her, and butting heads with the prejudice against women, and the Don't Ask, Don't Tell policy, she retired her hard-won Navy commission and joined the Central Intelligence Agency in clandestine operations. Over a quarter century she had amassed a record of achievement and educational commitment second to none.

She smiled at Chang, brushing her gray-streaked plain brown hair from in front of ordinary brown eyes. "Well, Mat, what we don't know can hurt us, and we don't know a damned thing about how pervasive this thing is. But the thing that led Pete and I to raise hell with you over this obscure report was the ARCTIC ANGEL PROJECT. Eventually we will have half a dozen facilities for this shield. But for now, all we have is one prototype as far out in the wilds of the Aleutian Islands of Alaska as it could be. It is in a place where we have no immediate backup if the Chinese or the

Russians or even the forces of Paraguay wanted to launch a sneak, small force penetration operation. We have been counting on the fact that, to the world, even our own forces, it doesn't exist. We have the facility ringed by every sensor we have in the inventory. But if someone finds out, the two-dozen guards there aren't much of a deterrent to a small group of trained commandos who can reach the facility undetected. Even if they call for help, it will take hours for a rapid reaction force to reach them."

"I agree with Jana," offered Wilson. "But of equal importance, is what she led with. We technology guys are always rattled by a phenomenon we don't understand. We don't have a clue about this submarine thing, and until we do, we can't guarantee any site close to the ocean can be secured."

Mat Chang ripped the end from a package of Lay's potato chips. "So, if this is real, we have three tasks. First, figure out where they have been, or are snooping on us. Second, work with the Defense folks to come up with a strategy for ARCTIC ANGEL without blowing our cover. Third, figure out what technology the Chinese are using to move a sub into our waters without a hint that it is there."

Pete Wilson stood up, brushing crumbs from his shirt into a napkin neatly folded in his lap. He folded the napkin over and over to ensure none of the crumbs fell out. He crossed the room, laying rather than dropping the napkin into a wastebasket. "This seems to be a fair assessment of the problem."

Chang smiled. If Pete just had a pencil protector in his shirt pocket the moment would perfectly describe the Technology Director.

Jana shook her head. "One more small complicating problem, gentlemen. Just in the last couple of weeks, we've noticed an increase in Chinese intelligence aircraft and snooper ships in the general area of the ARCTIC ANGEL facility. I'm not convinced that they haven't figured out that we are up to something out on that island. The main facility will be complete this month and the stealth laser platform is scheduled to begin movement from California to the facility in weeks."

"Then, we need to add a fourth item," continued Chang. "We need to figure out what the Chinese already know."

CHAPTER 3
VIRGINIA

CHANG AND DEPUTY Director Taylor had always had a great relationship, probably born of watching each other's careers. While Jana's career had been focused on European operations, many of them clandestine, Chang's area of expertise had been Asia. His grandfather had been a General in the Army of the Republic of China and after their exile to Taiwan had immigrated to the United States, somehow with a very substantial nest egg.

Jana remembered having a drink with Chang after her body language gave away her concern over a Chinese American running intelligence operation on China. Chang had run up a big tab on his credit card as Jana subtlety pressed him with questions. Chang's father had been a West Point grad who had retired in just twenty years and gone on to start a joint venture with a couple of officers who he worked with. The company integrated American and Korean technologies, all in the defense industry.

Chang had also sailed through West Point, and then spent three years bored out of his mind as an Army Intelligence officer. He'd negotiated an early release from his commitment courtesy of his new employer, the Central Intelligence Agency.

With the death of his father, Mat Chang left the agency to take over as president of the family firm. To his surprise that involved him more deeply in intelligence and on a level that a career CIA employee would never see.

When a former West Point classmate became President, Mat accepted an offer to head up the Central Intelligence Agency after he was assured of direct access to POTUS and gotten that man's agreement that he could slash the agency's red tape. Not only had Jana accepted the man's history, she had grown to consider Chang the most effective operative that she had ever worked with. She'd been elated when the President made him director.

He'd passed over a dozen more experienced career employees to pick Pete Wilson to run Science and Technology and did the same to slide his old friend Jana into the Director of Operations job. Wilson had been the Agency liaison to his company. No one in the world had overcome more to succeed than Jana, which made her, a can't fail appointment. She'd even taken up golf so that she and Mat could get completely away from the bureaucrats that both detested.

Jana pushed the tee into the soft ground, concentrating on getting her ball to rest on the tee as she struggled with her close-up vision, a function of head trauma from a mission a decade before. "Pete and I were a bit surprised that you signed onto the data that Lt. Gritt presented. It was plenty thin."

"Jana, my family has been battling the communists since the 1940s. Family members who stayed on the mainland after the retreat to Taiwan were never heard from again. This secret sub thing is just the kind of low-cost attack that they favor. Their espionage has allowed them to close a fifty-year technology gap in less than fifteen years. We're still ahead but only by a decade. Our next move will widen that advantage again, but only if they can't steal the technology before it is fully implemented. If this sub is real, we need to stop it now."

"Mat, I don't have anyone in mind that I trust with this project. The couple of go-to people I'd consider, are both buried in critical work." Jana relaxed, as she watched her ball sail about a hundred and fifty yards directly down the middle of the fairway.

Her old friend and boss lobbed a slight hook into the ruff about fifty yards further down the arrow straight manicured grass in front of them. "I was kind of thinking it might be a job for an old timer. We're looking for a high-tech system, but this looks like a good old shoe leather investigation. We just need to look at every site that may be vulnerable without raising an alarm. Of all the things we don't need right now is to risk the Chinese somehow figuring out that we are chasing their stealth boat. We need to ascertain the damage before they go dark on us. I'm thinking we give someone almost complete control, and back them with a small Special Forces team. We can use base security testing as a cover."

"You're thinking of Thad Walker, aren't you?

Mat smiled, as he tugged a pitching wedge from his golf bag. "Only because he never fails, and nobody outside of the few old timers left around the company, even know who he is."

Jana lofted a three iron up to within thirty yards of the green. She had learned to love working things like this out with Mat, each speaking a sentence only when they hit a shot. It allowed a lot of time in between to think through each piece of the puzzle.

"Pete has been combing through the reports on the Chinese surveillance of the Arctic project." Mat's next shot bounced twice and then ran well past the green. "He thinks it might be an opportunity to let them find what we think they are looking for."

Jana's wedge shot rolled up to within four feet of the pin. "I'm not sure that I understand that. Giving them anything on Arctic Angel seems damned risky."

Mat decided on a thirty-foot put rather than another wedge shot. He'd never mastered getting enough backspin to stop his ball from rolling well past where it landed. "He thinks we can give them just enough to think they know what they are dealing with; just enough that they quit digging." His shot came up ten feet short of the cup.

"Okay, but what's that got to do with Thad Walker?" Jana went ahead and putted in for her par.

"You both think that Arctic Angel is a logical target for the stealth sub. We're going to have to read Walker in on most of the project since part of what we need to do is secure that site." His put rimmed the cup and stopped six inches away.

"Agreed, but I still don't see how that fits into Pete's plan?"

Mat's ball finally dropped into the cup. Both of them began the slow walk to the next green as their security detail began to move as well. Neither wrote a score on their scorecard.

"I just think we put the two of them together and see if they can kill two birds with one stone. We use Angel as bait to study this sub and give the Chinese enough to 'think' they understand Arctic Angel."

"Let's call in the dogs," said Jana. "That's our usual five holes and you're playing like you hate this game."

"I do hate this game. I'd much prefer floating down the Madison in Montana with a fly rod, catching brown trout."

Jana laughed. "You going to Montana to talk to Thad yourself?"

CHAPTER 4

FLATHEAD LAKE MONTANA

THE DIRECTOR'S PRIVATE Gulfstream jet touched down on the long runway at Malmstrom Air Force Base in Great Falls. It taxied past a huge portion of America's strategic bomber force before stopping in a parking place well away from normal base activity. Since even he hadn't figured out that he was making this trip until the night before, Chang was traveling light, with no advance security. He and the two guards that had volunteered their time as a break from the hustle of D.C. and a ride on the plush private jet fanned out talking to a half-dozen military policemen who met the jet. A third very junior agent struggled down the ramp carrying the hastily thrown together luggage of four men.

The commander of the base met Chang near a waiting helicopter. "It's the best I can do with no notice," he offered.

"It will work just fine. I'm on my way to surprise an old friend and we will need to land in a small meadow next to his home on Flathead Lake."

The base commander knew better than to ask any questions.

"I may need the helicopter for a couple of days, if that is all right?" said Chang. "I'll have your crew keep you posted. If there is any ground expense, the Agency will take care of it."

The backbone of the Rocky Mountains stretched about halfway between Great Falls and Thad Walker's house on Montana's largest lake. That meant that they had to fly high, but the trip was only about 150 miles. It was still mid-morning as the helicopter began to circle the small field next to the house. Chang could tell from the air, that his old colleague was there as expected. Walker was a man of routine, and part of that was an early morning row out on the lake, in a boat he'd built himself. Walker was on the dock as they circled. A large dark dog stood on the shore barking.

Walker, now in his early seventies, met the men at the house as if a helicopter dropping from the sky was an everyday experience. He extended his hand to Chang but said nothing with the others around. The two men wandered back down to the dock as the two Air Force pilots found a place in the shade and opened a thermos of coffee. Chang's security detail spread out trying to look casual in their suits, in a place that never had seen a suit before.

"Well that was quite an entrance," offered Walker, working his way down the gravel path, his cane planted carefully next to his bad leg with each step.

"Time was of the essence," laughed his old friend. "I'm about to tell you a story and would appreciate your feedback. If that feedback includes any interest in helping your country out of a small jam, then we will talk about spending a day fishing to flesh in the details."

"It's a little early for the lake to produce well."

"If you still have that buddy with the tackle shop over on the Madison, I was thinking that we could saddle up that chopper and catch a half day floating the river. We will need to borrow his boat, since we can't really talk in front of him. I can row if you're too old to handle the boat."

"Well look what D.C. and dealing with that bureaucracy has

done to you – brought out the asshole that all of us suspected all along," said Walker with a laugh.

The two men sat on the dock, Walker pulling off his tennis shoes and dangling his feet in the water. He listened as Chang outlined the Chinese intelligence efforts, troubled by his old friend's description of their success. He smiled, as Chang pulled off his shoes, stuffing his socks in them as he rolled up his pants, plunging his feet into the brutally cold April water.

"Well, my old friend, just what would you have me do to help fix this fucking mess?"

"We're looking for an old hand that we can trust to find out how big the hole is and then help figure out how the Chinese are pulling this off. As part of the effort, we'd like to get some idea of what they might already know."

Walker's worn feet were getting really cold, but he wasn't about to admit that yet. He soaked them every morning to reduce the swelling. "Seems to me, to be a multi-team project that requires nothing more than spending whatever time is necessary, using whatever resources you already have available to dig and dig. Over a reasonable period of time, the details will paint the picture. Why do you need me?"

"Well, it's the last part that has us really worried. We are building out a prototype defensive system that will change the balance of power for a decade or two, maybe longer. The problem is that we're building it in a place that is really vulnerable to this Chinese technology. It could be very vulnerable. It's important enough to risk a shooting war, if either the Russians or the Chinese figure out what we are doing before the system is operational. We're trying to keep this completely secret right up to the time we finish testing. If this gets out, we're liable to have a division of bad guy troops landing on a beach secured by a handful of Air Force cops."

Walker pulled his blue feet from the water and began to massage the parts that always hurt as they warmed up. "You and I have discussed how difficult it is to keep a black project secret. I am assuming that you can't read me in on the technology that you want me to help secure. But I have to ask, why don't you just put a division of our people out wherever this thing is to protect it?"

"Thad, that could just be enough of a tipoff to ensure that we end up with a shooting war. We need an experienced lead, given whatever resources they require, to put together and run a plan to blunt the intelligence attack and buy the time to get our 'project' operational."

"Are you paying for the fishing trip and to reimburse Uncle Sam for the use of one of his helicopters and the security staff? I'm too old to get dragged in front of some congressional hearing to explain misappropriation of government assets." He used his cane to get to his feet. "I'm on a retiree's income."

Chang looked up at the new $80,000 GMC pickup parked next to Walker's home. He knew that his old colleague bought a new one every time the ashtrays got full, usually full of chewing gum wrappers, as Walker didn't smoke. "Yea, I guess so," Chang replied with a laugh. "I already pay about a hundred times the average taxes of most Americans, but yeah, I'll pick up the tab."

"Well, April's damned boring around here, I guess I'm in," replied Walker. His Gordon Setter, Winchester followed both men toward the house. Chang marveled at how the black and tan hunting dog stayed glued to Walkers left leg. He smiled, knowing of Walker's early life, one of constant chaos and how the man had overcome that. Thad Walker was the most thoughtful and disciplined man Chang new, just the man to take on a task with 90 percent unknowns. Even his hunting dog was trained to a cutting edge.

The dog trotted in front of them only when one of Chang's security men appeared at the top of the hill.

"Win, sit," ordered Walker who patted the dog on the head as he passed. "Friend," he said, pointing at the guard.

CHAPTER 5

MADISON RIVER NEAR BOZEMAN MONTANA

ONE OF THE nice things about fishing the Madison was that for most of the distance, a person floating the river had cell coverage. That worked out for Chang and Walker, as they took their time working the sixteen foot drift boat along the shoreline, casting mostly terrestrial bug pattern flies toward the bank, hoping to find the large brown trout that laid near the bank to pick off insects that fell from overhanging grasses and brush.

Taking turns rowing with the other in the front of the boat casting, they communicated with a boat in front and one in back, each rowed by a local fishing guide. The guides had little to do except row as the security people in front of each boat spent all of their time watching along the banks and directing their guides each time the two men in the middle boat called to let them know they were stopping.

"It's really nice of your buddy in the tackle shop to put this together with no notice," said Chang, as he carefully released a fourteen-inch trout. Winchester stood, head over the edge of the boat, nose almost in the water watching the fish swim away. He shook with excitement.

"Piece of cake," replied Walker. "It helps that I own the shop and, other than cover the expenses and taxes, he gets to keep any profits." He moved the boat further out into the current. "Don't even think about keeping a trout. Win will just pick it up and drop it back in the river."

The two men used fishing, much like Jana and Mat used golf. They had been fishing together since both ended up operating a very VIP float fishing operation on Russia's Kamchatka Peninsula years before as a cover for research on a new Russian radar system. The business still operated, now as a purely fishing venture. Chang's notoriety as director of the CIA meant that he could no longer fish there.

"Seems to me," offered Walker, as he slowed the boat allowing Chang to work a drift that was one of Walker's favorites, "that we either need complete specifications on this Chinese sub or the sub itself."

Chang smiled. This was the Thad Walker that he'd come to recruit. "Getting our hands on that sub would probably be about as difficult as any operation we've ever tried," answered Chang. "It has to be among the most carefully guarded secrets in the Chinese inventory. This caught us completely by surprise." He watched a couple of mallards working on a nest near a tiny side water. The president would never approve seizing a Chinese naval vessel so he would never ask. But if it somehow ended up running aground where it could be studied...

"Yeah, you're probably right," said Walker. "I suspect that even finding out where its home port is could take months if not years, and then we'd have to figure out how to penetrate their security. Might be easier to use HUMINT, Human Intelligence; good old fashioned spycraft. Maybe find a scientist or bureaucrat who worked on the project and pay them enough to change their life forever." He pulled the boat into the bank. "It's your turn to row." Win leaped from the boat to water a nearby tree.

Chang called his escorts, advising that they would be stopped for ten minutes. He stowed his rod along the side of the boat as Walker made his way to the casting rail in the front of the boat, carefully leaning into the platform to compensate for his weak leg.

"If you don't mind, I've got a couple of days of work to do before I can tear into this, and I need to arrange a sitter for Win," said Walker, as he tied a grasshopper pattern on his leader. "A bit early for hoppers, but sometimes the big old fish have such vivid memories that they hit it anyway. Let's go." He made a couple of false casts as the boat worked its way away from the bank. "I'll catch a commercial flight."

"Take your couple of days," replied Chang, but we can save a day if I send a plane for you. We can make it a night pickup in Missoula. I'll leave the guy you call the Kid to coordinate it and as your driver. As I recall you refer to anyone under fifty as Kid. I'll work on a location where you can take your dog."

"Yup, that's what I thought you'd say, replied Thad. "That would be a lot more comfortable for an old guy like me, and Win hates those big plastic kennels." He hooked a nice fish, losing it as he tried to release it anyway. Win glared at him just as he did when Thad missed a pheasant that Win had pointed. "It sure would be nice to take a look in that Chinese sub," he mumbled.

"What in the hell are you talking about?" offered Mat.

"I'm just thinking that we could kill several birds with one stone if we got out hands on that submarine. We'd learn how the damned thing works and I'll bet there would be a logbook with all of its missions, telling us where they have already snooped on us."

"But it would also change how the Chinese use it after we gave it back. It's not like the old days when we could just leave the crew in the middle of the Pacific without life vests."

"If it was easy, you wouldn't have come all the way out here," said Thad. He hooked a huge fish that began to run downstream, tearing line from his reel. "Or maybe you would have, just for the fishing."

CHAPTER 6

BEIJING

ONE THING THAT made General Quing's job a bit easier than his counterpart in the United States was that virtually all of the military intelligence operations were part of the Peoples Liberation Army. Every aspect of the Chinese military was part of the PLA, even the Air Force and Navy. While China had its share of inter-service rivalry, the intelligence operations had been centralized in 2016 into what was now labeled the Strategic Support Force.

Years before, Major General Dai Quingman had developed a military theory after watching U.S. operations in the Baltic and in the Middle East. He was the first Chinese general officer to recognize that information was often more important than bullets in war and that timely intelligence gave you a huge advantage at the beginning of hostilities and became more important as you tried to end them. He had been put in charge of what the military called 4PLA, the intelligence group that conducted electronic intelligence. 2PLA – the group responsible for HUMINT, human intelligence and spycraft – had resisted the turn to electronic intelligence for some time until someone finally pointed out that the group had trouble recruiting spies from outside of China, and all their operators looked Chinese. In between the two groups, 3PLA was responsible for clandestine operations. 4PLA had slowly become the tail that wagged the dog.

Those three groups developed rapidly improving capabilities to the point where their abilities began to rival and worry the leadership of Chinese Communist Party. In the early 2000's military intelligence was hobbled by party hacks and policies. They were afraid that the centralized intelligence was a threat to the Party. In 2016, newly powerful President and General Secretary of the Party, Xi Jinping ordered a reorganization and cut much of the red tape that was hobbling intelligence operations.

Quing's job was to work through the political and technical problems of integrating all military intelligence, and he was slowly succeeding in molding the new Strategic Support Force. The simple fact that the heads of all three former divisions were now seated in his private conference room proved that. Quing, though was struggling to pay attention as General Ling worked his way through the second hour of what his Human Intelligence group was working on.

"In the first three months of the year," rattled the director of Human Intelligence, "we have placed twelve assets into major American universities. We successfully recruited two American students who are studying here in China. We–"

Quing interrupted his subordinate. "General, all of your report is about assets, with very little about what they are telling you. As I noted when I set this meeting up, the field commanders, especially those of the Air and Rocket Forces are deeply concerned about the facility that the Americans are building on Kiska Island. We have gathered almost nothing through airborne and naval intelligence targeting the project. Just normal construction chatter about a facility on one square mile that the American's carved out of the Historical Park and Aleutian Marine Park."

"Sir, I have nothing new to report. The one asset that I have close to Boeing states just what he has been reporting for a year.

Boeing is contracting the construction of..." Ling referred to his notes. "...of a twelve thousand square foot concrete and steel facility with living quarters for thirty-five staff. The project includes a new port with modern docks and a new 10,000-foot airstrip. Boeing claims it is their first project for the American Park Service. My agent only has secondhand information on other Boeing employees who are actually working on the project."

"That we knew months ago," replied Quing. "Based on satellite photos, the project is almost complete. General Liu's aircraft detected minute trace amounts of radiation from one shipment that was moved to the site three months ago. We assume that the site will be powered by a small nuclear reactor. What in the hell is so important about this facility that the Americans would violate their own laws on disrupting parks and marine sanctuaries and their long-standing aversion to standalone nuclear power? General Liu's people have also detected signals that indicate a very unique radar being tested. It may be linking with the data from their new low earth orbit observations satellites."

"Sir," said Ling, "all I have is the same guess that I gave you when we discussed that nuclear reactor installation. Maybe this is the location of the new laser weapon that I warned you about three years ago. Boeing and Raytheon are working on a large aperture laser. With adequate nuclear power, such a laser could concentrate its beam and attack targets at great distances. The limitation would be the height of the installation and the curvature of the earth. Most of our analysts believe that the best use of such a weapon would be to target cruise missiles and aircraft." Ling snuffed out the cigarette that he hadn't touched in five minutes.

"Could such a laser be used to intercept intercontinental missiles?" Quing looked around the room, realizing that none of the people in the room were going to volunteer an answer. Finally, he turned to his director of electronic intelligence. "General, Liu, can you answer that question?"

"Maybe," was Liu's answer. A laser weapon will lose a great deal of power just penetrating the earth's atmosphere. I am no expert on such weapons, but any missile with a trajectory well away from the weapon would probably survive a beam that had to fight its way through our atmosphere. In the North Pacific, where the weather is often terrible, the beam would be even more degraded. Our newest technology allows us to change the trajectories of our rockets, making them hard for America to hit with their anti-rocket missiles." Liu toyed with the coffee cup in front of him. "But the Americans are damned good at technology or we wouldn't spend so much money and effort to steal what they engineer. A laser could retarget in seconds. If such a laser was capable of hitting high-flying rockets, it would change everything. For ultra-high-speed rockets, it wouldn't have to penetrate the skin as it would to destroy the electronics of an ICBM. If it just opened a minute tear in the outer hull, the friction of the missile moving at thousands of kilometers per hour would rip the vehicle apart."

The youngest member of the assembly faked a cough to be recognized. General Yang had come out of the Army's special operations, driven to complete two doctorates in the time given him to get one. He ran clandestine operations for the PLA.

"Yes, Yang," offered Quing with a wide grin. "You have a plan of how we can swoop in with one of your operations teams and answer all of our questions?"

Yang, just thirty-three and one of the military's rising stars, laughed. The generational difference between him and the others showed as his laugh was met with icy stares. "No, sir, but we could mount an EEL mission to see what we might find. Our EEL could put men on that island without any construction workers noticing. We could grab one of them and interrogate him."

"General Yang," replied Quing, "one of the things that we have worked out with all of our adversaries is to respect the game we all play. Part of that respect is a tacit agreement that we don't kill or kidnap theirs and they don't kill or kidnap ours."

"Sir, sometimes such sacrifices are necessary."

"Like when two of your operators on an EEL mission helped a healthy security man drown on that Guam project?"

"The Americans reported that he drowned, probably after falling into the ocean. The waters of the North Pacific are far more dangerous than those around Guam. One man who goes missing won't stir up any suspicion."

"Perhaps Yang, but how will you select a construction worker with the knowledge to tell us what they are building and how threatening it is? If one doesn't help much, do you propose to grab another and then another until you can piece together a picture. Won't several missing men create just the security apparatus that could stop you when we have a legitimate target on that island? Won't it send the American's on a mission to understand your EEL?"

"Respectfully, General Quing, if the Americans build a laser weapon that can shoot down our missiles, cruise missiles and aircraft, then we are rendered impotent. Where are we then, sir?"

"General Yang, that would probably leave us right where we are now, as a strong regional power rather than a Pacific-wide power. It would leave us naked, our strategic deterrence very weak. Our work would increase, as the party demanded that we develop comparable weapons and defenses for theirs. Your team's ability to penetrate their security around that island might be our only way to do that quickly. Don't piss away our only advantage by forcing the enemy to build a wall around a facility that you may need to target later. I am not saying that is acceptable, but that is my answer to your question."

CHAPTER 7

MARYLAND

THE PRESIDENT SIGNED off on the importance of the mission to understand the new Chinese threat, offering the use of the Camp David Retreat as a site to put together a strategy and flesh out a plan. It was the best that the D.C. intelligence community could offer as a work site. Thad Walker had a well-known hatred of hotels and high-rise buildings, and an even more well-defined dislike for secure rooms which he found claustrophobic.

Thad had learned to sleep almost anywhere, which allowed him to use the four-hour flight to D.C. to rest. Win had never been in a helicopter before, but he'd flown a lot and slept right next to Thad as they were whisked off to the Maryland Presidential retreat. The two took an hour walk around the facility, familiarizing his dog with the place and introducing him to several security people.

The first briefing began as Thad wolfed down a roast beef sandwich, carefully stripping tiny pieces of meat from the edges and slipping them under the table to his waiting friend. "Tell me Lieutenant Gritt, do you have a copy of the underlying data that led you to your conclusions?"

"I do, sir." Gritt tapped a couple of keys on his computer that sent six compact files of data to a small printer that was hard-wired to his laptop. His laptop and printer had never been connected to the Navy's intranet or the Internet. Every document had been scanned into the device rather than transferred. It was cumbersome, but completely secure. "I'll print them one at a time for you. Do you want them sorted in any specific way?"

"Call me Thad, Lieutenant, and the answer is no. I just want to sit next to you with a highlighter and mark up the documents to make sure that I understand how you arrived at your thesis."

"Sir, my first name is Chad," replied Gritt, handing five sheets to Walker.

"I recognize the name, son. I bumped into your father a time or two. As I recall, your family has a long history of righting wrongs."

Chad smiled and nodded. "That goes back to the 1820s, sir. I had a German ancestor who commanded a warship in the war for independence." He plucked the next file from the tiny printer that he'd carried from his office. "Most of us were Army or Air Force at some point, most of my family were pilots, but since the 1940s many of us were involved in intelligence. I graduated from Annapolis but couldn't get into flight school because of my eyes. They are good enough for a private pilot's license, but not for military flight status."

"Mat Chang told me that you have a master's in engineering."

"True, sir, I have a master's in electrical engineering and am working on a PHD in electro-optics."

He handed the third and fourth reports to Walker, who had lofted his body from the overstuffed chair next to the rock fireplace in the VIP cabin and headed to the door to let his dog out.

"Just let him roam," said Walker to the security man near the front door. "He'll let me know when he wants back in." He turned back to Gritt. "Just what are you specializing in, I mean, I'm not quite sure what electro-optics is all about."

"Well," replied Gritt, slipping a paper clip on the last of six reports, "it can go several ways. I can specialize in using electronics to work on ways to see minute things more clearly, or I can use optics and electronics to communicate more efficiently."

Thad reseated himself. "You mean like improving fiber optic signaling?"

"Yes, sir, it might be that." Gritt took a seat next to Walker, plucking four different colored markers from his briefcase. He noted the look on Walker's face. "Or using lasers to communicate over long distances without the need for cables, or even using lasers to communicate with moving objects rather than radio which can be jammed or intercepted."

The two men started with the report on Newport News Naval Shipyard. Chad waited as Walker quietly read the five pages, making no effort to interrupt.

"Chad, is your educational background how you started putting this all together? For example, do you think that the Chinese used some laser communications to send the data from what you think was a camera on the end of that cable?"

"I think my education helps; as to the laser on this, no. I think that they planted a camera, well-camouflaged and probably smaller than a box of matches on shore and then recorded what the camera picked up on a large capacity storage device on the ocean floor at the other end of the cable." He opened an envelope from his briefcase and handed Walker a one-foot section of cable.

Walker turned a piece of cable no thicker than pencil lead over and over in his hand. "When I heard cable, I though you meant a fairly large cable, like you use for the Internet or to hook up a television."

"The cable is designed to deliver just enough power to drive the camera and the signal is carried by the fiber optic thread back to a storage device. The cement block at the other end would allow for a box with power source and recording device. When the Chinese got what they wanted, they just plucked the camera back off the beach and unbolted the controlling box and hauled it away. There are a hundred sources that would tell them when the carrier they were watching would be launched."

"Wouldn't they be concerned that we would find the cable and put two and two together?"

"The cable is very interesting. Our lab confirmed that the coating is water-soluble and would decay over four years. With the coating gone, the copper wire would corrode in weeks and the action of waves and tides would probably break up the glass fiber. We just got lucky. If whoever placed this device hadn't buried their trash so that a dog could dig it up, we'd have never known that it was there."

By dinner that evening, Gritt had convinced Walker of his analysis. The helicopter that came to pick up Gritt brought Director Chang and both of his deputy directors. Each carried a small suitcase. Chad and Thad shook hands as the young man climbed into the helicopter that would whisk him back to CIA headquarters in Virginia where he'd parked his car.

As the chopper lifted off, Walker turned to Chang. "Lieutenant Gritt will be my direct assistant, if you can arrange that."

"Done," replied Chang. "The Navy has a lot of egg on their face over the security breaches." Chang picked up the light Cabela's jacket that he'd purchased for his trip to Montana. "Let's go get some dinner and you can brief me and my staff on your first day. I think you know them both. We plan on staying tomorrow and another day if you need us."

Before they could get out the door, Chang's phone rang. His face turned almost white and then beet red during the one-minute conversation. He turned to Thad, "the Navy just sent your young Lieutenant Gritt a message. He forwarded it to me. They just discovered another breach. He is sending us a secure copy of the report when he gets back to the Pentagon."

CHAPTER 8

WASHINGTON D.C.

GRITT COULD ALMOST feel the anger bleeding from the report as he opened the secure file on his desk computer. The author was the commander of one of the Arleigh Burke class destroyers operating out of Okinawa. That morning he had been handed supposedly secret orders for a mission similar to one that was becoming routine over the previous three years. It was part of the game.

The Chinese had created several man-made islands in the South China Sea, supposedly to claim sovereignty and to protect resource development rights from conflicting claims of five other nations in the region. What had followed was rapid militarization of the islands including PLA attack and defense aircraft on airfields built on dredged landmasses.

To counter the Chinese claims, the United States had continued to sail its warships within sight of the disputed islands to maintain international rite of passage through what had been unclaimed ocean, and the rights of the other countries to the resources. Usually the missions were planned out over several days, and while the Chinese bitched and screamed, they just watched the American ships pass by.

This mission had been a spur of the moment sailing, triggered by spy satellite pictures of unusual construction at tiny Bing Atoll that had never been part of the Chinese land grab. The orders had come directly from the Pentagon, requesting a sail-by with photographs and electronic surveillance. The American ship was underway in less than an hour.

They had been at sea only eight hours, by the GPS, only two hundred nautical miles from their homeport when the bridge picked up six Chinese destroyers on radar. A half-hour earlier, American surveillance satellites had downloaded photos of the ships. They were racing to get between the American ship and the target atoll. As they closed on him, the radio came alive with warnings. The commander of the Chinese ships was warning him that all six ships had "severe steering malfunctions," and that they "would certainly collide with the American ship if it closed on Bing Atoll."

To intercept his ship, the commander calculated that they would have set sail at almost the same moment that he did. He pulled up the satellite photo that had launched the mission. Other than two transport ships anchored at the atoll, there were no other ships within hundreds of miles of the remote site. Someone had been reading his mail. After playing the game for three hours and the Chinese coming within feet of colliding with his ship, the commander had been ordered to retreat. The final decision had been made when the Chinese commander had indicated that, "If your ship is damaged, we will consider it a requirement of the Law of the Sea to board your ship and render assistance." Nobody in the U.S. Navy wanted a bunch of Chinese technicians crawling all over a Burke class ship.

Gritt added his own comments to the bottom of the report and fired it on to Walker. "It appears that the breaches we have been discussing include American bases on foreign soil." He was about to add a warning about code breaking when he realized that he had no idea of whether the orders had been encoded. The report, the first of immediate repercussions of the security problems, was enough.

Gritt had just parked his prized 1960 Corvette in the tiny garage of his Georgetown townhome when his phone rang. The caller gave no name, but Gritt recognized the voice.

"Pack enough clothes for a week's stay. Civilian clothes would be appropriate. Be here at seven for a short briefing and to pick up anything you need from your office. Be ready for a shuttle pick up and a ride back to where you were this afternoon. Do you understand?"

"That is affirm, sir," he replied. He looked at his watch. It was already a little past two in the morning, the beginning of a very short night.

CHAPTER 9
SEATTLE

THE TINY CESSNA 150 had been reserved only a couple of hours before. Molly Wang, a petite former flight attendant had called ahead, begging the owner of the small flight operation for use of the plane. "My instructor has the afternoon off," whined Molly, "and I am getting close to being ready to solo."

"Hell, Molly," replied the owner, "I didn't think you were even close to solo. I haven't seen you or Andy in weeks."

"We fly wherever Andy happens to have some time off. He's been up in Bellingham a lot lately, so I've been driving." Molly took a minute to check the tiny notepad in her purse. "We like your planes better, they are cleaner and better maintained, but I need to finish this before I graduate."

"I'll personally make sure the plane is ready," replied Pete Johnson, a retired Air Force pilot from the old school. Pete would have canceled out some other renter to accommodate Molly if he'd had to. She was his only renter that always arrived in a form fitting dress or short skirt and silk blouse. He felt a little jealous of her instructor, often wondering if the instructor had figured out that placing Molly between him and the sun might answer the question. 'Did Molly wear a bra over her ample breasts?'

Dr. Andrew Burgess had worked for Boeing for more than two decades. He helped do concept design on commercial aircraft, which meant that he spent most of his time flying his desk. A love of flying was what led him to study aeronautical engineering, and flight instructing was an opportunity to actually fly. He made a really good living at Boeing, and often offered instruction for nothing to students who interested him. Molly fit that definition on several levels.

First, she was really bright, a straight-A student in chemistry at the university. She spoke three languages, including Spanish, which after buying a condominium in Puerto Vallarta, Mexico, Burgess had been working on himself. Finally, to a guy in his mid-forties, a single dad with a special needs' son and full-time grandmotherly caretaker at home, he found the beautiful girl from Taiwan charming and after twenty hours of instruction a bit more than that. They had first met on a Boeing plane on a trip that Burgess was dreading to Taiwan. She had shown him special attention that made the eight-hour flight tolerable. At the recommendation of his seatmate, he'd intentionally left a business card in his seat as he deplaned in Taipei.

To his amazement, he'd actually received a call from the young woman almost two years later, pleasantly surprised that she had quit her airline job and gone back to college, Doing very well in Taipei that she had been accepted at the University of Washington where she studied chemistry with a plan to become a doctor. They had a couple of lunches together when she'd first arrived. It had been Molly's idea to start flight training.

While Molly had been on the phone reserving the plane, he'd reserved a room at the DoubleTree Inn, a twenty-minute drive from small airport on the southern shore of Lake Washington. He'd been troubled by some of Molly's questions early in the relationship, but their time together had become the highlight of his life. Besides, she never asked any questions about critical aircraft design, or other trade secrets. Taiwan was an ally, so Burgess never considered disclosing his contact to the company.

"Andy," offered Molly as they maneuvered up the Skagit River Valley, practicing slow flight, "we are studying the use of laser technology in chemistry research. You mentioned that Boeing was part of a group working on new laser technology. I believe that you mentioned that they were actually managing some construction for a laser project." Flaps out, engine working hard, Molly managed to keep the plane under control, making slow turns with the airspeed barely above stalling.

Burgess laughed. "Yeah, a couple of the guys that I sometimes have a beer with are involved in that right now. Both of them are somewhere in the wilds of Alaska, but one of them will be back at the end of the month. Why do you ask?"

"Well, I was just kind of wondering if you knew someone who would be able to help me take a deep dive into lasers. I'm thinking of making that the focus of my application for a master's degree before med school. I'm way ahead of my original schedule and need to start thinking about my advanced degree soon."

"We can discuss it at dinner," replied Burgess, a bit of concern in his voice. He wasn't sure that he wanted to share Molly with any of his colleagues.

"I would appreciate that," offered Molly as she slowly advanced the throttles and reduced the flaps on the small Cessna as she'd been taught. She turned to Burgess and smiled.

"Let's head back," replied Burgess. "We will do a couple of stalls on the way."

Molly rolled the plane into a slow turn, headed south and switched radio frequencies to listen to the recorded weather and traffic broadcast for the area around the airport. "Are we having dinner at the Thirteen Coins tonight?"

"If that's where you want to go, I'm in."

By nine, the two had finished a bottle of Merlot with their meals, seated at the counter overlooking the cooks performing their ballet in front of several grills and preparation areas. Molly leaned across the divide between their two wingback chairs, resting her hand on Andy's thigh. "If I can do my masters here, I'll be staying in Seattle for a couple more years."

"I'd like that," replied Burgess, pulling enough cash from his wallet to cover the bill and a big tip. "I have an early morning meeting."

"Then we need to get going," offered Molly, "I wouldn't want make you late."

CHAPTER 10

SEATTLE

MOLLY GOT BACK to her university district apartment just before nine the next morning. She needed to change into clothes more appropriate for class and then jog the half-hour to campus before her 10 A.M. class. The tiny feather that she had inserted between the door-jamb and the door had blown into the landscaping across the sidewalk. Molly had never studied the craft of espionage; the feather trick had come from a book that she'd read years before on a trans-Pacific flight. She used it to prepare herself for what she was about to encounter. She stood on the walk trying to calm her breathing. She struggled to insert her key into the lock, finally using both hands to control the shaking.

Sitting on her couch was a slight Chinese man from school. Like Andy, she'd met him on the same Cathay Pacific flight to Taipei. He'd been sitting next to the nice American. Pa Huang was a political refugee from The Peoples Republic of China. He was a self-described deserter from the PLA, who like most people with his background had been welcomed by the Nationalist Government on Taiwan. He was only eighteen when he fled China, traveling through Hong Kong where he'd requested asylum. His father, a colonel in the Chinese Air Force, had been a tyrant, demanding that his son choose a military career instead of following his heart into music. His acceptance in Taiwan had been cemented when he produced a file of documents stolen from his father, documents that defined the capabilities of China's latest fighter-bombers.

The documents had been verified by cross-checking the information with other sources. But they had also included information on the Chinese efforts to intertie ships and aircraft with a fully integrated data capability, something that neither the American nor Taiwan military thought China was capable of. He'd been debriefed by both countries and then been offered a full ride to a university in the United States where he could study music. On both sides of the pond, he'd been called in to help verify low-level intelligence from time to time.

Molly and Pa had dated a few times when she had Seattle layovers. He'd introduced her to the joy of pot, finally talking her into carrying a couple of pounds in her crew-cleared luggage when he went back to Taipei for a break. That had been the beginning of both the best and worst part of Molly's life.

A month later, Pa had taken Molly to lunch and suggested that he had friends that would be happy to support a very bright young woman's dreams of a university degree. They had already funded a grant at a University in Taipei and Pa suggested that Molly apply for one of five scholarships. Accepted, she quit her airline job and became a full-time student.

A year later with exceptional grades, Pa had encouraged her to apply for a scholarship in America, indicating that he knew that the University of Washington, where he was a junior might look favorably on her. Accepted in months, after extensive screening by the U.S. State Department, she found herself with her education covered by a scholarship, but without the money to travel or live.

Pa's friends had again stepped in, with a job that required Molly to keep a journal of her experiences with the goal of writing a book that would be made available to future students moving to American schools. She would be paid with two round-trip tickets each year and a monthly stipend of two thousand dollars. Pa agreed to introduce her to some other Chinese people he knew in Seattle to help her adjust. "You have met other Americans while with the airlines," he'd mentioned, "perhaps some of them could become friends."

Molly had carried the card of the nice older man she'd met on a flight two years before in her purse, coming close to throwing it away numerous times. In Seattle, she had used the card to call Andy Burgess, looking for any familiar face in her new city. For six months, everything was perfect, right up to the point where Pa showed up with a friend one evening. Molly recognized the man who she'd seen with Pa a couple of times.

The friend ordered Molly to sit down, literally squeezing her arm so hard that she almost screamed. He then then opened a file folder and laid out six pictures. One was of Molly accepting the pot that she had carried for Pa. Another showed a picture of her handing him the package at a restaurant In Taiwan. The third was Pa with a uniformed man with a label that indicated the man was a full colonel in the 3PLA Chinese Communist military intelligence unit. Molly was shocked to see that it was the man in her apartment. The three other pictures were of Molly in other social situations, all of them involving some action that could be interpreted as spycraft.

"Wang has compromised my life," whined Pa, "and unless I do what he asks, I will be arrested and perhaps even executed as a spy. He is the friend that has been helping you, and now he expects you to also do what he asks or the pictures of you and what you were doing will be leaked by Chinese intelligence in a way that both the government of Taiwan and the Americans will find it. You will be arrested for transporting drugs into Taiwan and investigated as an agent of China."

Molly had erupted in tears, right up to the moment when Wang slapped her.

"We do not ask much of someone who can offer so little," Wang said. "But we will find things that you can do to help us learn what we need to know. Ask Pa, go ahead and ask him if we have ever requested that he do anything that might lead to an attack on either the U.S. or Taiwan."

Molly had looked at Pa, who shook his head.

"All of China is one country, and the government of China simply wants to keep all Chinese safe."

From that moment on, Molly's life had been directed by that man, often through directions delivered by Pa. It had been his idea for her to ask Burgess about flying lessons. It had been his idea to select rental aircraft from several different companies, a decision that would make it very difficult to bug her conversations with Andy. Acoustic listening devices aimed from the ground couldn't intercept conversation in a light plane. Changing planes regularly ensured that anyone who took an interest in Molly and Andy would have a difficult time placing and servicing recording devices. Other than maintain her relationship with Burgess, she had been asked for little until she had been directed to find out what Burgess knew about lasers. From the moment that she had first been recruited, which was the word that Pa used instead of blackmailed, Molly's mind had raced with how to end this nightmare. Nothing seemed possible.

She was worried about her own life but also about what might happen to the kind middle aged engineer who in Taiwan would have been fully accepted as a patron of the young woman, but in America, probably thought of as a bit of a lecher and perhaps someday as a spy. She liked Andy. He was a better lover than the men her age. He treated her like a princess while assuring her that he understood that the relationship had an expiration date. Someday she would move on with her career and eventually find a life partner, but not now.

"What did you learn about the laser project that Boeing is working on?" asked Pa.

"Not much more than we already know. Andy's two friends are both in Alaska right now. One of them will be back within the month. I asked Andy to meet him, to see if he could mentor me on lasers as part of my master's degree application. It didn't dawn on Andy that a masters was a strange diversion from medicine. We will have to figure out how to deal with that when the time comes."

"Did he agree to introduce you?"

"Not in so many words, but he will do it. I believe that his only concern is that it might interfere with our relationship. I did my best to assure him that one lover was all I had time for."

"You are a master at getting what you want out of men."

Molly looked at Pa, fidgeting on her couch, "What will it take from me to get out of this mess that you have created for me?"

"There is nothing. If you fail, then both of our lives are destroyed," said Pa. "I was on the flight where you met Burgess specifically to develop a relationship with him. I failed because you commanded all of his attention. You got yourself into this, and I suspect that you will be called upon to 'help' for the rest of your life, just like I am."

"You realize that once I meet this other man from Boeing, that he will probably not offer much that is specific about the project. All I am going to learn will be general information."

Pa lit a cigarette, something that Molly hated in her apartment. "Once you size him up, we can develop a plan to find out more. We will research his life. Everyone has a weakness."

"Just so you and Wang realize, me sleeping with Andy's friend would probably set him off. He is very bright, and it won't take him long to figure out that I played him. That could only lead to problems."

"I will pass on your concerns. In the interim, you will become a respected doctor just as you dreamed instead of the daughter of a factory worker, a girl in a uniform, a short skirt with lusty businessmen always pestering you for dinner."

Molly walked over to where Pa sat, gently taking the cigarette from his mouth and crushing it out in the soil of a grape ivy plant. "I will play this game with you, but you are wrong on one thing. Someday, I will figure out how to rip away the net you have thrown over me."

Pa smiled. "Perhaps you won't need to. What could a medical doctor offer that would justify her future service? In the interim, and even if you are released, remember that the people running this operation will destroy you if you turn on them. Either that or just kill us both."

CHAPTER 11

CAMP DAVID

GRITT'S ARRIVAL THE next morning interrupted a meeting between the three top executives of the CIA and Walker. The guard who escorted him to the dining room warned him "those gray hairs might be a bit touchy that morning since the four of them had been up late into the night requesting a second bottle of Knob Creek Bourbon at midnight." Gritt had seen how different people in the Navy answered the stress of critical threats and shrugged off a bit of discomfort in the "process" being used in Camp David.

Chang rose as Gritt stepped through the door, Winchester issuing a slight growl before recognizing the newcomer.

"We're having bacon and eggs, a good old camp-ground high grease and cholesterol breakfast. Join us if you'd like or the chef here can probably make almost anything appear."

Chang extended his hand.

Gritt shook it and then circled the small round table greeting Wilson, Taylor and Walker. "I'm a guy who grew up in hunting camps in Alaska. Bacon and eggs sound great."

A waiter in a white linen coat finished refilling coffee cups, handing a full one to Gritt who was still standing. "On the way; ten minutes at most," the waiter offered, as he left the room.

"Thad asked for you to be his number two on this project," said Chang. "The secretary of Navy has loaned you to us for as long as we need you and for as long as you will stay. For the next week you will be here and after that it will all depend on the plan. That okay with you, Lieutenant?"

"Yes sir." He turned to Thad. "Just what will I be doing, sir?"

"Figuring out just exactly what we are dealing with and then fixing this damned mess."

Gritt slid into the fifth chair at the table. "I'm a bit out of my league here."

"We don't think so, son," replied Thad. "The first task is to put together a team. One or more people to help with the following." He looked down at a graph pad that he preferred over a standard yellow pad. "We need someone who can help us envision the sub configuration. We need someone to map out all of the spots where we are vulnerable. We need a special ops person to help develop a plan to visit every site to uncover any breaches without alerting the world to what we are looking for. Finally, we need someone with extensive China experience to see if there are any Irish Pennants on the Chinese side, threads that we can pull to unravel their secrets." Chang flipped to the next page of his pad. "With any luck, we will also need to recruit one of the special operations teams to provide a little muscle where needed." He went back to his breakfast, hoping that the starch, protein, and grease would soak up the unused alcohol still twisting his stomach.

"What do you want me to do, specifically?" asked Gritt, as the waiter slid a huge plate of eggs, bacon and hash browns in front of him, and picked up the empty plates of the others.

"By tomorrow we will have a half dozen resumes for each of these tasks. You will help us select the team, but once they are on board, you need to understand that many of those selected will outrank you or will come with lengthy resumes." Walker stopped and studied the young officer. "As of this meeting, we will ignore rank and operate on the same model as the Israeli Air Force. You are the quick and nimble one in the group, the one without any specialty to defend, you will lead our attack."

Gritt hadn't eaten more than two Cliff Bars since he'd left the day before. He finished chewing a mouthful of egg-soaked potato before responding. "Okay? And then?"

"Once we get the new people working on their tasks, you and I are going to start brainstorming how we can take all of the bad guys success and use it ourselves. We will develop a library of what they know. If we can't do that, we will figure out how we can let them continue to snoop, but only see what we want them to see."

"Didn't the U.S. do something similar when we found the Russians snooping into our tech companies back a few decades?" asked Gritt.

Walker smiled at the others. "Yup, son, and the way we handled it was to allow the bastards to continue to snoop, but only on things we wanted them to see. We loaded Russia with technology that either had a virus we could exploit or that would fail in a critical situation. They never completely recovered."

The five of them spent the entire day pouring through resumes, finally settling on two candidates to head each of the tasks. They brainstormed interview questions that would help arrive at final choices, questions that would test a candidate's willingness, time commitment, and abilities without disclosing the problem or mission. Chang's personal administrative assistant made up a sixth for dinner that night. She spent the rest of the night on the phone contacting the candidates and arranging transport to Washington D.C. for those from out of town. By midnight she had six candidates scheduled. Each had been enticed by the same simple message. "The President of the United States is interested in meeting you and seeing if you are willing to commit a few months to a project that is one of his highest priorities. Your trip and the visit will be completely confidential and not to be discussed or disclosed to anyone. If you are selected, you will start immediately, and any problems created by your absence and new tasks will have to be taken care of later. Are you willing to be in D.C. tomorrow afternoon to find out more?"

The last candidate to arrive was Army General Lisa Johnson, the youngest general officer in the American military and current intelligence liaison to the Nationalist Government on Taiwan. Her trip to D.C. had required her to strap herself into the second seat of a Navy F-18 Hornet fighter that raced across the Pacific, refueled in the air by Air Force tanker aircraft launched from Fairbanks and Washington state. From Naval Air Station Whidbey Island, she somehow managed to get her cramped and tortured body working well enough for a bathroom break and a light meal before a second F-18 began the long trip to D.C. She arrived in the nation's capital just in time for the second helicopter shuttle to Camp David.

That night, all six candidates were registered for rooms at the Country Inn and Suites only a mile from Andrews Air Force Base in Maryland, where the helicopter rides to Camp David originated. The six candidates were back in their rooms before ten that night. Two Air Force vans arrived the next morning. One took the three candidates that would not be part of the team to a breakfast at the White House where the President thanked them for their time and assured them that they might be called upon later. The other van drove the selected candidates to a mall where they were told that they needed to purchase enough casual clothing and other needed items to spend ten days back at Camp David. Two hours later they were on the helicopter back to the Maryland retreat, each studying a suggested script to advise their work and family that they would be gone for a couple of weeks, possibly more.

Joining Gen. Johnson was Dr. Macey Davis, a former Navy

captain and now head of bio-technology research at Woods Hole National Oceanographic Institute, and Col. Bob Phillips. Bob was career Air Force and a member of the team that kept track of America's nuclear weapons and a former member of the team that scoured the world for locations of other countries' nuclear arsenals. The three sat on the helicopter staring at each other trying to figure out what they had in common.

Landing at Camp David, they were welcomed by Gritt, and Chang's assistant. Each was asked to sign a detailed non-disclosure agreement, reflecting that their government would have no qualms about making their lives a living hell if anything about their pending mission leaked.

Their first briefing from Chang was short and extremely concise.

"You three were selected to assist your government contain a highly technical Chinese intelligence effort. Within a few days you will be read into a new American defensive system that may change the overall balance of power in the Pacific, one that is vulnerable to the Chinese intelligence effort. The team being assembled will be on a first name basis with no emphasis on rank or prior service. Our sole focus will be on the threat. Any questions?"

Chang didn't wait for an answer before continuing. "Lisa, your initial task is to develop a dossier on who in the Chinese government may be responsible for the technology and on any potential human targets or database targets that we can engage to get a hard reading on the technology itself. If you can't identify specific people, start defining a list of target facilities."

Turning to Macey, he continued. "You three are about to see a presentation from the Navy. It represents what I personally believe is an accurate assessment of the Chinese technology and the types of targets they are attacking. Our belief is that the espionage has been facilitated by the use of a truly unique and undetectable submarine. Your initial task is to take what little we already know and research just how this underwater vehicle operates, its characteristics and systems. Please prepare your best guess at just what this thing is. Once you get a read on how it is being used, you will start work on how we can confirm just how this thing operates."

"Bob," continued Chang, "you are probably America's best mind on finding things that aren't supposed to exist or in evaluating disclosed things that have been under-counted or otherwise concealed. Your task here is to evaluate what the Navy already knows, and then develop a model for where else the Chinese may have already penetrated or are likely to attack. We already have one site in mind. If we can find the pattern, we can probably limit the damage from existing snooping and develop defenses or counter measures for future sites." Chang turned to Walker. "Thadius here will be the point man on this effort. He will be the one you go to when you need resources or access. His job is to turn this pile of shit into fertilizer. That is, to figure out how we make this obvious failure actually work for us. Barring that, he is tasked with simply stopping it."

"Mr. Gritt here will be your go to for resources that you cannot access from here. By tomorrow I will have a specialist on cover stories available here who will help you develop correspondence without disclosing any part of the mission." Chang popped the tab on a can of Pepsi and consumed a third of it. "Mr. Gritt, you may commence with your slide show."

Macey turned to the other two newcomers. "And, that ladies and gentlemen is how you cut all of the fluff and bullshit out of a briefing."

CHAPTER 12

BEIJING

LING SAT IN the deep, padded chair in his office overlooking the sprawl of Beijing. The offices of PLA2 were utilitarian and large enough for the staff that tracked China's international human intelligence efforts. His superior had made clear that he expected a more accurate and comprehensive analysis of the new American facility on Kiska Island, which most analysts believed was a laser weapon facility. Ling had already discussed the problem with General Liu, requesting as much electronic intelligence as Liu's group had on the subject, and asking him to retarget his limited resources to that subject. Liu had just stared at him, finally making it clear that he was already working the problem. Ling was more than willing to share any success with Liu but wondered if his counterpart felt the same.

Neither of them wanted to involve the young hothead, Yang unless it was critical. Yang was already the fair-haired boy of the party. His boldness, what some regarded as recklessness, might just turn this difficult problem into a crisis, especially if special-forces people that he loved to deploy were caught or his EEL submarine detected.

Ling began to tap on his computer keyboard. A rudimentary plan was forming in his head; one that required research into what foreign assets could be brought to bear on the problem. He was deeply worried that the two assets already tasked in Seattle lacked the depth of contacts to give him what he needed to keep the director off his ass. Perhaps it was time to call on one of his deep plants, a professor at San Diego State. She'd been a grad student there and through extraordinary effort managed to land a visiting professor's job after finishing her doctorate in computational sciences, adding it to her doctorate in philosophy from China's prestigious Zhejiang University.

Lia Chen had not been one of his original recruits, more of a target of opportunity. Her unique combination of studies created opportunities in California's liberal education environment. Combining philosophy and mathematics made Lia a real novelty, her classes were packed, and she embraced that with about 75 percent of her heart.

The other quarter of her heart belonged to Ling, not as a lover or anything close. Lia's twin sister's passion was science, specifically biological sciences. She had been part of a team that identified the virus behind a deadly outbreak in Huludao Province that went from unknown to killing hundreds of people in three months. If the disease was not controlled, there might be a worldwide pandemic. Lia's sister made the mistake of making the risk public, meeting with a group from the World Health Organization then touring China. The news of the epidemic got out before the regional government or national government was prepared to deal with either the disease or the public fear. That had been three years before. Charges of "creating a public panic" landed Lia's sister in a local prison that housed mostly violent criminals.

Ling had seized the opportunity to add a charge of "assisting foreign powers in defaming China." He'd leveled the charge privately, only to Lia and her sister in a meeting where the sister was released from solitary confinement for the first time in six months. Lia had agreed to "help China in any way," as long as the new charges were not filed; they would have extended the existing sentence of ten years to twenty.

Up until this moment, Ling had never called on Lia. But San Diego was home to America's foremost corporation developing laser weaponry. Ling didn't know whether KRATOS TECHNOLOGY had anything to do with the new Kiska facility, but most of his analysts believed that the site had something to do with laser weaponry and the San Diego corporation was America's expert in the field. They had surprised the world ten years before when they rolled out a fully field-ready laser system now deployed across America's Navy.

Before he would approach Lia, Ling needed to ensure that she recognized how important her new tasks were. He picked up his phone and asked his assistant to track down the man he referred to as Ma. Ling knew the man's full name but had developed a habit of using only his nickname. He'd removed Ma from the military hierarchy by making him his special projects director. Ma was not the kind of man who you would choose as a friend, but he had never failed. Twenty minutes later his phone rang. Two hours after that, Ma was on a flight to Huludao.

The credentials that Ma presented to the prison warden gave him anything that he wanted. What he wanted was a private room with one chair. He wanted the prisoner Lou Chen in the room within twenty minutes and some form of stand where he could place his phone to record a conversation with the prisoner.

Lou was escorted into the room wearing simple cotton pajamas, which emphasized her frail body. Her buzz cut hair did nothing to hide her sunken eyes and cheeks.

"Miss Chen, started Ma, "we are going to have a short conversation, one that will reach your sister within days."

Lou began to smile.

Ma slapped her across the face, and then backhanded her again, leaving her cheek and nose bleeding; her left eye swelling. "Do not misunderstand me," spat Ma, "this conversation will have only one purpose and that is to assure that your sister does exactly what General Ling asks of her."

Lou Chen pulled her hands from her bloody face, glaring at Ma through her tears.

"Good," said Ma, "now tell your sister just what life in this hole is like for you. Make sure that you mention what happens if we think you are not doing exactly what is asked of you. Let her know that your treatment will be her responsibility." Ma reached out and grabbed the young woman's nose and twisted until he heard it crack.

Ten minutes later, Lou Chen was on the way to the infirmary, and Ma was on his way to the airport. Even with the traffic, his entire stay in Huludao was less than three hours, and he was confident that the video of his meeting with Lou would insure her sister's cooperation. This mission would take him back to California, his second favorite place in the world.

CHAPTER 13

LOS ANGELES

THE CHINESE CONSULATE in Los Angeles could have sent a car to meet Ma at LAX, but he'd already informed them that he preferred to drive. He liked the small, boutique car rentals, where he wouldn't have to choose from a Ford something or a Toyota whatever. His expense budget for this mission was virtually unlimited. An hour after leaving customs he dropped his tourist style aluminum suitcase behind the seat of a Corvette and guided the car out of town and onto I-5 and headed south. He'd avoided any contact with the consulate hoping to avoid the mandatory FBI surveillance focused on the facility and staff.

Two hours later, he steered the car into a secure parking lot in San Diego's North Park district, handing the keys and a $20 bill to the young man who ran to meet him. A minute later he entered the pass code he'd memorized that let him into the cozy garden suite he'd rented online. He knew that it would be available since it was owned by one of his agents. He'd made only one stop on the drive, a five-minute diversion to pick up a couple of burner phones. Ma was tired after the long flight. He popped another of the pills disguised as Bayer aspirin that PLA-2 offered to all of their field people and dialed Dr. Chen's number.

"Dr. Chen, I'm an associate of your sister, and when I left her yesterday, she asked if I would track you down while I was in San Diego."

Lia sat quietly, her phone next to her ear, instant fear spreading across her face.

"Lia, can you hear me?" asked Ma.

"Yes."

"Good. I know your last class was more than an hour ago. I suggest that I pick you up at your apartment in a half-hour. I'd like to take you to dinner. I prefer someplace outdoors, overlooking the ocean. You figure out where we are going while I'm on the way. Dress like we are celebrating."

Lia began to overcome her shock, at least enough to answer. "Okay."

Less than thirty minutes later her phone rang again. "Dr. Chen, I am waiting in the black Corvette in front of your building. Please leave your phone on and in your apartment when you come down."

Lia slid into the seat of Ma's rented sport car, strangely surprised by Ma's tall-lean physique and movie-star looks. His English was almost flawless.

Ma handed her the second burner phone directing her to a discreet online address. "Click on the icon at the top left and enter 91919," he ordered.

Lia was shocked at the site of her sister flashing onto the page. The initial few seconds were terrible, but it got worse. After a break of only a few seconds, Lou's face reappeared; this time blood dripped from her lip and cheek. Her nose was clearly broken, making it hard to talk, as she wiped the blood running down her upper lip and into her mouth. Lou's message could not have been more clear.

"You didn't have to hurt my sister to get me to cooperate," she whispered through tears and chattering teeth.

"Dr. Chen, neither I nor our country have time to discuss or debate what needs to be done. We need for you to be completely focused, and you must understand that you cannot fail." He carefully unfolded a handkerchief he'd slipped from an envelope and handed it to Lia. "Here, wipe away those tears, we're supposed to be celebrating."

Lia unfolded the cloth, revealing large reddish-brown stains. She almost snapped her neck, as she recoiled from her sister's dried blood.

"Now that I have your attention, you must focus on what is needed," said Ma.

Ma waited for the pretty thirty-year old woman with her American-style short bobbed hair to calm before he turned the key. More horsepower than any normal human could use in a city rumbled to life. "Now where are we having dinner?" he asked.

Again, the parking valet gladly accepted the keys and a twenty from the obviously wealthy Asian couple, as they entered a large restaurant's packed waiting area. Ma extended his arm to Lia as he approached the podium.

"How long for a waterfront table?" he asked.

"Without a reservation, probably two hours," answered a tan blonde woman.

Ma slipped a hundred-dollar bill into the woman's hand and pointed to the reservation list. "I swear that Dr. Chen's reservation is there somewhere. Would you please see if you can find it?"

The woman slipped the bill into the pocket of the tight shorts she wore and picked up two menus, waving to a man across the room. "Robert is our wine steward; he will be happy to recommend something exquisite for your special occasion." Turning to the man who approached the podium, she continued, "Robert, these folks are celebrating, and I am sure that the gentleman will be very generous if you could escort them to table nine and suggest something appropriate for their occasion. I am seating them in Margaret's section."

Ma peeled two more bills from his clip and discretely handed it to the woman. "If possible, we'd appreciate a little privacy for the next hour or so."

Their corner table overlooked the Pacific; potted palms and flowering vines giving them a small amount of privacy on the crowded terrace. Ma smiled as the couple at the closest table left and nobody bothered to buss it. "I thought all you people worked to keep a low profile," chanced Lia. "You, on the other hand like to make an entrance."

Ma smiled. "Perhaps being a little bold and right out front can make the other side less suspicious." He unbuttoned the second button of his shirt and used a napkin to wipe the sweat from his brow. "It's a bit warmer hear than in Huludao where your sister lives. Shall we order?"

Lia struggled with her shrimp scampi, her appetite disappearing with Ma's phone call and even more after meeting him. His description of some kind of doomsday weapon that the Americans were developing that would render China's arsenal worthless, virtually ensuring an American attack seemed like nonsense. It didn't make any difference. Lia knew that how she responded to Ma controlled her sister's fate and probably her own.

Ma seemed to be enjoying all of this. He finished his meal of snapper almost before she had started, without even slowing his conversation. Other than keeping his voice low, he seemed to care less about the other patrons around them. "This Kratos company is right here in San Diego. Our analysts believe that they must be deeply involved in the development of any new American laser weapon. Unfortunately, we have no sources inside the company so I cannot direct you to any one person to confirm their involvement. Finding someone will be your first task. Then we need to know the capacity of the new weapon, what it is capable of doing. Finally, we need to know when it will be operational.

Lia tried again to chew, struggling to eat. Ma ordered her to eat, explaining that they were supposed to be celebrating, and she just sitting there would eventually draw attention. She swallowed, fighting to keep the food down.

"I am not capable of deciphering the exact scientific workings of any such weapon," she said. "Laser technology is a unique engineering challenge, one that I am not competent in."

"For now, we are not asking you to determine how the weapon works, only to define what it may be able to do. You may, of course, use your exceptional engineering mind to learn about such technology, and someday we may need for you to dig deeper. But for now, the task seems fairly simple."

"How do I figure out who might offer the information you require?"

"Use your research skills but be careful not to dig too deep. Don't leave a large footprint, one that will trigger a response to your search. Subscribe to technical journals and websites. Read the paper. Americans can't keep their mouths shut. You will find what you need." Ma lifted his glass of chardonnay. "You and your sister really don't have any other options, do you?"

"I will do what you ask."

"And, Dr. Chen, do not try to deceive me. We have other sources researching the same information. What you give us will be checked against what they send. All of it will be reviewed by the technical staff at PLA-4."

"Do you have any questions?" asked Ma as he pulled up in front of Lia's apartment building after dinner.

"No."

"Good." Ma pulled the second burner phone from his pocket and handed it to Lia. "In the next couple of days, someone affiliated with the Chinese Consulate will contact you on this phone. They will be your primary contact. They can answer questions and offer limited support, but this is your project. I entered my new phone number in the memory under the name of Mark Me. Do not contact me until you have a hard target. Prepare for any call you make on this phone and under no circumstances talk for more than one minute. Do you understand?"

"Yes."

"Finally, whoever you target must see the relationship as personal. It may be collegial or friendship or whatever, but they cannot feel that what they tell you is a violation of their security. It is very important that the Americans do not know we are targeting this island project in the Aleutians."

"I understand." Lia pushed the door open and stepped onto the curb. Her fear and anguish were slowly giving way to anger. She stared at Ma through the open window. "Pretty fancy car just to drive a few hundred miles and deliver a message."

"Oh, I'm not leaving San Diego just yet. I have an old girlfriend from college who lives in the area. I'm taking a few days off to see her. We may take a road trip. I will check in with you before I leave the country." Ma waved out the window, as he pulled away, just as if he were an old friend.

There were lights on in the top floor, end apartment of the North Park project, as Ma made his way to his rental. He'd left the window shade next to the front door open a few inches when he left, a battery-charging unit with an unusual blue LED on the table. It was a signal that he was back in San Diego, the only city on the west coast where the PLA had a real operating intelligence operation.

The head of the cell was his old college girlfriend, a San Francisco woman with no real interest in politics but an insatiable appetite for wild sex and an even greater appetite for money. Polly McGregor was almost thirty, five-ten, and the epitome of the tanned surfer girl. She was a partner in and senior tour guide for a firm that specialized in bringing Asian groups to beaches, deserts, and the national parks of the Southwest. The job gave her a reason to travel across the region and to make contact with any group or company that might be of interest to her clients.

She'd met Ma at UC Berkley where she was a student in the Asian Studies department while Ma was a foreign exchange student in the American Studies program.

She spent the monthly stipend she received from the Chinese government traveling the world, sampling beaches at expensive resorts. They negotiated higher fees for more important work.

Ma hadn't even closed the door when Polly called, "I'm in the bedroom, lover."

CHAPTER 14
MARYLAND

GRITT WAS SHOCKED by how fast the team was jelling, constantly pushed by Walker's, "Let's all think like what we are doing might stop world war three." Chang and the two deputies were back in their offices, his admin assistant the only one still with the group that now called itself Team Walker. The young naval officer, Chad, was a perfect offset to the graying Thad, his analytical approach balancing the older man's instincts honed by five decades of service. The staff referred to them as the Chad and Thad couple except when presenting to the CIA senior staff when they used the formal, Lt. Chad Gritt and Senior Officer Thadius Walker.

They'd moved to a suite of offices in a vacant building surrounded by landscaped grounds near Andrews Air Force Base. The firm that had previously occupied the building had suddenly moved, almost as if someone had directed it. Within three days of the move, the six had become a staff of twenty as other recruits went through the interview and screening process.

Gritt and Walker sat in the tiny break room. Walker munched on a donut while the younger Gritt spread cream cheese on a whole-wheat bagel.

"I never realized just how many people in this country have high security clearances," offered Thad. "Seems they multiply like flies on a hot summer day. Twenty years ago, only a handful had clearances."

"Seems a little nuts to me too," replied Gritt. "We filled in the team without submitting a single one to a screening. But it saved time, weeks probably." He finished his bagel.

"General Johnson will have three operatives ready for cover stories by next week," added Gritt. "Two of them will be traveling to Huludao Province in China as tourists working on a travel book. The shipyard in Huludao is where the Chinese build submarines. The other will be attending a communications product fair in Beijing as a sales engineer. We will pump up his profile with stories about his former work at a company that is an MIT partner. Maybe we will add a stint at DARPA. Lisa is working on selecting the company now."

"That's fast work. It matches the General's profile. Maybe we will get lucky and one of our fishermen will land a contact who can help," replied Thad. "What's on the agenda for our afternoon session with Macey?"

"He's been brainstorming and the submarine designer brought in from the Navy Weapons Lab have a couple of concept drawings they want to show us."

"Great," offered Thad. "I'll take Winchester for a walk and be ready to go by two. In the interim, we need to refocus our attention on how we completely turn the tables on the Chinese."

"I agree, but I think any plan is a bit premature until we have more data," answered Gritt.

Walker used his cane to lift his body out of the plastic chair. "Perhaps, but the real data we need is in the two briefing papers that Director Chang and Jana Taylor sent over. The PLA has been pretty damned consistent in how they handle these problems. Once they get their teeth into something that they see as a real threat, they will pull out all of the stops to penetrate the project. If they can't learn enough by hacking, they will move to more aggressive research."

"They won't want to start a war," replied Gritt.

"Hell, son, you can count on them leaving a line of crumbs that point right at Russia or North Korea. They are really good at that, but if they see a big enough threat, they aren't above a little skirmish. I'm not kidding when I say we may be able to stop world war three."

"Well as of today, the Chinese just seem to be casting a wide net. Based on the penetrations we know about; I doubt that they have seen anything that scares them shitless."

"We may have to sweeten the bait," replied Thad. He called to his dog.

"Jesus," replied Gritt, "the Air Force is already going nuts about our involvement with that project in Alaska. What can we offer that won't send them into convulsions?"

"Young Mr. Gritt, the services always are nuts about their next big project. I'm not quite sure how you were allowed to take your concerns to the Agency, but the Navy allowed it. Our job is to protect the good old USA, and Director Chang, myself and the President could give a damn if what we are doing tromps on a few toes." Walker's dog raced through the open door almost losing part of its tail as Walker slammed the door behind them.

At two in the afternoon, Dr. Macey Davis and the new engineering assistant Oliver Levitt flipped the page on an old-fashioned chart pad and began.

"Thad, Chad, we think this damned Chinese sub is probably one of three configurations. The first two concepts we will show you, depend on the vehicle being deployed by some kind of mother ship. That would dramatically shorten the range requirements of the silent sub by eliminating the need to haul food, supplies and the fuel for long ocean crossings."

Macey flipped to the next page on the chart pad. "The other concept is far more complex but can literally move anywhere in the world on its own. It would need two types of propulsion, probably powered by some kind of small nuclear power system: one for high speed but still very quiet; and the other virtually silent for final approach to guarded targets."

The third page had a crude drawing that looked like a fat fish with a really long tail, a dorsal fin and large pectoral fins.

"This is one concept," offered Macey. "The propulsion is accomplished just as a fish swims, by moving the tail back and forth. Steering would come from movement of the fins. Twenty years ago, this configuration would require mechanical internal workings, probably powered by electricity. Today, with advanced engineered materials, introducing and eliminating electrical current directly into the materials could trigger the movements necessary to propel the sub. There would be no sounds whatsoever from the drive train."

Oliver Levitt rolled his wheelchair to the front of the room. "If the sub only had to cover relatively short distances, it would not need fresh water or oxygen producing technology, or the capacity to preserve food. In other words, with the exception of some way of flooding the buoyancy tanks to submerge or blowing them to rise, there would be almost nothing to hear."

Walker pointed at the drawing with his cane. "How fast could this thing move and how far could it go?"

"It depends on the size, but our thought is that it would have to be small, probably only big enough for a crew of three and the clandestine operators needed to do the job. Let's say a maximum of five or six people. Then my best estimate of speed would be five knots max and a round trip range of maybe three hundred miles."

"What would the mother ship look like?" asked Chad Gritt.

Anything from a large fishing trawler to a massive container ship could be configured to launch this sub from a specially designed moon pool in the bottom and recover it the same way. My bet would be a container ship that could be legitimately sent to nearby ports. It wouldn't trigger any questions." Macey flipped to the next page. "This is a different design, one using graphite materials with a propulsion system that would charge water coming into the front scoop of the sub and using electrical charging of the water to propel it from the back, providing propulsion."

The drawing looked like a 1950s MiG aircraft without wings, a huge opening in the front and nozzles that could be directed in the back. The top would probably be some clear material to facilitate observation.

Levitt picked up the conversation. "This would be easier to build and control, and like the other design, it would be very quiet, although probably not as quiet as the first drawing. The propulsion system has conceptually been around for decades. It is basically what Tom Clancy wrote about in his fictional *Red October* submarine. Depending on size, a mother ship similar to that we discussed earlier would be required. Specs would be similar due to the amount of space needed to house batteries."

Macey continued, "The limitations of these designs would be as follows." He moved to the next page. "Limited range, limited space, limited depth, probably less than fifty feet, limited capacity to carry crew or operators." He moved to the next page. "For a long-range boat, the quiet operation will require some form of propulsion system with baffles to control the noise. They will probably require some form of system that uses stationary vortices generators distributed in an enclosed space rather than a traditional vortices process using a spinning propeller. Such a system would require a lot of continuous electrical power, probably a small nuclear plant. The British have perfected ducted propeller propulsion systems that spin a propeller by moving a magnetic field around a ducted shield rather than a motor and propeller shaft. It could be very quiet compared to traditional propulsion, but there would still be some water cavitation noise. Such a system would allow greater top speed, but we do not consider it practical for this submarine."

The drawing looked like a traditional submarine without a propeller with two long tubes along the sides instead. While neither Gritt nor Walker really understood the idiosyncrasies of the vortex discussion, they got enough of it to recognize that no spinning propeller meant quiet.

Oliver picked up the conversation. "With limited size, this could be built to be very quiet, but you would still have the noise consistent with a reactor and power generation. This could get you from China to the West Coast in five days." Oliver shook his head slowly. "With our best technology however, this design could be detected. They would have to either carry long range mini submersibles for the final approach or there would have to be able to shut everything down and use batteries to power a final approach propulsion similar to the second boat we showed you. Overall, this design would be the easier to defense but we will have to substantially upgrade our sensor arrays."

Thad Walker looked over at Gritt with a smile. "What we know from this briefing is that this thing the Chinese built can do what we expect it does, but we really don't know how."

He turned back to the briefers. "What's your best guess?"

Macey looked over at Oliver Levitt but answered himself when Levitt remained quiet. "With at least six confirmed penetrations and not a single report of anything unusual, I'm betting on really silent, perhaps like the first drawing. If that is right, we can work on defense measures, but the best way to find this damned thing is to work the Mother Ship angle."

Walker stood, Winchester moving when he did. "You keep working on possible technology part of the day. See what else might work. Then I would like you two to begin thinking about detection measures." He turned to Chad. "We will task General Johnson's new hands to work the mother ship angle. Back in the

1970s, Howard Hughes built a ship called the *Global Explorer*, supposedly to explore for mineral nodules on the sea floor. Instead it was used to lift a wrecked Russian submarine. The world had no clue of its actual purpose. We need someone who thinks like that to help us define what this ship would look like, where it was built, and how to pick it out of the thousands of ships at sea. We will also need someone who can do a deep dive into the data to figure out if we can find one ship that was close to the areas that we know were penetrated within the timeline we are studying."

The young lieutenant rose, offering his hand to the two briefers. "Keep us in the loop daily. I'd like one or both of you to help me screen for the right folks to work on the new tasks." He turned back to Walker. "We need to give the agents that Lisa is recruiting something to look for before they go to China."

As the two briefers left the room, Walker motioned for Gritt to take a seat. "I'm going to read you into a top-secret project that I know just enough about to be dangerous. I'd like your feedback on whether it might be enough to prompt the Chinese to consider it the threat that would trigger their historical response. Based on this briefing, I am slowly coming around to thinking that we may have to actually get a look at the Chinese sub."

The younger man settled back into his chair, as did his mentor.

"To date we have touched on the Alaska facility. The truth is that it will control the most powerful narrow-beam laser ever built. It is designed to clear a swath almost three hundred miles wide of incoming missiles. It can hit high-flyers, cruise and even hypersonic missiles."

The younger man leaned forward, his hand covering his chin and cheek. "If we really have such a weapon, is it worth risking it to go after this sub?"

"Perhaps not the missions we are discussing with this team," replied Thad. "But while Director Chang and his team was here, Pete Wilson discussed an alternate use for that damned sub. "What if they convert it to a remotely guided device and load an atomic bomb on the thing? They could penetrate and park it in the harbor of any major city in the world. They win by simply announcing that a half dozen of these things exist and that attempting to penetrate into the sub or move it will detonate the bomb."

"We'd lose the first nuclear war without a single detonation," mused Gritt. "We could retaliate, but no president would risk losing New York, or San Francisco or Seattle."

CHAPTER 15
BEIJING

THE DIRECTOR OF the Strategic Support Force had been summoned by China's President. While China worked to modernize its Navy and Air Force, both with an eye on dominating Southeast Asia, it had staked its defense against the United States on a three-tiered missile approach. First were the traditional intercontinental ballistic missiles. Second were long-range cruise missiles or sea launched shorter-range devices. Last was a strong commitment to development of hyper high-speed missiles, capable of low altitude speeds of thousands of miles per hour. Such missiles were almost indefensible using traditional technology.

President Xi Jinping leaned across his huge desk, his eyes almost cutting through General Quing. "General, 50 percent of our military hardware budget is invested in missile technology. That was done to deter the Americans from interfering with our policy of dominating all of Southeast Asia and the waters along our borders. You seem convinced that the Americans are building a defensive laser site. If your assessment is correct and the Americans are building a laser that renders that deterrent worthless, we can count on the Americans interfering with our regional strategy.

Most of our neighbors will be afraid of China's power, and some can be bought off. However, some including our rogue province of Taiwan and Viet Nam, will push back if they have American backing. We will have to completely rethink our deterrent strategy and postpone our regional push until we can convince the Americans to stay on their side of the Pacific."

"I understand, Mr. President. Our analysis is based on really sketchy intel, but it is the only thing that seems to make sense."

"Do you understand that it also makes us vulnerable to their missile technology?"

"I understand, Mr. President. Perhaps it will require that we slow our regional ambitions until we develop counter measures."

"General, the problem with waiting is that the other nations in our region are developing rapidly, growing more wealthy. Within a decade, four or five of them together may develop conventional military strength to stand up to China. We will have lost the opportunity to control the petrochemical and mineral resources of the region, especially those in the South China Sea. We will have to pull our fishing fleets in closer to our own borders. In other words, we will feel the pressure of our own population developing with fewer resources than our planners feel we need." President Xi leaned back in his chair, his eyes still penetrating. "We need to know just what we are facing before the Americans perfect this one installation. Once it is fully operational, they may have the resources to clone such a site over and over, building an impenetrable laser barrier."

"We may need to develop new strategies to deter the Americans, sir," said Quing.

The President ripped his glasses from his face and threw them across the table. "That, General, could take another two decades. The Americans are much better at protecting their secrets than they were before they saw us as a threat. In the interim, we may not meet the development needs of our country. Already the American trade policies of the last decade slowed our growth and by moving their production elsewhere increased the development of the other southeast nations we have been discussing. Our country and the party are vulnerable to an unhappy population."

"Sir, I understand the complexity of the problem," replied Quing.

"Then, General, give me a hard report on just what the threat out in the Aleutians is. With that, we can plan. With that, we can develop counterstrategies. Perhaps it is worth a small confrontation to stop this menace and a larger confrontation later. With that report, I will not need to find a new director of the Strategic Support Force."

CHAPTER 16

SEATTLE

MOLLY WANG HAD debated how to dress for her lunch. Andy Burgess had called, announcing lunch reservations at a fancy waterfront restaurant, and he was bringing his friend who had just returned from Kiska Island. Molly finally decided on college kid attire, a pair of fairly tight jeans with a couple of holes in the legs and a fairly sheer black blouse over a black bra under a yellow cardigan style sweater. She needed to get this Chet Williams' attention without risking her relationship with Andy.

She found the two men leaning against the rail, talking and staring out at a Washington State Ferry on its way to the other side of Puget Sound. She loved Elliott's Oyster House but was pleased that they had waited for her outside on the wharf. Andy turned, grasping her hand. She thought he was about to kiss her on the cheek, but instead he turned to his friend.

"Chet, this is Molly."

Chet was younger than she had imagined, perhaps early thirties. He was tall and really thin, his clothes draping his body. He had bright blue eyes and flaming red hair, bottled up under a Seahawks ball cap. He extended his hand, meeting hers with a surprisingly firm grip. "It is a pleasure to meet you Miss Wang. I understand that you would appreciate a little coaching on lasers."

Molly wiped her brow with a Kleenex. She'd seen a bank sign on her way down from the train station that read seventy-nine degrees. It gave her just enough excuse to casually unbutton two more buttons on her sweater, revealing a bit more of her sheer blouse. "I would really appreciate it. I am contemplating making laser use in chemical and biological research the subject of my master's application." Molly caught Chet's momentary glance at her chest. He turned away; his face flushed.

Andy had missed it, his gaze momentarily trapped by a new Boeing 787 overhead, on approach to Sea Tac Airport.

"Let's eat, I'm starved. I had two early classes this morning and I haven't eaten all day," offered Molly.

Their lunch went about as Molly figured it would, with Andy anxious to please her by encouraging Chet into offer some tutorial. What she hadn't expected was Chet's shy demeanor and admission that he would be pleased to help any friend of Andy who he considered a very close buddy. Molly had done enough homework to engage in a rudimentary discussion of basic laser technology and Chet had confirmed what little she knew. Chet acknowledged that he had been working on a project in Alaska but offered no details.

They left lunch with an agreement for Chet to meet her Saturday morning at the public library up the hill from the waterfront. She'd learned that Chet was a bachelor and just watching how he was around a woman, she realized that it was not because he wanted to be. The man was painfully uncomfortable talking to a woman. "I want to make sure that Andy and I don't miss my flying lesson that afternoon," she'd said, realizing that Chet would never do anything to offend his buddy.

Their meeting at the library began with Chet discussing five pages of sketches and notes that he had compiled. She learned that there were different kinds of lasers and that some of the simplest, like penlight lasers, could be powered by small batteries. Others needed more power, with the most powerful including some that could actually reach the moon requiring a lot more energy. "The focus of the beam is all a function of the aperture of the laser itself," said Chet. "You need a really large aperture to create a tight beam that can maintain that focus over a distance."

Molly learned that some lasers produced a beam that was invisible.

"That could be useful in a military situation," Chet volunteered.

Molly casually asked about Alaska, learning that Chet had loved his time there, especially the stark beauty of the treeless windswept mountains of the Aleutians. As she slowly steered the conversation to Chet himself, she began to realize that the man craved wilderness, but almost desperately wished that he had someone to share it with. She also realized that he was fiercely loyal and that he found her relationship with Andy "incredible."

"What do you do to relax?" she'd asked, "I mean where do you go on vacations?"

"In the summer, I love backpacking and time in the mountains. In the winter, I try to find some very secluded small hotel in Mexico or Central America where I can snorkel or just sit on the beach and read."

"Always alone?" she'd asked.

"Almost always, unless I can tack on to some friends' plans."

Molly realized that she was not going to get anything of substance about the Alaska project from Chet, simply because there was no reason for him to discuss it. He would never consciously violate security commitments. After ninety minutes, she began to pack up her things. "Do you suppose we can meet again next Saturday and discuss the use of lasers on a tiny scale, the kind that can be used to study elements or even help create new substances?"

"It would be my pleasure, Miss Wang," he replied.

Molly began the long trudge up the hill to the light rail station.

She'd left her car at the apartment just in case, extending the meeting by suggesting that they grab an early lunch somewhere away from downtown. Even if she was ordered to seduce Chet, it would be an act of last resort, and based on her read of Chet, impossible anyway. It was clear that extending the meeting wouldn't help her learn about Kiska. She tugged her phone from her purse and dialed Pa's number.

"I have little progress to report," she offered, intentionally keeping the conversation vague. "I learned a lot about the subject but nothing about the application."

"Perhaps my friend and I can help you flesh in what you know," offered Pa. "We can come by this evening."

Molly smiled, as she stepped onto a northbound train. "I won't be available until Monday. I'm going flying, and I suspect that we will find something to do later." As concerned as Molly was about the situation that Ma had created for her, she still enjoyed rubbing his nose in her relationship with Andy.

"Then we will see you Monday evening at the regular time," replied Pa without a hint of jealousy.

❧

Andy rented the plane for two days. Molly had just enough time to pack an overnight bag before he picked her up. He'd rented a small oceanfront house in Westport along the Washington coast north of the mouth of the Columbia River. It gave Molly the opportunity to fly a complex map route out to a distance that would qualify for her cross-country solo later in the spring.

They finished the afternoon with a long beach walk.

As Andy built a fire in the woodstove, she opened a bottle of wine to go with the oysters, crab and vegetables they had picked up earlier. "How did your session go with Chet?" he asked.

"It went well. We're going to get together at the library again next week to discuss laser use on a micro level." She poured wine into two mismatched glasses she found in the cupboard and started toward where Andy had a small flame under a pile of kindling. She handed him a glass. "He is almost giddy over you and I being together. I think that he must be really lonely."

Andy stood and closed the door of the metal stove, the glass window in the front casting dancing shadows and lights across the floor. "Chet is as nice a man, as you could ever meet. He is just painfully shy unless he is talking about something that he knows inside and out."

Andy held out his glass, tapping Molly's. "Here is to us, even for a few months."

Molly stepped onto her toes and kissed him on the neck. "Have you ever been on one of Chet's trips?"

"Once, to a tiny village on the Sea of Cortez. The guy is an expert swimmer and diver, and he knows everything about the ocean and its creatures."

Molly grabbed Andy's hand and dragged him over to the kitchen counter. "Speaking of sea creatures, how about opening a few of the oysters?"

CHAPTER 17

SEATTLE

MOLLY FELT SORRY and a little disdain for Pa, but she feared his friend, who had somehow now become a part of her life.

Molly briefed the two men on her meeting with Chet Williams, realizing that most of what she had learned was about the man and not the project. "He is very shy, but I believe that he is an expert at almost everything he takes up. He really loves diving in Mexico or Costa Rica and places like that. I will keep trying to learn more about Kiska, but I don't think I am going to get much that helps. I am sorry."

Pa looked over at Wang who finished a cold Bud Light that he'd found in Molly's refrigerator. "You may have learned enough to help. I am going to contact a friend who recently arrived in the States. We will be back to you on Thursday or Friday before your next meeting.

⁂

Ma rolled over, trying to find the burner phone in the jumble of clothes and sheets. Only three people knew the number. Polly rolled over giggling, his phone between her breasts.

"One kiss on each nipple and you can have the damned thing."

"The things that I have to do," mumbled Ma, as he paid the bribe. "Hello," he mumbled, as he answered the phone.

"It's me," replied Wang, "I'll be on an Alaska Airlines flight arriving at 3:40 this afternoon. I'll meet you outside the check in doors."

"I'll be the guy in the Corvette," answered Ma.

"Is your friend Polly still around?"

Ma paused a few seconds, enjoying Polly blinking her lashes along his neck sending shivers down his spine. "Yes," he finally answered.

"Good," answered Wang. "She's the reason that I am coming down. See you in six hours."

"Who was that?" asked Polly. "It must have been an important call. I couldn't stop you from taking it."

"It was my primary contact, from Seattle, he's coming down this afternoon."

"Wow," exclaimed Polly, "is it that Pa guy? I can kind of get off on trying to do Ma and Pa at the same time."

Ma shook his head at her humor. No, it's a guy you have never met, Pa's boss."

Ma actually felt that he saw disappointment in the woman's face.

৩

The two men found an old-fashioned diner only a half hour from the airport.

"I'd like to catch a flight back tonight," offered Wang. "I wouldn't have come down, but one of Pa's recruits in Seattle had made contact with an engineer on the Kiska project. It doesn't look like she will be able to develop the kind of relationship that will yield any real information."

The two men occupied one of only three tables in use, both slowly working on cheeseburgers and fries as they talked.

"Still, that is progress. It is the first contact that we have developed with first-hand knowledge of the facility," replied Ma. "Can we help his retirement enough to give your recruit any leverage?"

"No, but perhaps your friend Polly can help. Our recruit describes the man as tall and gangly, lonely, and as shy around women as any man she has ever met."

"I'm not getting the connection," said Ma.

"Among the man's passions is anything to do with beaches and especially diving and snorkeling. When he is talking about any subject that he is an expert in, he's at ease. Your friend Polly is also a real beach nut, isn't she?"

Ma had briefed his top agent on the west coast on the resources at his disposal only two months before, when the Kiska issue had boiled over. They were thin on resources and both men realized that developing any real intelligence might require a rifle shot instead of a shotgun approach.

Strangely, Ma felt a touch of jealousy. "Yes. She could be just the one to help with this."

"I have a meeting with our recruit on Friday, and she is meeting with the target again on Saturday. Perhaps it is time for your Polly to have a new old friend in Seattle; one she just has to visit this weekend."

"Do you have photos of your agent and the target?" asked Ma.

Wang pointed at Ma's phone.

Ma opened a secure site that he and Wang used to exchange information. He studied two pictures for a few seconds. "Do you have any other ideas?"

"None right now."

"I'll track down Polly this evening. I think she will consider this a real challenge, especially if it includes adequate rewards. I'll call you in the morning and if this is a go, I'll post a picture and travel information."

Wang finished his burger and sat back in his chair. "If I am making your visit here in the states a little less pleasurable with my request, I am sorry."

Ma shook his head. "I have other concerns right now. Let me get you back to the airport. Are you on Alaska again?"

"No, I don't want to leave a clear trail, so I am flying Delta with a stop in San Francisco. I'll leave my Alaska return open for our next visit."

CHAPTER 18

VIRGINIA

THE LIMO SENT by Director Chang weaved its way through heavy traffic, finally rolling to a secure private entrance to the CIA headquarters. Walker and Gritt were escorted to the small conference room adjacent to the director's office where Pete Wilson and Jana Taylor met them.

"We'll wait for the director to finish his phone call before we get on to business," said Wilson. "I called this meeting after your man Bob Phillips briefed us this morning. He presented his initial assessment of where the Chinese have penetrated. Thanks for sending him so promptly."

"Col. Phillips felt that his findings might be scrubbed by some of the folks in your science and technology group," replied Thad. He smiled as he extended his hand first to Jana and then Pete. "Oh, by the way, we are all doing just fine."

Gritt found a chair next to Jana, a bit amazed by how this old hand was dealing with the top tier of American intelligence. 'When you have already cemented your legacy and retired, you have a lot of latitude,' he thought.

"Will Col. Phillips be returning with us?" he asked.

"Probably depends on the next hour," replied Jana.

Chang sailed into the room carrying only a yellow pad. "Hello all. Let's get to it."

Pete handed out a copy of Phillips' summary to the other four people in the room. "This is potentially a damning document. We will know as quickly as you can get a team out to confirm what Phillips surmises. He was a great pick, and his van Gogh mindset keeps his analysis and writing concise."

"Vincent van Gogh?" asked Gritt.

"Phillips is a huge art fan, and a bit of an expert on the artists and art of the early twentieth century," replied Chang. "The artist mentioned often described his technique as 'exaggerating the essential and leaving the obvious vague,' a fairly good approach for sorting out what is really important."

"You will all note that Phillips' report indicates that we are vulnerable in about sixty locations around the world. That includes about twenty-five on U.S. soil," said Wilson. "Using the exaggerate-the-essential strategy, he has ranked the sites based on what he feels are the most critical to the Chinese for technology, military awareness, or political reasons. He also made a couple of assumptions, the most important of which is that this Chinese sub probably has not been operational for more than ten years and that each mission would require planning, time to practice a mission, and execution time. He figures that we are already compromised at between eight and twelve locations."

The sheets provided had a dozen locations highlighted. "These are the first sites to be investigated," continued Wilson. "My troops ran up an additional red flag immediately after the Phillips briefing this morning. They are most worried about a site missing from Phillips' list."

"Hold it for a minute," interjected Jana, "shouldn't we send out the cavalry to, at least, investigate the submarine base in Washington, Diego Garcia, and those targets in Japan and Taiwan? We have a lot of intel that those are the locations most troubling to the Chinese."

"We will get to those sites in a minute," replied Wilson. "Tell me, do you all agree with Col. Phillips' assessment that the Chinese probably started with a couple of easy to penetrate sites to test the technology and then moved immediately to the sites that most concern them?"

Four heads nodded. "Good, my folks feel that he is probably spot on. Now if you look at the first four or five sites on the Phillips list, what do you see?"

In less than a minute, Director Chang flipped the pen he had clipped to his pad into the air. It came down and skittered across the conference table. "Every one of the priority sites deals with our military ability to interfere with their Southeast Asia doctrine. They are either sites where they need to track day-to-day activity close to the area of operations or where we may forward deploy weapons systems that give us a big advantage."

"So that first conversation that you and I had back on the Madison River is once again our highest priority," offered Thad. "Mr. Gritt and I have already been kicking this around."

Wilson opened a can of 5-hour ENERGY and chugged it. "It's been a long couple of days, and tonight looks like it will be a repeat." He took a deep breath. "Yup, there is no more critical site on our map than the laser facility being built on Kiska. Other than site prep and the construction of a couple of big buildings along with movement of crates of things being moved into those buildings, Chinese satellite surveillance will have shown them nothing. Their recon aircraft and ships are now frequenting the areas around Kiska. They have to be chomping at the bit to nail down the threat. By now they surely have figured out that the site is perfectly positioned to defense missile launches from northern China, Korea, and southeastern Russia."

Jana Taylor leaned back in her chair; her cheeks flushed a bit red in her otherwise makeup-less face. "It wouldn't be just that damned sub that we have to worry about. I'm sure that their hackers have been furiously trying to penetrate this project. The Chinese don't have much of a HUMINT intelligence presence in the States, but it is here. If this analysis is correct, and I think it probably is, they are pulling out all of the stops to penetrate every company with a hand in the Arctic Angel project."

Chang rose and wandered over to what is the probably the most secure window in the world. "Our original fears of a Chinese operation against Kiska are now going to dictate that we play defense. We must keep the Chinese away from verifying the threat until it is operational."

Gritt pointed over at Walker. Walker pointed back. "Go ahead, son, and share our thoughts on this Arctic Angel problem."

"We briefed all of you earlier about some ideas of how to use the Chinese snooping to give them faulty or misleading information. We won't know just how to do that until we have an inventory of what they have planted. We need to begin sending teams immediately to survey the sites. Our reading of Col. Phillips' report certainly gives us the sites to prioritize." He opened the laptop that had become part of him and tapped a couple of keys. "We probably need to be read into the hard data on this Kiska site before we can recommend a final course of action."

"I will need to get Air Force sign off before I can assure you that is going to happen," replied Chang. "But let's assume for a minute that you get that; what do you think it will say?"

Gritt just shook his head, unsure how to answer the question.

Walker, smiled and leaned back in his chair realizing that the conversation had just drifted into a category that he called *sniffing poop*. "Here is what I think we will learn. The site has at least one high-powered – probably nuclear-powered – laser." He paused a moment. "Or maybe more than one. It is supported by some form of aerial surveillance or detection capability that can detect enemy missiles at any height or speed and direct their demise at the speed of light. Everything within range would be toast, which forces our enemies to go around the site to hit the good ol' U.S.A. That would only work until additional sites are built."

Chang started to laugh. "That would make for a damned important target for the Chinese. The faster they can define the threat, the faster they will begin developing countermeasures, maybe even weaponing this sub."

"I agree; we need to protect this site at all costs," added Jana, "at least long enough to insure it works and get more sites built to wrap a laser net around the country."

Walker turned to Chang. "I noted your word 'will' when you mentioned counter measures. I am going to make the assumption that word has significantly different meaning than 'they may have to' or something similar. At any rate, our thought is that we may be looking at this all wrong."

He had the group's attention. "As we discussed earlier, we may want to use the Chinese surveillance system to feed them bad data. Thad and I believe that the Kiska site is too valuable to compromise, but it is also the perfect project to feed the enemy misleading information. Even more, nailing down this sub could be more important than one more source of misinformation. With the right bait, we may kill two birds with one stone. We can protect the actual capabilities of the site while luring the Chinese into using their secret sub in a way that we learn enough about it to keep it from being weaponized. Even if they know we've compromised the sub, they won't know that we have identified the locations where it's already planted devices. If we can detect it, the threat of using it to park nuclear weapons in our harbors is greatly diminished."

Jana leaned forward, folding her hands on the table. "Sounds logical to me, but just how in the hell do you manage the situation closely enough to control the movement of this sub without risking technology that Uncle Sam has invested billions in?"

Walker reached behind his back, retrieving a small leather pouch. He opened the Velcro opening and laid a plastic reproduction of a snub-nosed Ruger 9mm pistol on the table. "This ladies and gentlemen is a 3-D reproduction of a deadly close-in weapon. Most of you would perceive it as a threat if it was pointed at you."

Chang glared at Walker. While he was trusted and fully cleared, it still bothered Chang that Walker had managed to carry a weapon into the executive offices. But he didn't say a word, knowing that his old friend would explain it.

"If I wanted you to worry about this, I would do just what I did," Walker said. "I would let you know that I am carrying it and that right this minute you are completely vulnerable. I wouldn't do any more than just show this to you. You might try to wrestle the weapon away from me. In fact, I know enough about all of you to know that you would try it if you thought it would save your own life or that of our colleagues. What you don't know is that this weapon is completely operational but flawed. Also, the first bullet is designed to blow up if you happened to wrestle the gun away from me. It probably wouldn't kill you if you pull the trigger, but the weapon would be destroyed along with your hand."

Gritt had no idea that Walker was planning this show. He sat frozen for a few seconds before commenting. "I would have no choice but to try to keep you from killing us all."

Walker went back to his notes for a second. He jacked the first round out of the gun and passed it to Pete Wilson. "Someone in the department you now head built this bullet twenty years ago. I carried it for years. Never had to use it. Never lost my gun to a bad guy. As most of you know, I could never point a gun at anyone and pull the trigger. Like young Mr. Gritt says, someone would likely step up to try to stop me from shooting because they think I would shoot." He pointed at Gritt. "You want to finish your briefing?"

"The key is for us to show just enough of this Arctic laser thing to ensure that the Chinese have to act. They aren't going to drop a nuclear bomb on the island or launch an all-out invasion of Kiska. After all, we still advertise that what is being built is part of the development of the Maritime Park." They will use their best tools to define the risk."

He looked over at Walker. "We had discussed letting them steal some fake reproduction, but until just now, I didn't know we'd make the damned thing blow up. The technology that we fed to the Russians decades ago led to major failures in several of their systems, even an explosion of a pipeline in Siberia." He'd already developed a great respect for Walker even as the man continued to surprise him. "If we do this right, they will use all of their tools, and when they still don't have a clear picture, they will use the sub. We just need to be ready to learn everything we can about it when they do."

"What are the risks?" asked Chang.

"Well," started Walker, "we may already be a minute late and a dollar short. If they have sniffed out enough about Kiska to have operations underway, they may already have what they need. We need to screen every government and contractor's data system for breeches. We need to make sure critical players understand the risk. We need to screen for soft contact by Chinese operatives." He turned to Jana. "That's where you can help us. We need to know just how your Operations Group would attack this problem right up to the moment when the decision to use the sub becomes mandatory."

"I hate the word mandatory," responded Jana, "but I assume you think whatever plan we develop will be similar to that of the Chinese."

"I'm sure that your group is developing parallel strategies to ours," replied Thad. "You are working on how to get a hard finding on the Chinese sub. We could take that plan and reverse it to anticipate what they are doing to us. That lets us mix a little offense in with a defense."

Mat Chang tilted his head, studying the ceiling of the room. "Ladies and gentlemen, when the President asked me to take this job, he had only one direct order. Her told me that the primary role of the intelligence community was to avoid a catastrophic war at all costs. Let us keep that in mind as we make decisions." He took a minute to study the people in the room. "With the exception of Lt. Gritt, every one of us has seen a carefully crafted plan go to shit in seconds. We do our best now, but in the end, it may be a final field decision that keeps us out of a conflict with the Chinese."

CHAPTER 19

MARYLAND

THE LIEUTENANT COMMANDER could have passed for any normal all-pro linebacker in the NFL. His muscles literally rippled the front of the pull over shirt he wore, and his arms were the size of some men's legs. His demeanor however was completely the opposite of that you would expect from a man who physically could tear your head off with his bare hands.

"I was told that you gentlemen have an assignment for my team," he said as he slid into a chair across from Gritt and Col. Phillips. "Team Four has been on the beach for months now, so a little jaunt away from Little Creek will be welcome. As much as we appreciate time home with our families, little league practice and school chorus presentations are growing a bit tame for us."

The man pulled a stick of Dentine from his shirt pocket, unwrapped it and popped it in his mouth. "How can Seal Team Four help you gentlemen?"

"Carl," started Gritt, "the old stodgy guy next to you is an Air Force colonel. He goes by Bob. I'm Navy like you. My name is Chad. Bob and I are working on a major intelligence fuckup, primarily from what I can see, a Navy fuck up. We need your guys to help us get a hard read on how big the screw up is without telling anyone what you are actually doing. We will be the only two people who need to know what you find. I'll let Bob here explain the problem as he probably has the best read on the scope available."

For thirty minutes, Bob Phillips briefed the Commander on the defined penetrations of American facilities and on his list of other probable targets. "Commander, I know better than to tell you how to attack this problem," said Phillips as he wrapped up, "but in the name of speed you may need to divide up your team to cover the plowed ground as quickly as possible."

Carl stuffed a third stick of Dentine into his mouth. "What are we looking for?"

Gritt handed the Commander several captioned photos, explaining where and how they were found. "You will know it when you see it. The areas to be searched are all adjacent to where men in your profession can slip out of the water to plant the device. For the devices to work, they need to be able to send their findings out over commercial data circuits or using some transmission or recording like they used at Newport News Shipyard."

Carl stopped taking notes. "You know that we have devices that can send burst transmissions to satellites or even to cell phone sites for transmission."

"You're right," replied Chad, "I guess you are looking for anything that isn't supposed to be there. Something that your commanders would ask you to plant to study China or Russia."

"Based on your security strategy, I understand that no locals are to be informed on what we find."

"That is correct," answered Chad. "Your cover will be that you have been directed to do thorough base security sweeps. Notify Bob here of when you are departing to each target. He will ensure that the proper introductions and clearances are transmitted to the base commander prior to your arrival. He will also arrange transport. We will use military transport to every site that you cannot drive to. Again, Bob will set it up."

"How soon do we start?"

"This afternoon would do," offered Phillips. "I suggest that you start with a thorough sweep of the Newport News location. The fiber-optic cable in the photo is still in place and you may find additional installations. You will report to me in person as your team members use your own secure communications to report to you."

"Are the folks at Newport News expecting us?" asked the seal leader.

"They will be in two hours," replied Chad. "The base commander will know; you will try to avoid contact with existing base security as much as possible. We need all of this done within a few weeks. Then, we may have a secondary mission for you, but that is still being discussed."

"I'll rally the troops this afternoon, and brief them," said Carl. "We can mobilize in an hour for a normal mission, briefing and planning on the fly, but it would be better if we spend the evening planning how to best work this problem and then use Newport as a test run tomorrow. I'll call you in the morning to let you know when to notify the folks at Newport. In the interim, you should check on access to our secure data system. It will save me a lot of time if I don't have to drive over here for each report."

The man rose, shaking the hands of the other two in the room and headed for the door, already on the phone to his team."

"How'd that go?" called Walker as Gritt passed his office.

"We're up and running."

"Give me a second," replied Walker. Gritt stepped into the office and closed the door.

"General Johnson has her two agents on the way as of this morning. I haven't met either of them, but I don't need to." He handed Gritt a slip of paper with two names. "Spend a couple of hours this afternoon and look up these two people. Tell me how good a job our folks did in creating and aging their online profiles. Lisa doesn't expect to leave them in place in China long enough to generate Chinese research into their profiles here. The Taiwanese gave Lisa a few targets in China, locations with ties to their submarine fleet. I am not optimistic that we will find what we are looking for, but we have to try."

Gritt folded the paper and slipped it into his shirt pocket. "I just hope that we don't run up a red flag with the Chinese. General Johnson's people can't tip them off that we are looking for that sub."

"She made it clear to her agents that they were to tread softly. If they identify a target that might help us really define the objective, then we will flesh in a plan."

CHAPTER 20

SEATTLE

MOLLY AND ANDY finished a flight lesson just in time to beat the Saturday rush hour traffic. It really didn't matter what day of the week you tried to drive in Seattle anymore. Between three in the afternoon and seven the traffic was terrible. Andy left the airport on the south end of Lake Washington, his vintage 1970 Jaguar weaving through traffic as it skirted the eastern shore of the lake. "Are you sure that you can't call Chet and reset your meeting this evening?" said Andy. "You just had a study session with him this morning."

Molly swallowed hard, her heart racing, as she wrestled with her deceit. She reached over and ran a single finger from the top of Andy's ear, tracing it slowly down his neck and under the collar of his shirt. "We can fly again tomorrow, and I don't have any plans after that. But I promised your friend Chet that you and I would have a drink with him this evening. He may be the loneliest human that I have ever met. And he is really helping me with my laser study."

Andy maneuvered the car onto Interstate 90, headed west toward downtown, delighted to be heading the opposite direction, as the bumper-to-bumper traffic moving the other direction. "I was kind of keeping Elliot's as a place for you and me."

"Your friend doesn't get out much, and since he was there with us earlier, it was an easy place to meet," said Molly.

A half hour later, Andy found an isolated spot in a parking lot only two blocks away from the Seattle waterfront. He had memorized a list of parking places downtown where he could park his prized car without worrying too much about it getting dinged. "Is there anything special I need to do or say or am I just along to deliver you to your new tutor?"

Molly punched him in the arm. "He's your friend, and he's taking his time to help your girlfriend. It would be nice if you offer to buy."

"That's what I thought," said Andy with a laugh, as he opened the door to their favorite bar and restaurant. Both of them stopped to scan the bar, looking for Chet.

"There he is," said Molly pointing toward a table way in the back, along the windows. They started through the crowded waiting area, paralleling the bar.

"Molly, Molly Wang, is that you?" came a voice from the bar. A tall blonde woman pushed out of a small crowd of men that surrounded her. "It is you!" The woman wrapped Molly in an embrace. "God how long has it been?"

Molly disentangled herself, stepping back. It was really starting. She and Polly had rehearsed the night before, but then it was just acting. "Wow, Polly what are you doing in Seattle?" She forced a smile then turned to Andy. "Polly, this is the man in my life, Andy. Andy, this is Polly McGregor, an old friend from San Diego." She waited a moment, as Andy took in the view. "Polly is one of the most fun people you could ever travel with. She's a tour guide in the Southwest when she isn't roaming all over the world on her own looking for the perfect beach." Molly hesitated again. "Perfect doesn't mean private when you travel with Polly. Her friends call her Hots, and she attracts a crowd."

"I can see why," mumbled Andy. Polly was dressed in a pair of form-fitting black jeans, with roses stitched in colored thread on the back pockets, and a black pullover turtleneck sweater. Her blonde hair was pulled back into a ponytail. Andy couldn't help staring and thinking, *her figure is the kind of perfect that leads women around the world to scream about how every woman was beautiful.* "Maybe once you get to know them, that is true," said Andy.

"What?" asked Molly.

"Nothing."

Andy looked back at where Polly had been sitting and smiled. At least five men turned watching her every move. "Would you care to join us?" he offered without asking Molly. "We can save you from that pack of circling wolves. That is if you want to be saved."

"That would be very nice," replied Polly as she slid past the entourage and picked up her mai tai. "I came up for a meeting with a new overseas tour operator, but he was delayed in Hong Kong, so I'm just killing a couple of days. It's nice to bump into a friend."

A moment later, Molly introduced her to Chet. "My Andy here is teaching me to fly airplanes," offered Molly. "His friend Chet here is helping me prep for my master's degree application." Molly hesitated, as Chet almost stumbled getting to his feet, his hand working to overcome paralysis, as he tried to accept Polly's extended hand.

"What are you drinking?" asked Andy. "Molly and I usually order a Tanqueray and tonic here. Chet can I get you a refill of whatever you are drinking?"

"I'm on my second mai tai," said Polly. "I'll hold off a bit."

"If you two are having a gin and tonic, I'll join you," replied Chet.

They settled around the table, as Andy waved at a waitress.

"You and Chet have a couple of things in common," commented Molly, as she placed her hand on Polly's arm. "You both are searching for that perfect beach and gin-clear warm water."

Chet had managed to take in everything that Polly presented in just a second or two and busied himself with staring out the window at the seagull screaming from the railing overlooking the bay. His face was slowly losing some of the red that had accompanied his handshake.

"That's really cool," offered Polly. "I really like most of the people I've met on quiet beaches." She smiled at Andy. "Most of the guys are real gentlemen, not like the bums you meet on crowded city beaches where they just sit around undressing you with their eyes, as you walk by. I go to the ocean for the water and the swimming."

"Where have you been?" asked Chet, turning back to the table but carefully avoiding eye contact with the stunning blonde.

The waitress arrived with the drinks. "A toast to friends and beaches," offered Molly.

Polly sipped her drink before answering. "Oh, I've been all over the south Pacific. I kind of like Rarotonga in the Cook Islands because it is really private. There are some great getaways in Tahiti, but it's very expensive there. Some of my clients have been raving about some of the small villages in Central America. I've been all over Mexico and Costa Rica, but I haven't been anywhere else down there. I've got a couple of weeks off coming before the summer tour season kicks off, maybe I will try to find one of those secluded villages."

"Aren't you frightened to go into one of those isolated villages by yourself?" asked Molly.

"It's always nice to have a friend to explore with," replied Polly, "but other that the local guys who hit on every blonde that comes by, I've never had any trouble. Usually some wife or girlfriend will come along fairly quickly and set them straight."

Andy was laughing as he addressed Chet. "Do you have any recommendations for Molly's friend?"

"Perhaps," answered Chet finally getting over his paralysis. "I go to a couple of spots that are friendly. You have to put up with a clean local hotel. There are no five-star hotels where I go, but the people are really nice, and the food is good. If you like to dive or snorkel, the locals normally leave some of the shorelines and reefs alone. They don't fish them so that they can produce fish for the nearby areas where they earn their living."

"That sounds wonderful," offered Polly. "What countries do you prefer?"

"I have a spot in Nicaragua and another in Panama. I try to visit each at least once a year."

Polly reached into the tiny clutch purse she carried and produced a pad and pen. "Nicaragua and Panama," she said as she wrote. "I wouldn't know where to start looking." She turned to Molly. "I saw some incredible oysters come from the oyster bar when I first got here. Maybe if I bought a couple of dozen for us, I could tempt your ocean friend here to stay long enough to give me some pointers."

"Well, Chet?" said Molly. "Are you up for a few oysters to help a fellow beach nut?"

"Sure," answered Chet. "I have a lot of information stored on my phone. I even have some pictures."

"We can stay for the oysters," chipped in Andy, "but Molly and I have a morning plane rental, and I will not fly with a hangover."

"I thought the rule is eight hours from the bottle to the throttle," said Molly.

"That's the legal definition, but the old saying about aviation kicks in where the law drops off. Aviation is terribly unforgiving to errors in judgment, and I don't think worth a damn with a hangover."

"Chet can stay and show Polly the pictures." She reached over and took Chet's hand. "As shy as you are, I'm sure that a few more minutes with a beautiful woman would be welcome."

"Sure, I'd be happy to share about the villages I visit," replied Chet, still having a hard time looking across the table at Polly.

"I'd be happy to buy a little dinner for us after Molly and Andy leave," offered Polly. "I've been guiding tours for fifteen years, and the best leads I ever get for great places often come from quiet discussions like this. The really good ones, I keep for myself."

"I'd enjoy dinner with you," managed Chet.

"And I will have another mai tai," added Polly. "But I need dinner soon. Three drinks make me a little tipsy, and oysters make me horny. I wouldn't want to embarrass Chet here or myself."

CHAPTER 21
SAN DIEGO

LIA CHANG WAS a bit shocked by how easy it had been to look into Kratos, the company building America's laser weapons. Deep inside, she had hoped that the task was impossible. American companies published annual reports and websites. Many referenced key employees being recognized for business or professional success or peer recognition. None of the sources she searched made any mention of specific projects that the company was involved in, rather they used terminology such as, "involved in a significant project for the Department of Defense," or "part of a corporate partnership helping to defend America."

Within three hours Lia narrowed her search to a Dr. Tom Parks, when she found a post on his Facebook page noting that he had recently returned from a trip to Alaska. Thumbing back to older posts, she found he'd written a rave review for a San Diego area cider bar. Newtopia bragged that it was redefining American cider. Her target was referenced in one of the bar's posts as their most loyal customer, and his post indicated that he stopped for a cider every evening on his way home. "It's just the thing to help me empty my mind of the data that commands me all day. Their cider gives me a chance at a real life outside the office." The idea of actually spying on the man made her stomach squirm, but not like the pictures of her sister had.

Lia blew through her last class, dismissing her students with a research list and an assignment for a short paper. She grabbed an Uber, arriving at the bar a little after 5:30. The small industrial like tasting room was starting to fill with people just getting off work. Lia found a small table near the back and spread the small briefcase of things she carried onto the table and ordered a cider. She nursed the excellent drink for over an hour before she saw the man she was looking for come through the front door, looking for a seat. Parks was medium height and weight, probably in his early forties, with blond hair that he obviously never combed. He was dressed in jeans and a bright red t-shirt. The man was an all-American technical geek, so different from the engineers in China that he seemed almost a different species. Catching his eye, Lia moved a couple of files from the table into her canvas case and pointed at the spot she had just opened.

"I wasn't being very courteous," commented Lia as the man approached. "I've been here for a while, working, and I hadn't noticed that I was, how do you Americans say, hogging the space."

The man slid onto a stool like strange foreign women inviting him to sit with them was an everyday occurrence. "Hi, I'm Tom," he offered. "Your drink is about empty; may I buy you a refill?"

"That would be very nice of you." Lia extended her hand. "I'm Lia Chen. I teach at San Diego State. A couple of my students were raving about this place. I thought I'd check it out." She finished the small amount of tawny fluid in her glass and handed the empty glass to the man.

Tom Parks took ten minutes to make his way back to the table with the drinks, as half a dozen patrons stopped him to chat. "I took the liberty of buying you one of my favorites. It has just a hint of marionberry, which offsets a really dry brew. It's my favorite."

This man likes to show off what he knows, she logged. For the first time in her life, she was a spy. She had known that the Chinese government had her under their thumb for a reason, and this was it. She stared at her phone almost expecting one of Ma's pictures of her sister to appear.

The man seated himself. "I'm an engineer myself. I spent some time in academia, but I like the practical challenges in the private sector. It also pays better," he added with a laugh. "What do you teach Miss Chen?" He glanced at her left hand. "It is Miss isn't it?"

Lia found herself fighting continuing butterflies in her stomach. She paused before answering. "Yes, it is Miss Chen. I studied here in the States and then back in China and then again here. I've studied statistical computation and philosophy. San Diego State offered me a visiting professorship to fold the two fields together. The classes have been very well-attended. But as a former student yourself, I'm sure that you realize that I didn't take much time for other things like personal relationships." Lia sipped the new drink. "This is really good." She closed her laptop and slid it into the canvas briefcase resting on a stool next to her. "What about you Tom. Are you single or should I head for the door before some jealous wife bumps me off my stool?"

"Divorced, or rather within a few weeks of being divorced. I'm probably hard to live with. I really love my work, and I just can't leave it in the office. It didn't work for a traditional Midwest girl who only wanted a house with a picket fence and a couple of kids."

"I get that," replied Lia. "Maybe if I end up staying in the U.S., I'll take a shot at some kind of permanent relationship." She sipped her drink and smiled. "Probably not if I end up back in China. I'm just a bit too independent for most of the educated men I know." She looked toward the windows realizing that what she had just said was the first time that she had ever admitted it. "What field of engineering do you practice?"

"Electrical engineering," replied Tom. "I have a doctorate in electrical engineering. I've always had a fascination with how you take a steady reliable stream of power and convert it into momentary bursts of extraordinary energy."

Lia knew that what he was saying was important to the mission that Ma had imposed on her, but she didn't understand. Her face showed it.

"Think of it like a fast-steady mountain stream. I study how to build a dam in the stream for only a moment. Then I let the water I've dammed up loose all at once. That burst has a lot of power, and it can do amazing things if you can control it."

"The mathematician in me would like to see the data behind that kind of thing," replied Lia. "The philosopher would like to understand how it helps man understand who he is."

"It's not really that difficult," said Tom. "The math is simple. The tough part is working with materials engineers to find substances that can handle the process."

Lia looked at her watch.

"Am I boring you?" asked Parks.

"No, not at all. I am fascinated," replied Lia. "My stomach just reminded me that I haven't eaten since breakfast, and I was wondering what time it was. Do they serve food here?"

"Usually there is a food truck parked nearby, but we can do better. That is if you'll allow me to add dinner to that drink." He pointed at Lia's mostly empty glass.

"I'm kind of dressed for work, not a date," replied Lia.

"Then we will define dinner as a scholarly discussion," answered Parks. "Do you have a car?"

"No, I took an Uber."

"Good, we will take mine and after dinner, I can call you a ride. I wouldn't think of embarrassing myself by asking if you would like me to drive you."

"Maybe the answer wouldn't embarrass you," replied Lia, "but calling Uber is probably a better idea for tonight."

CHAPTER 22
BEIJING

BEN ROTH HAD been a last-minute addition to the large contingent of Americans attending the commercial communications fair in Beijing. The leader of the American delegation, a deputy secretary in the Department of Commerce had inserted a full-page single sheet description of Ben and the new startup company that he had founded to the glossy catalog that Commerce had prepared for the exhibits and conference. She'd even pressed another of the conference attendees to cut his lecture from one hour to a half-hour in order to give Ben time to address the people gathered from around the world. Her offer to the head of another struggling start-up had been simple. "Dr. Roth believes that this conference may be a make or break opportunity for his company. He's offered to reimburse you and your staff for one-hundred percent of you travel costs if he can steal a half hour of your time."

Ben was really a little-known professor of communications who actually did lecture at MIT and who really did work for America's premiere military technology think tank, DARPA. That made creating his persona both easy and challenging. Stripping away the areas where Ben was working on highly classified projects took some time.

Adding projects where his "startup' would attract meeting participants who knew something about the stealth sub was easier.

General Johnson and her tiny staff had brainstormed the communications difficulties that they thought the Chinese might be having with their sub and created phony break-through technologies that would solve the problems. They had built Ben's speech around the concept of communicating highly private statistical data from underwater production projects, like offshore oil fields. The key was the ability to communicate even if terrestrial connections were broken, for example by an earthquake or storm and the ability to deliver data in a secure way that neither competitors nor nosy government agencies could even detect, let alone read.

He had been speaking to a group of about two hundred for fifteen minutes when he dropped the idea that he hoped would lead to a contact with someone familiar with the stealth sub. "One of the things that our small team has been working on is the ability to communicate in our secure way with mobile systems. For example, let's say that you run a mineral excavation company and you invest the millions in autonomous underwater exploration machines, machines capable of making their own decisions as they follow a promising streak of detected minerals along the floor of the ocean. You may want continuous data on just what the system is doing. You may want to redirect the device based on analysis that was unavailable when the mission launched. Our technology may allow you to do both of those things without your competitors even knowing that you are communicating let alone reading the communications."

Ben took a minute to slowly turn his body, sweeping across those assembled so that the tiny camera embedded in the pin on his lapel could scan the faces and actions. Inside a room in an adjoining hotel, a colleague from DARPA read the data from the screen of a tiny laptop disguised as a cellphone. Each time the computer's facial recognition and human movement software found someone that it considered deeply engrossed in the speech or who was frantically trying to take notes it captured that person's image and tied it to a database allowing Ben's assistant to identify the person.

Ben continued, "Now I know that none of you would intentionally do this, but let's just say that your rover somehow decided to cross over into a block of underwater real estate that was not allowed by your exploration permits or inadvertently crossed a border." He paused waiting for the laughter to subside. "You wouldn't want that mistake picked up by some government agency before you could remedy the situation. You wouldn't want them to even know that the rover was on the wrong side of the line. Our prototypes indicate that our signal is almost undetectable. Our algorithms are virtually undecipherable even if the signal were somehow detected. Our signal uses very little power and bounces around anything solid, like rocks on the seafloor. Using direction-finding technology to track it is almost impossible. I can't give you the specifics, but we have testing data to back up this statement; data collected in environments where agencies were working hard to detect any penetration."

Again, he paused and scanned the room before continuing.

"The reason I am here is that the perfection of this technology and scaling is going to require a substantial amount of new capital for us. What we are working on is not the kind of project that your big worldwide communications companies are investing in. They don't need it. But we believe that there are companies with either the need for our technology, or who can see the markups that those who do would be willing to pay. If you are one of those firms, we would be interested in in talking with you about capital or even a partnership. If you are, my email address and cell phone number are on the flyer in your catalog. I'm Ben, and I thank you for a half hour of your time."

Ben took a seat near the back of the room, as the final two speakers used up the balance of the three-hour block dedicated to "Non-Mass Market Technologies." He knew better than to use his cell phone to check with his assistant to see if there were any obvious interested parties. The Chinese would be monitoring and probably recording every cell phone call from the conference. They would have seen the incredibly weak signal from his camera but would have no chance of deciphering it with only a few seconds of data to work from.

⁂

Four days later, he and his assistant plopped themselves into the business-class seating on a Boeing 777. The American Airlines flight would get them to Los Angeles just in time to catch flights to Reagan International. In the three days after the speech, all six people that the computer had flagged approached them. None of those people turned out to be leads to the Chinese submarine, though. In fact, Ben guessed that at least two of those who made contact were Western intelligence plants that, like the two that profiled as Chinese intelligence operatives, were very interested in figuring out how to counter this new threat. Their profiling had not been successful in identifying the remaining two, but one was clearly Arabic and the other from Ukraine. The trip yielded no real leads on the submarine.

His trip had succeeded in one phase of his mission. His open participation in the conference had triggered no unusual Chinese surveillance.

Perhaps the newly created corporate offices in Maryland would generate a call. The offices were in the same building as Team Walker operated from, with its own entrance and no windows. A sign on the door made it clear that access was by appointment only and the hall in the back of the offices allowed the occasional Walker team member to enter or exit the offices. Anyone watching would see activity, but to find out what was going on inside required that someone called first. The only source of that secure phone number was the flyer offered at the conference in Beijing.

CHAPTER 23

HULUDAO CHINA

MARGARET DAWSON AND her traveling companion, Peggy Wilson, had been interrogated in depth before their travel visas had been approved by the Chinese government. China never made it easy for writers or journalists to travel in that carefully controlled nation. Margaret was the first to receive approval, the government interested in increasing tourism even if they were not quite sure what the Huludao region offered. "That's what I want to find out," offered Margaret. She had tapped on the keyboard of the laptop she'd carried to the interview launching a travel website that she had written for "years."

The site had been built in less than ten days, by a team reporting to General Johnson. The same team had also created a full historical record of Margaret Dawson. It wasn't bulletproof but would stand up to the scrutiny needed for a two-week trip.

Peggy Wilson was a novelist in real life, with three published thrillers, all set in exotic and historical places. For the first twenty years of her life she had been a covert CIA operator, switching after retirement to writing. Her previous covert history made creating a cover story easy, and with two decades of records, it could withstand a deep study if the Chinese decided her visit warranted research. Her first request for a Visa had been rejected, with the advice that "only writers who respected China's unique history" were allowed. Four days later, she had been accepted for a second interview, this time carrying a story outline of how American Army operators had helped the Chinese Communist Army under Commander Mao defeat a particularly evil Japanese general near the end of the Second World War. It had taken another week, but the Chinese Government had approved the book concept even offering Peggy access to a PLA publicist for assistance. They had been especially intrigued by Peggy's research into how the Japanese had forced the Chinese industrialists in the Huludao region to cooperate in developing and building Japanese weaponry. She had obviously done extensive research. Many of those Chinese industrialists never saw their families again.

The two women managed a quick room service dinner before collapsing into two comfortable beds. The trip had taken more than a full day from their carefully planned departure location of New York. A note slipped under their door overnight indicated that a representative of the PLA would be waiting for them the next morning in the lobby.

Chi Wi stood near the entrance to where the hotel's free breakfast was served. He carried a clipboard with Peggy Wilson's name on it, but that proved to be unnecessary as the travelers were the only western women staying in the hotel.

Chi was a little over six feet tall, dressed in a blue suit with a red tie. "I studied journalism in Hong Kong," he offered. Chi helped the two women select from an endless list of foods, none of which resembled ham and eggs. "My undergraduate study was in World War II history." He turned toward Peggy. "When your resume and your book outline reached our offices, I asked for this assignment. Most Chinese history only teaches about the horrors of the Japanese occupation or the struggles between the Nationalist forces and the Communist forces after the war. It was refreshing to find an American who was studying how our two countries were actually allies in defeating the Japanese. I was especially interested in learning of your research on General Mukai."

Chi turned to Margaret. "If you would like, I have a friend who speaks reasonable English. She is a world traveler herself and has offered to introduce you to our city if you would like a guide." Chi produced a sheet of paper folded lengthwise from his lapel pocket. "I have taken the time to prepare a list of sites that might be of interest to you. I suggest that you start with the Great Wall. Huludao is the only place where it passes directly through a city. Then you must see old town, where we have preserved the old Ming Dynasty city.

"I suggest that you rent a car service through the hotel here. Having a driver to avoid finding parking will save you hours each day."

"Having your friend's help would be delightful," responded Margaret.

Chi slipped his iPhone from a pocket and used the voice access to place a call. He scribbled a note onto a page in a tiny notepad he carried and handed it to Margaret. "Give this to your driver. It is the address of my friend Chunhua. She will be waiting for you in one hour."

"Are you sure that I can get a car?" asked Margaret.

"The hotel is charging you twice what they charge locals. They will take good care of you. The driver is similar to your Uber service. The hotel will have advised the driver that you are Western, and he will also be charging you twice his normal rate, with a kickback to the hotel."

Margaret hesitated, recognizing that all of their expenses were being covered by Team Walker, but also cognizant of her official status as an independent travel correspondent. "That sounds a little expensive for me."

Chi laughed. "Your room charges are less than $50 U.S. per day, about a quarter of what it costs for the most basic room in your home of New York. The car will also be a fraction of what you would pay at home. My countrymen will be happy that they are skinning you Americans while you will think China a bargain. Perhaps before you go you will want to have dinner at one of our five-star restaurants. That will be more expensive but still a bargain."

Chi waited for both women to make a trip to their room before walking them to the front desk. "Ms. Dawson here needs a car for the day," he said to a woman sitting at a desk at the end of the counter."

"I have the names of several competent local guides," replied the woman.

"That will not be necessary. I have a friend who has offered to spend the day with her."

The woman at the desk frowned but picked up the phone and began dialing.

Chi turned back to Margaret. "My friend will not charge you and please do not insult her by offering. She is doing it as a favor to me."

"May I buy lunch or something like that?" asked Margaret.

"Of course, that would be very nice of you. By the way, Chunhua means spring flowers in our language."

A green Toyota rolled to a stop just as the three people pushed through the front doors of the large unflattering Communist era hotel. Chi stepped up to the drivers open window, and flashed some kind of ID. "This is your driver. I will allow my friend to introduce you to him in the name of saving time."

As Margaret pulled away, he turned back to Peggy. My car is over here. Where would you like to start?"

"My research indicates that the local region is very rich in minerals. The mineral wealth and the refining were what made this region valuable to the Japanese. I don't know if it would be possible, but I would love to talk to someone who knows about that wealth, especially the exotic minerals that made the Japanese intent on keeping Chinese industry operating during the war. Then I would like to explore the conditions where General Mukai held their families."

"I read two of your books after I learned that you were coming," answered Chi. "The books were amazingly accurate, with settings so real that I felt that I was part of the story. I can now see why." He again slipped his phone from his pocket and this time used the memory to dial a number. His call lasted only seconds.

"The head of the local institute on mineral research has agreed to giving you a half hour. After that, we will drive over to the park where the internees' camp used to be. They have an exhibit of items and photos of the camp as it existed during the war. To give you some context we can then have lunch at a restaurant in one of the mansions where the families once lived."

Peggy stopped and reached out touching Chi's arm. "How is it that your bosses and you personally have agreed to help me this way?"

"My bosses just want to make sure that you aren't an American spy. After reading a couple of your books, I don't believe that you are. The story of Huludao and General Mukai and especially of how your American Military advisors arranged for arming a division of Chairman Mao's army to defeat Mukai is important. It is little known in my country or yours. Perhaps it will lead to better relations."

Only two miles away, Margaret extended her hand to a perfectly groomed twenty-something woman who slid into the backseat of the Toyota next to her. Chunhua introduced herself as Chi's sometime girlfriend. "Please call me Chun." Margaret asked no questions about that, but she could have sworn that Chi wore a wedding band.

"What would you like to see first?" asked Chun.

"Your friend Chi gave me this list," replied Margaret, handing Chun the paper. "He suggested that we start with the Wall and Old Town. And then I would like to visit the area where your commercial shipping operates. If you have seen my website, you probably notice that tourist travel on large freight ships is a specialty for me. It appeals to the adventurous travelers that subscribe to my site."

Chun's puzzled look was quickly replaced by a smile. "Can you help me find your website?" she asked, as she produced a small tablet computer from the bag she carried.

As she opened the computer, Margaret caught just a glimpse of some kind of official seal in the corner of the screen before Chun moved on.

"The first two requests are easy," answered Chun. "If I can get a better idea of what this travel by ship is, I will try to help."

"That's all I could ask for," replied Margaret. She didn't know if Chun was police or an intelligence operative or something else. Perhaps the opening screen on every computer in China had that official seal. But Margaret's pre-trip briefings kicked in. She pulled out her own carefully prepared smartphone and called up the address of her website showing it to Chun.

"This is in English. You will have to translate it to route to my site. I'm quite proud of the site and would be interested in hearing your ideas on extending it to potential followers in China."

CHAPTER 24
SEATTLE

POLLY "HOTS" MCGREGOR slid into the first-class seat on an Alaska Airlines flight back to San Diego. Her mission to somehow get close to Chet Williams turned out to be an enjoyable experience. The man was painfully shy, but also impeccably polite and courteous. Polly had employed every trick she knew to seduce him that first night. What the man lacked in experience he made up in gentle energy and endurance. The next two days he had returned to work but both nights the couple finished long romantic dinners at his home overlooking Lake Washington.

In just over a week, Chet would meet her in Los Angeles, and the two would be on their way to Guatemala and a tiny beach town that was his favorite. She had learned little about the project that Chet was working on, other than it was the one on Kiska Island.

The seven-day trip to a place where she would have his undivided attention, offered a better possibility of fulfilling the mission that the Chinese had given her. They were paying her a $10,000 retainer, masked through her company. If she produced a concise description of the Kiska project, one that allowed the Chinese to measure the threat, they would forward an additional fifteen thousand from a shell corporation headquartered in Singapore. The retainers would be non-refundable deposits for tours that would never happen. Polly had already decided that they would post the first two-thirds of the second payment before Ma would get anything, but for now she kept that to herself.

Ma met her at the airport in his rented Corvette. "Well?"

"You will have to wait a bit. I'll be traveling with Chet next week. For now, all that I have for you is that he is involved in a project on Kiska Island. Your team has targeted the right guy."

Ma looked frustrated, but quickly transitioned. "Can I buy you some dinner?"

Polly leaned back in the uncomfortable seat and closed her eyes. For a moment, she conjured up a vision of Ma's boisterous and selfish lovemaking and then a vision of Chet's gentle concern over her satisfaction. "No, I think that I need to catch up on laundry and then get a good night's sleep. Taking the time for the Seattle trip and another week for the trip to Guatemala out of my late spring booking season will require some serious overtime before I meet Chet."

Ma's disappointment showed in his tightly clenched teeth. "I am now second to your laundry. Remember, you are being paid well for this effort."

Polly faced the man as he weaved through traffic on the way to the apartment building where both were staying.

"You can't forget who is calling the shots here," he continued, as they pulled into the parking lot. Ma handed the attendant the keys, and a $10 bill.

Ma was fun, and the business relationship was exciting, but his domineering attitude was wearing thin. He needed her more than she needed him. "I'll add a chapter to my report when I get back. You might find it interesting, Ma."

"What in the hell are you talking about?"

"It will be the lessons that your mark, Chet, could give you on how to treat a lady."

CHAPTER 25

SAN DIEGO

LIA CHEN SETTLED into the wicker chair at a table overlooking the beach. If you could call this a date, it was her third with Dr. Tom Parks. In the previous two, starting with her contrived meeting at the cider place, it had become clear that Parks was a bit of a lady's man. At least four beautiful women had stopped them on the way out to say hi. At their next "date," a dinner at a restaurant at his golf club, every single woman in the room knew him.

Lia proposed a mid-week early lunch at the Hotel del Coronado. At their first meeting, she'd thought that he was attracted to her, and after a couple of dates, she still believed that. But her rail thin five-foot-four-inch frame was not the kind of sexy of the other women she had observed. Perhaps it was her Asian heritage that attracted Tom, some kind of unique Asian experience, but she was beginning to think that the man had all the sex he wanted. Perhaps he was one of those guys who believed that a really bright woman was more interesting. At least she was hoping that was the case, as she watched him approach her table.

"I've taken a few minutes out of my schedule to do a bit of homework since dinner," she started, as the waitress departed with their orders. You've never come right out and told me, but your company works on lasers for the Navy among other things. That would explain your comment about finding materials that can handle the energy bursts you create. I have some family in Huludao. That's a coastal city in China that is renowned for its mineral deposits and refining."

"I know a little about Huludao," replied Tom. "Our counterparts on the Chinese side have laboratories in the city. They are fortunate in that they have access to large quantities of rare earths. We work with tiny samples because the U.S. doesn't produce much of these really expensive materials."

Lia had deliberately worn a pink embroidered Chinese blouse over her wispy silk pants. She'd spent an hour on makeup that morning, emphasizing her Asian eyes and round face. If she couldn't attract Tom with her curves, she was willing to use her exotic features and intellect. She just wanted this nightmare over, and that required information acceptable to Ma.

She caught him sneak a peek as she reached for the coffee pitcher across the table, the sun glinting off from the ocean behind her. "I really like our technical discussions. I guess that I find them intellectually challenging."

Tom accepted a coffee refill from the petite woman. "Anybody ever tell you, Miss Chen, that you have a sexy head?"

"I don't think that any man has ever said the word *sexy* to me. It is kind of empowering isn't it?"

Their conversation continued over breakfast. Eventually Lia steered it back to lasers. "I read that it is hypothetically possible to build a laser that can damage a target hundreds of miles away. I understand that we have built lasers that can actually hit the moon. That must take a lot of energy. I've even looked at a couple of the formulas, but I find it hard to believe that any material could possibly control the energy to trigger a burst."

Tom sat back in his chair. This woman was getting to him in a way that he had never considered. His recent security briefing had touched on subjects that foreign powers wanted to understand. But Lia's conversations were all generic. Besides, what kind of spy would announce that they were an intellectual scholar from China? "Hitting a target a hundred miles away is all a matter of the aperture of the laser and generating enough energy. Hitting the target with enough energy to damage it would be the tough part. Most traditional missiles or aircraft would require you to hold the beam steady long enough to penetrate the vehicle hull and then damage what was inside. That and accurately tracking a target so that you could even aim the damned thing is a bitch. Remember that a laser beam can only travel in a straight line, and the curvature of the earth would limit the range." He paused and watched Lia for a moment. "Overcoming the technical material issue turned out to be easy. Probably not as easy as it would be for your Chinese scientists with their massive supplies of rare earths, but not as hard as I thought it would be." He paused again, watching the petite woman add three teaspoons of sugar to her coffee. "Can I change the subject since I have already said all that my job will allow on the subject of lasers?"

"Of course. I am sorry to dominate the conversation with technical talk. In my classes, most of the conversation is about the philosophical challenges of technology. I guess that I am still a bit of the pure scientist that I started out to be."

"Okay, how about a major change in the conversation – nothing technical or philosophical, nothing about mathematics?"

"I think I would like that."

"Would you sleep with me tonight?"

Lia giggled. As much as the espionage part of this terrified her, the actual give and take with Dr. Tom Parks was kind of fun. "Only if the good doctor can generate and direct adequate energy to satisfy his target."

CHAPTER 26

SAN DIEGO

LIA'S REPORT WAS almost all speculation, but it was well-reasoned. Kratos was involved in designing, if not actually building, a laser with the capacity to clobber a target a long distance away. They were using rare earths to control the energy bursts necessary to fire the weapon. They had mastered the capacitor problem. The fact that Dr. Tom Parks was now working on the use of lasers to communicate discretely seemed to indicate that his work on a long-range weapon was complete.

Ma reread the report, sitting in a secure communications room at the Chinese Consulate at 500 Shatto Place in Los Angeles.

Next, he turned to the really loose report from Peggy. She had demanded another $10,000 before handing him the four sheets of handwritten notes. All that she had been able to confirm was that Chet worked in terrestrial tracking for Boeing, "whatever that is." And, that he had been assigned to a project in Alaska in a place where there was little to do. He had taken his diving gear with him on the last trip. "He loved diving in the harbor where he was working. There were a lot of old-World War II wrecks." Ma read on, as she rambled. "He thinks that precision weaponry like today's would make that kind of destruction obsolete." She included one quotation from Chet: "All of the major military powers will soon have the ability to target ships and planes at distances that could never have been contemplated during the Second World War."

Ma decided the report had nothing of value. Perhaps what he did get would be enough. He'd told Polly that she could wait until hell froze before he would authorize another $5000. It pissed him off that she intended to continue her contact with this Boeing engineer, especially after she told him that Chet would never violate his secrecy commitment.

Ma had no hard evidence of what was going on at Kiska Island, but he had what he was going to get. He sat down with a cup of heavy black coffee from an urn that had been steaming for hours and began to encode his report to General Ling: "The Americans were building a laser on Kiska. They had mastered the problem of capacitor capability to handle the enormous bursts of energy needed to make the laser lethal. The device was designed to hit targets a long way from the base. They were using a targeting system designed by their best targeting experts. Finding out more from the sources at his disposal could take another year if the information could be gleaned at all. That is unless he was authorized to coordinate an operation with General Yang's operations group to actually seize a couple of Americans on American soil to force them to disclose the secrets of the new facility." Ma knew that Ling would never approve such an operation. He used a match to light the two underlying reports on fire, dropping them into a wastebasket on his way to the communications center.

His miniscule report on the way, Ma thanked the two people in the consulate that worked for General Ling, and slowly made his way to the rented Corvette parked in the adjoining lot. His flight home didn't leave for several hours, so there was plenty of time to return the car, check in for the flight and relax over a couple of drinks at the airport. He had the ten-hour trip home to figure out how to deal with Ling who would be furious over how little he had accomplished in six weeks. His job would be to convince Ling that the report was enough, that the Kiska Island facility was just what the PLA had concluded. Perhaps Ling would give him a further assignment to quantify the risk, hopefully in the United States.

CHAPTER 27

HULUDAO, CHINA

TO MARGARET AND Peggy, the old Chinese city full of traditional activities and loaded with ancient buildings, all within the shadow of The Great Wall, was a smokescreen. Peggy had pages of notes that would allow her to actually write the book about General Tsuyosi Mukai and the two American Army intelligence men who had secretly helped the Communist Army drive him out of China. Margaret had hundreds of pictures and pages of notes, all of which would make travel to Huludao interesting and for many, exciting. She was especially surprised when Chunhua took her to the beautiful Longwan Beach where people with more tolerance for the mid-sixty's temperature were actually swimming. But underlying all of that was a secrecy portrayed by staring faces.

They found the only time they could exchange notes was during a brief walk each evening before their handlers arrived for some staged dinner event. Both assumed that their room was bugged and that people seated near them for meals were listening to their conversations. They carefully inspected their clothes before each walk to ensure there were no bugs. "The engineering and technical ability to build the type of submarine we are looking for certainly exists here," said Peggy. "They build all of China's nuclear subs here and my visit to the metallurgy research facility was an eye opener. They are working on hundreds of new alloys, even some that seem to merge materials and biologics."

"All I know for sure," replied Margaret is that the few actual scientists or engineers that I have come into contact with are amazingly closed mouth about what they do. I don't know what Chunhua actually does for a living, but her presence literally closes any conversation beyond, 'How do you like our country?'" Margaret reached down and picked up a wrapper from some kind of candy and slipped it into her pocket. It was the first piece of litter she had seen.

"What about a ship to transport that submarine?" asked Peggy.

"I have pictures of several ships in the harbor that are certainly large enough, and one of them only seems to leave the harbor about twice a year. She opened her phone and scrolled to a picture of a huge container ship, the *CCL Atlantic*. I asked if there was someone that I could chat with about tourist passengers, but nobody seemed to know whom that ship belonged to. My bet is that it has something to do with covert operations, maybe with the sub. It will require some more digging by the folks back home, but I found nothing like a smoking gun."

"Not much to show for our trip, is it?" added Margaret.

Peggy stopped. "Sometimes in this business that's all you get. Analysis of dozens of snippets is what we work from. We almost never produce a smoking gun. The intelligence that led to the death of Bin Laden came from more than 200 reports." She stopped to see if the two men who followed them each evening were still a block away. "Remember, above all else we were not to tip off the Chinese that we were looking for that sub."

"We better get back," said Margaret. "Chi is taking us to dinner at his favorite spot tonight."

The restaurant was in one of the old mansions surrounding

the industrial area of the city, overlooking Liadong Bay. Entering, Chi introduced the two women to his boss who greeted them with a warm smile and handshake. The man was introduced as "Boss" and not by name.

"Have you each acquired the information that you need to complete your projects?" asked Boss.

"We would like to stay longer, in your beautiful city, but the answer to your question is yes," answered Margaret, "and now it's time to go home and go to work."

"And, before I forget," added Peggy, "I want to thank you for the help that your man Chi has provided. When the book is done, I would like to send each of you a signed copy."

Boss turned to Chi. "He is one of our best men. I've read his daily reports and appreciate your thoughts on his work. I am sure that you can understand that in a region like Huludao where much of our industry, especially that focused on our military is centered, we must take precautions. You have been within a few minutes' walk of several of our most important facilities. For us not to have monitored your trip would have been stupid."

Peggy couldn't resist herself. "You do know that China has an excellent reputation for espionage in America. Your hackers are constantly searching through our business and government computers trying to steal our technology and secrets."

While Chi, leaned back in his chair, his face a bit ashen, Boss took her comments in stride. "You are right of course. It is not just computer espionage that we practice. We use every means at our disposal to keep track of you, your technology and policies. Like you, we have developed advanced means to steal from you, just as you steal from us. Why you focus on us, I don't know, since you are far more advanced. We are masters at copying things. Perhaps you should be proud that we invest so much studying your country and stealing your excellent ideas. In China, copying someone else is considered flattering." He paused, twisting his tie back and forth. "You have nothing that we cannot steal...eventually. At least today we do not kill each other over some idea that will be obsolete in a few years."

"Perhaps that could be the subject of my next book," offered Peggy with a smile. "I could call it *Stealing Anything We Want*, or something like that. If I write that book, I'd like to come back to interview you."

"And I would answer any questions that would not get our friend Chi here to arrest me."

Boss waved to a waiter who circled the table pouring an excellent dessert wine as two other people quietly removed the dishes from an extraordinary seafood-based dinner. He turned to Peggy and smiled. "Even retired old pros, who move on to new careers, can appreciate how much better it is to use methods that don't leave bodies in the streets."

CHAPTER 28
MARYLAND

BY THE TIME the two operatives sent to Huludao returned, the facility in Maryland was humming with more than thirty people. Like most intelligence operations, the Chinese submarine project was talking on its own life.

Gritt met Walker, as he and Winchester returned from a walk. He handed the older man a penciled organization chart with dozens of erasures and new entries. "One of the reasons that I retired," said Walker, "was that the intelligence community was getting cumbersome, so full of bureaucrats that it was becoming impossible to get anything done."

Gritt just shrugged, folding the paper and slipping it into a pocket.

Still, the findings demanded even more digging. Seal Team Four had worked its way through the first six sites on the list prepared by Col. Phillips. With the exception of Newport News, where no additional penetrations were discovered, every site had been compromised. Following orders, the Seals hadn't revealed any of the devices to local commanders, nor had they interfered with them.

Their daily reports reflected efficiencies by the Chinese that surprised everyone. Their search had been extended to the next ten locations on the list.

Thad and Chad, as the two men directing Team Walker were now being called, were on their way to CIA headquarters, and a meeting with Director Chang. "The trip to Beijing was a bust," offered Chad as the two rode in the back of a black Chevy SUV with a soundproof barrier between them and the driver. "The dummy office we set up, however, may be paying some dividends. Just yesterday some man who described himself as a Chinese businessman living in Indonesia left a message that he might be interested in investing in Roth Technologies, that is if the information forwarded by a friend who had been in Beijing was accurate." Chad stroked another key on his laptop. "Ben Roth is going to meet with the guy this evening at his hotel in D.C. I'll have one of our team in the hotel to get some photos. Maybe we can identify this Indonesian businessman."

Thad made a couple of notes on his graph pad. "I don't think the director is going to give us the time to plant seeds that take months to develop."

Chad nodded. "The report from Huludao is a bit more promising, but still gives us no hard confirmation on the sub. Your old colleague Peggy Wilson indicates that the Chinese appeared to know that she was a retired agent, which means that they already had a file on her but still allowed her trip to happen. She felt that the man running her surveillance was almost daring them to step over a line. She felt that her primary contact, a guy by the name of Chi, almost relished any attempt to penetrate the secrets of the Huludao complex. The Chinese showed them enough secrets to keep us occupied, but only what they wanted to disclose; kind of like bait."

"Sounds a lot like what we are doing," replied Thad. Were there any hard findings?"

"Only the name and photograph of a ship that seems to leave port just a couple of times each year. If it is the mother ship for the sub, that means that they have run far more operations than we thought possible. I have Bob Phillips tracking down the ship's travel to see if there is any correlation with what the Seals are finding. Maybe it is important, or maybe it is a red herring. The Chinese actually allowed access to one of their most secret technology labs where they showed Ms. Wilson a number of metallurgical innovations. They have the materials technology to build the sub."

"That's good," replied Thad. "As to the mother ship, if there is any correlation, any additional trips may give us some new locations that have been compromised."

"The thing is, after three months we only really know what we knew to start with. There is some device out there that is allowing the Chinese to penetrate really good security around critical maritime installations. The use of this platform is very professional and there may have been more penetrations than we suspected. That's not much to show for twelve-million dollars' worth of effort."

"Hell kid," replied Thad, "don't worry about the money. I suspect that we will spend a lot more on this before we finally nail this sub."

"Is that why we are making an unscheduled trip to see the Director? Are we looking for more funding? Were damned near out of the first fifteen million that he gave us."

Walker closed the folder where he kept his notes scrawled on a graph pad. "No, we are going to tell Mat that if they haven't already penetrated the Kiska site they are going to try. We are also going to tell him that Kiska is probably our best bet to really understand and nail this Chinese stealth sub."

"I doubt that they have already penetrated the site," replied Gritt. "Two thoughts. First, there is really nothing to see or monitor yet except a pile of steel being erected, some groundwork being completed including the road up the mountain and tons of concrete being poured. All of the important stuff is going on inside of the facility and even that is still in the installation phase, not operational."

"And your second thought?" replied Walker.

"The Chinese continue to do surveillance with their intelligence ships and flybys with aircraft. For the first time this week, one of the new intelligence aircraft based on their new C919 airliner design was spotted and monitored by a couple of F-22's out of Anchorage. The Air Force is now flying some long-range missions over Kiska to keep an eye on the Chinese. That Chinese jet was just over thirty miles offshore and was trailing some kind of sensing antennas."

"I asked for the Air Force monitoring," said Walker, as he again opened the folder in his lap. "We need to make the Chinese really anxious to figure out exactly what we are doing on Kiska. The fact that we would run a couple of relatively short-range fighter planes out there with tanker support has to say, this is important."

"So today is our hard pitch to the director?" answered Gritt.

"Yup. We want him to convince the President to dangle the Kiska site out there as bait where we can at least get some underwater pictures of that sub. Pete Wilson's technology group is working on new underwater sensing measures to learn even more about that craft. If we know they are going to plant some kind of monitoring devices, we can counter them even if they succeed in planting surveillance equipment." Walker paused, staring out of the dark tinted window next to him. "I just wish I knew what the Chinese were up to in Huludao. Like us, they are dangling bait, they must want us to target something."

The meeting room was just as it was the day that the Navy came to the agency with the exception of Walker. For an hour Gritt ran through the findings of the Seals and of the two covert operations in China. Over the next hour, Deputy Director Wilson discussed the technology group's ideas for additional sensing and monitoring of the sub inside the security area around Kiska, including underwater low-light cameras. Director Taylor offered a couple of ideas on additional covert operations but warned that her resources inside China were very thin and that losing any of them would leave her almost blind.

"We have no short-term ideas on how to nail down this sub using the means that we are all comfortable with," said Mat after two hours of sitting.

"That's about right," replied Walker, "it's about time to try something that makes us uncomfortable or just throw in the towel. We want to make penetrating Kiska critically important to the Chinese that they throw together a plan to target the site. Perhaps they will make the kind of mistake that will make this easier, but as long as we are prepared, we can mitigate any penetration and get a solid read on the sub."

"What do you need to start planning this?"

"I need drawings and expert support on just exactly what this Kiska site really is and your authorization to launch the operation."

"I'm inclined to give you both," answered Mat. "But tell me, what if we ratchet up the Chinese concerns to the point that they invade the site before it is 100 percent operational. Can we protect it?"

"They aren't going to start a nuclear war over this," replied Walker. He turned to Gritt. "Tell the Director about the conversation with the mystery guy at that dinner in Huludao."

"On the last day the team was in the city, their handler set up a dinner and introduced his 'boss' not by name but only as 'Boss.' Whoever this guy was, he is not referenced on our portfolio of local intelligence people. Anyway, he emphasized that they stole information from us, and we stole information from them, but today it is civilized, leaving no dead bodies."

"I want someone from your team out in Kiska before we pull the trigger on any operation," said the Director. "Make it someone who can really analyze the risk and be prepared to tell me how you would defend an overreaction by the Chinese. Not a full-scale invasion, more like a raid. In the interim, I will take this to the President for final approval, but you can start planning."

Mat and the two deputy directors silently packed up and were out of the room in seconds, leaving Chad and Thad sitting alone.

"Wow, what was that all about?" asked Gritt.

"That, Kid, is how the director says; if this goes south your ass is grassed."

An escort arrived a few minutes later to walk the two men to the waiting limousine. Seated, Gritt stared at his closed laptop but said nothing. "Don't worry Kid, they can kill you, but they can't eat you," offered Walker.

Chad looked over at his mentor who had a huge smile on his face. "What don't I know?"

"The director and I go way back. He knows that I would prefer to shoot for the moon."

"Shit oh dear," said Gritt. "Just what does that mean?"

"If the Chinese are thinking exactly what the director thinks, that's an opportunity."

CHAPTER 29

MARYLAND

WINCHESTER DROPPED A tennis ball at the feet of his owner, as he and Gritt walked from the limo. Thad braced his bad leg and lofted the ball off into the trees. It took only seconds for the huge Gordon setter to emerge with his prize, racing in front of the walking men before dropping the ball again.

Walker leaned down and scratched the dog's back between his hind hips. "Win's almost ten now, and his joints are getting a little achy." He flipped the ball to Gritt. "Just like mine. My throws aren't much of a challenge anymore. Let it rip."

The men stopped to watch the dog as it raced through the trees like one of those border collies doing an agility course. "I work to keep in shape," said Walker, "and to keep Winchester in shape. Fall is our favorite time of year and living in Montana gives us easy access to some of the best pheasant hunting in the world."

Gritt was a bit surprised by the banter, especially since they had a cautionary green light for the Kiska mission. His feeling must have shown on his face.

"Kid, I just want this mission to be over by the end of August so that Win and I can head home. I figured out years ago that we weren't going to nuke each other. All this happy horse shit is just that. This mission, like the last three or four that I did, is important right now, but in the long run just an exercise."

"Then why do you do this?" asked Gritt. "If I was retired with a home on Montana's largest lake, I think I would be tempted to spend my days just soaking up the Big Sky Country."

Walker turned toward the meeting cabin where General Johnson was waiving at them. "Because Kid, this is just so damned much fun. The Russians were better chess players, but the Chinese are just fucking unpredictable. That is a hell of a challenge." He paused for a moment. "And maybe, just maybe, this time it is really important."

"What do you have for us, Lisa?" asked Thad as he shook General Johnson's hand.

"My friends in Taiwan are picking up chatter about some major meeting of all of the heads of the PLA intelligence group next week in Beijing. There is no chatter about other issues important enough to pull in all of the big guns. It has to be about Kiska."

"Thanks Lisa," replied Walker. "Please round up your guy, Ted Leonard, and Col. Phillips and that guy who runs Seal Team Four. I'd like a short meeting in a half hour, after I feed my dog."

"Mr. Walker," replied Lisa, "his name is Carl Quinto. He's part Tlingit and part Filipino from Alaska and quite well thought of in the Special Forces community."

Walker turned to Gritt. "Another Alaskan, no wonder you two get along." He turned back to Lisa. "Would you have Ted confirm that the new runway in Kiska is operational and see if it can handle a Gulfstream? Tell everybody that we will be gone for a couple of days."

Walker whistled at his dog and headed toward his cabin. If the Director's emergency meeting with the President had gone as well as he expected, there should be a secure file waiting on his computer.

A half-hour later he was still perusing the two pages that Mat had forwarded, a little confused by what he was reading. "Grab a coffee, everyone," he muttered. Walker rolled up the pages, lit them and dropped them into the fireplace.

"The director has asked us to do a site visit on Kiska before he gives us the final okay on using that new facility as bait to lure in the Chinese sub. He wants us to ascertain just what defenses we need to defend the site against an armed raid." He accepted a stick of gum from the Navy Seal sitting next to him, unwrapped it, and popped it into his mouth. "I want to figure out exactly how we can use any Chinese mission to complete ours."

He turned to where General Johnson and her assistant Ted were parked in two overstuffed chairs. "What's the skinny on the runway on Kiska?"

"Finished and operational," replied Ted Leonard. "Eight thousand feet in length and reinforced to support cargo jets. They rebuilt the old Navy runway. The Air Force has not yet published approach maps and procedures, but they are available."

"Good, we've discussed this possible mission a couple of times, and we will have about ten flying hours to discuss it further. We will be stopping in Seattle to pick up some guy by the name of Markus. I don't have a last name, but he is the project manager for the Kiska installation. He, the Air Force, and Boeing are all dragging their feet on us using their prize as bait."

He handed out a copy of a single sheet that he had printed only a few minutes before. "These are the initial tasks for each of you when we arrive. I've left a lot of room between my thoughts to add yours as we fly."

"When do we go?" asked Gritt.

"That, Kid, is up to you. Get us something fast, something that can accommodate up to ten of us. I'd like to be gear up before eight, tomorrow morning. We will be chasing the sun; even with a stop in Seattle we should get to Kiska in time to work a few hours."

He handed Gritt a tiny slip of paper. "When you get the plane scheduled, call this Markus guy and let him know when we will be in Seattle. He may be bringing along one of his guys. Find out and then have him contact Kiska and arrange someplace for us to use as a meeting room and a place to sleep. The heavy construction is done, so there should be some camp housing available."

CHAPTER 30
BEIJING

THE REPORTS FROM General Ling were disappointing. The small amount of information gleaned from his operator Ma's weeks long trip to the United States had yielded just enough to justify sending them on to the electronic intelligence group for their opinions. It had taken only two days for the technical engineers to respond with three possible scenarios. The only one that mattered was their first possibility, what they labeled as worst case.

"Our professional opinion is that the Kiska site is a large aperture, atomic-powered, pulse laser. Such technology is possible for the United States and within a few years to China. Such a device set on top of a mountain in the center of optimal flight paths of any missile deployed from our primary strategic mainland bases could render as much as 90 percent of our land-based deterrent irrelevant."

The lengthy report went on to site several experts that all agreed that the most difficult part of such a site would be building the computer integration that allowed American satellites monitoring any launch to work effectively with targeting radar and optical tracking technology to effectively aim a laser and hit Chinese missiles.

"Such integration would be especially difficult if the laser was tasked with intercepting an attack that combined low level cruise missiles, high altitude intercontinental ballistic missiles and ultra-high velocity missiles. A laser on Kiska would have to target each type of attacking missile, switching altitudes as well as swinging through various flight paths from north of the site to southern flight plans while cycling the power of the power plant into enough energy to fire on multiple targets that came within range. Our own laser scientists' question whether the Americans can aim a laser accurately enough to penetrate the outer hull and damage the important stuff." He paused for a moment. "But with enough power it wouldn't take a long burst." He paused again. "That leaves a massed attack of all three types of missiles as a possible solution. But a massed assault would test the integration beyond anything China can presently accomplish."

The head of human intelligence looked at a new report provided by one of his most trusted and secret sources, a deputy in the renegade territory of Taiwan's defense ministry. It indicated that the Americans would soon begin construction of a similar facility on their Midway Island. Such a facility could intercept missiles launched from bases in central China.

The one on Kiska was probably originally designed to defend against Russian launches. China's offensive American launch strategy had always been to launch from the northern border in an attempt to fool the Americans into retaliating against China's northern neighbor. If that option was blocked, then China might have to actually use the missiles positioned in the mainland bases, bases originally built to distract the Americans from the carefully hidden northern bases. It would be impossible to blame the Koreans or Russians. If the U.S. succeeded in building both laser interceptor sites, and if they really had mastered targeting and long-range attack radar, both China's northern and mainland deterrent was nothing but wasted money and effort.

"General," started Director Quing, "did any of your human resources report any information on computer science experts working on this level of integration?"

The HUMINT head tapped on the keys of his laptop, using a search engine to isolate any such report. "No, sir, not directly. We have made contact with one of Boeing's top targeting engineers, a Dr. Chester Williams, but our profile does not state specifically that he is an expert in computer integration."

The director of PLA intelligence operations laughed; his response clearly intended to insult his colleague. "What do you think a targeting expert in today's world does? Perhaps you think he figures out how to look down the barrel of a weapon before pulling an old-fashioned trigger?"

"That is enough Yang," spat Director Quing.

The human intelligence resource director fought his urge to reach across the table and strangle the arrogant young deputy. "What I am saying is that this Williams man is not himself the computer expert we are looking for, but it would make sense that he would have such people working for him."

Quing turned to the head of Technology and Electronic surveillance. Your teams report outlines their speculation that this Kiska site is a laser interceptor facility. How confident are you in that assessment and in their forecast that the Americans have achieved some such computer integration?"

"Perhaps our analysis on the last page of the report offers some light, sir. We estimate that the Americans will have invested at least one hundred billion dollars in this facility. It is not in their nature to spend that much of their budgets to only accomplish part of the task. If they didn't think this was a solid shield their congress would have canceled the project long before they began deployment. All of the production is centered in only three states meaning that congressional support would have to be based on actual defense calculations rather than jobs."

Quing, who had been standing since the others arrived, finally sat down. "They are confident in something. Since we used one of the planted sensors to successfully turn back one of their destroyers that penetrated our South China Sea area of domination several months ago, they have now begun sending destroyers into that critical area three or four at a time, often entering from different directions. The arrogant bastards are challenging us in our own backyard. So far, we have been able to intercept all of their attempts, but their efforts indicate that they are losing all fear of our nuclear deterrent. My speculation, which I have shared with President Xi, is that this Kiska site is changing how they look at the balance of power in the region." The man's energy forced him to stand again. "If we were to send in the EEL and a small team to steal the secrets of this site, what would they be looking for? How much of the critical technology could they slip aboard the EEL for out scientists to analyze?"

He turned to the director of Technical and Electronic intelligence. "General, can you answer that for us?"

Before answering, the General took a moment to make contact with his strongest ally. Both of them hated Yang and both worried that his rash arrogance might land China in a shooting war with the United States. "Comrade Director," he started without looking at Yang, "perhaps photographs or manuals found on such a raid will offer hard data on the laser itself and the reactor configuration, including the architecture of the pulse controller. Photographs of any radar found, or manuals of that system, would be helpful. But the devices themselves would all be far too large to remove or transport on the EEL. The actual data integration probably is taking place in small powerful desktop computers linked through one additional computer that would use all of its computing power just to ensure that the other devices talk to each other. This small local network would be controlled by a man or men who could look at a tiny amount of critical data fed to them by the controlling computer and make decisions. I suspect that once the humans approve an intercept on any missiles, the computers will use artificial intelligence to keep up the attack until the skies are clear or the missiles are out of range."

"I understand," replied Quing. "Still, you haven't answered my question. Could a team carry away enough of this system to allow us to learn to defeat it or at least duplicate it?"

"Sir, my best guess is that we would need to carry away technical manuals and training materials, as well as four or five small computers, perhaps small enough for one man to carry each of them."

Quing turned to General Yang. "General, the president wants to neutralize this threat. I want a plan to use a small force to infiltrate the Kiska site. You will need enough men to subdue the tiny force of guards at the site and then the operators. That same force must be adequate to carry away any technical manuals you find and the computers that your comrade here has just described. You will carry cameras and photograph anything of importance. With the actual computers we can reverse engineer the controller software."

"When do you want us to go?" asked Yang. In my conversation with the President early this week, he seemed very anxious."

Quing sat back in his chair. Yang's disclosure that he was talking directly to the President was way out of line. It could have been the President who initiated the conversation. Still, Yang needed to be put in his place. "I didn't ask you to do anything but develop a plan. We don't know how soon this site will be fully operational, so time is critical. Have a plan on my desk in ten days. I will discuss it with the President. He will tell us if and when he is willing to risk 27 percent of our international trade to steal the Americans' secrets."

The Director of Electronic Intelligence bolted to his feet. "General Quing, this may be considered an act of war by the Americans. I urge you to convince the President to allow us more time to use other means to measure this risk and to counter it."

Quing thought about revealing his intelligence on a second American laser site on Midway Island and just as quickly rejected revealing his private source of information. The president had made it clear that his initiatives in the South China Sea were becoming financial necessities. "General, time is also our enemy in this situation." He turned back to Yang. "Do you understand my orders?"

"I do sir," answered Yang, "You will have a plan in ten days, and we will be able to launch a mission two weeks after approval. We will smack the Americans fast and hard. They won't know what hit them." Yang rose to leave.

"One more thing, General," said Quing, shaking his head. "All of your offensive weapons will be non-lethal. We will leave no American bodies."

CHAPTER 31

KISKA ISLAND

THE NORTH WINDS funneling through the mountains were only gusting to twenty-five, and the pouring rain allowed a full two miles of visibility below the solid overcast only a thousand feet above the roiling Pacific. While the CIA had access to its own aviation fleet, as did many branches of the government, Gritt's boss in Naval Intelligence had pulled some strings to get Team Walker the newest executive aircraft in the Navy's own fleet. The Grumman Gulfstream G700 was so new that it hadn't yet been given a Navy aircraft type. The two Navy pilots jockeyed the plane from side to side and up and down as they made the approach to the newly paved runway on Kiska. Always fascinated by aviation, Gritt sat strapped into a fold down seat in the cockpit as his two Navy colleagues greased the sleek jet onto the stormy runway.

"If this place isn't the end of the fucking world, you can walk there from here," offered the copilot, as they taxied behind a pickup truck sent out to guide them to parking next to an unfinished hanger. "Your group have raingear?"

"I sure as hell hope so," Gritt answered, folding the seat and starting back into the luxurious cabin. The ground crew had configured the cabin with ten soft leather seats, all of which folded almost flat for sleeping. A couch configured with a coffee table filled the open area in the spacious jet. The soft recessed lighting offered the same amount of light that one would find in a romantic, very expensive, restaurant.

The navy steward who had provided VIP service for the last ten hours was already up and delivering the six carry-on bags that the passengers passed to him eleven hours before as they departed the airport only minutes away from their offices. The two men who had joined them in Seattle had both kept their bags stored where they could keep an eye on them.

The one who only introduced himself as Markus was no more than five feet six and a bit on the chubby side. His bald head glistened in the soft light, a function of the sweat that he continually wiped from his face. His blue eyes and black Tom Selleck style mustache were constantly darting. Throughout the trip he had carried on a conversation with his seatmate, Chet Williams, only answering direct questions posited by the other travelers. It was clear that he hated flying and beyond that was furious that he was even on a trip that might risk the Kiska site, his baby for the last seven years. He's left it up to the terribly shy Chet to answer most of the questions that Team Walker had for them.

To the team, it had become clear that there were secrets about the Kiska site that some of them would never know. As each member dug out the raincoats that had been the first item on the recommended packing list it became apparent to Gritt that most of the travelers were unprepared for Aleutian weather. Most were going to get soaked just getting from the jets air-stairs to the waiting van.

The van driver was a stunning red-haired woman wearing an Arizona State University sweatshirt. The travelers were surprised when she introduced herself as Major Olga Tvorshik, the head of the base security detail. "I've been out here for just over five months," she said, "since the sensitive equipment arrived. My orders indicated that a specialized team from Washington was coming in, and I am to accommodate your visit." She turned to the tall passenger from Seattle. "Nice to see you again Mr. Williams."

Walker smiled as the tall shy man nodded before turning away from Olga's attention.

"I assume that you all use civilian titles here," Walker commented, as he introduced himself and the other travelers. His team as well as the flight crew wore civilian clothes.

"Yes Mr. Walker. But we slip up quite a bit. The inertia of a military chain of command is hard to overcome." She pointed out the windshield, as the wipers struggled to clear the driving rain. "The camp is about a half mile from here, right above that large cement and glass building on the side of the hill." She pointed at a building about the size of a high school gymnasium built on a small hillside plateau just northwest of the airstrip. The building looked like a modern Frank Lloyd Wright building with stylish cement walls, and tall-thin glass windows on three sides. From the way the windows were fitted into the walls, it was clear that the wall thickness was measured in feet. The glass windows were narrow enough that even with the glass removed a person could not squeeze through the opening. The roof was also heavy cement, flat, and it overhung the walls by several feet all the way around the building. Behind the building six modular trailers made up the construction camp.

Behind those trailers, a smaller concrete building with no windows stood on a ledge carved into the side of the mountain. A road connected the two buildings and continued up and around the mountain disappearing into the low hanging clouds.

The entire developed site was only a little larger than two football fields and was completely surrounded by a heavy cement and steel fence topped by razor wire. Each corner of the fence was anchored by a short-roofed tower, open to the weather on the two sides that faced away from the compound."

Olga closed with, "Mr. Gritt, can you give me a short briefing on your mission as we drive?"

"Mr. Quinto, working with Mr. Phillips, are here to study how an enemy recon team might approach this base from the water. Anything your security people can do to accommodate that would be greatly appreciated."

"I've only got fifteen people on my staff," said Olga. "If your people can wait, I would suggest that I loan you a couple of old hands and our boat tomorrow. The winds are supposed to lay down and even with the roads built by the Japanese during occupation and the Navy later, the way to study approaches to this island is by sea."

"Do you two have that?" asked Walker. "Spend the afternoon looking at the approaches to the compound itself and the pre-planned defenses."

"Can do, Boss," replied Quinto. He looked at Phillips. "You up for a boat ride tomorrow, Colonel?"

Phillips nodded. "I could use some better rain gear," he commented.

"Two-thirds of the workers on the project have gone home," replied Olga. "Many left their rain gear in the barracks. Most swore they would never come back. Take your pick."

"Lisa here," continued Walker, "and her assistant Mr. Leonard would like to take a look at your security sensing plan and the monitoring station. They will be working with a team that will be joining you next week. Those guys will be adding underwater monitoring that is still classified. They will need help from you or the contractors to place their gear based on the survey that Mr. Quinto and Mr. Phillips complete."

"The folks from Raytheon are still here, calibrating their systems. I'll introduce your people to them."

"That leaves me and Mr. Gritt here along with our two guests from Boeing," continued Walker. I'm told that the facility C.O. is now on site. I'd like for you and her to join the four of us in a completely classified meeting. Since what we have planned will impact your lives and career, you should be part of the decision making."

"What do you mean, lives and career?" asked Olga, as she waited for a gate to open and then passed into a short concrete tunnel. She stopped the van, as that gate closed and a second allowing access to the compound opened.

"This is one of those hero or goat operations," interjected Gritt. "We all come out with presidential citations in our files or looking for other work."

Olga stopped in a garage and waited until the door behind her closed before opening her door. "What are the chances that this ends up on the goat end of the spectrum?"

"Mr. Walker here has been doing these types of operations since the Viet Nam war. When this op came up, they called him back from a very cushy retirement. That was good enough for me," answered Gritt.

A tiny radio on Olga's hip beeped twice. She pulled it from her belt and read the text on the screen. "Yea but based on the numbers on that plane that you just flew in, you are only risking an Annapolis education. I'm risking one from the Air Force Academy." She showed Gritt a text with a complete profile of the Gulfstream and its pilots. "My boss and his boss were very curious about this trip. They have been doing some digging. In general, they don't like the Navy poking around Air Force installations."

"Speaking of those three guys putting the plane to bed, can you have someone swing down and pick them up in an hour? I'm sure they would appreciate a drink or two before we shuttle them off to some lodging where they don't need a higher security clearance," said Gritt.

Walker stepped in front of Olga. "Major, in less than an hour you are going to be read into a project that even the Secretary of the Air Force will only find out about after we succeed or fail.

You need to shut down all back channels until I personally, or the President, give you permission to discuss this. Am I making this clear to you?"

Walker wasn't sure what kind of response he would get, but it wasn't what he got.

Olga's lips twisted into a sly smile. "Yes Mr. Walker, and perhaps as curious and intrigued as I have ever been."

Olga could probably earn an amazing living as a model if her Air Force career fizzled, thought Gritt. He'd dated a model working in New York for a couple of months, that is before she pulled the plug and moved to Elko, Nevada, to get away from it all. Maybe that was why Olga was on Kiska.

The base commander, Colonel May Washington, could not have been more opposite. The woman, in her late fifties, had short graying hair, carried an extra twenty pounds on her five-foot-ten-inch frame, and probably had never used makeup. Her eyes were some shade of gray behind glasses with lenses so thick that looking through them from the outside blurred her face. She stormed into the huge unfinished ground floor of the main building like a truck driver trying to cram a pit stop and cup of coffee into the time it took to refuel an eighteen-wheeler. Only the smile on her face was soft and warm.

"Ladies and gentlemen," she announced, "welcome to the Kiska National Memorial Park Visitors Center." She extended her hand, first to Walker and then to the rest of the group in order of her perception of their age. "I've been busy working with the technical staff calibrating our equipment for the arrival of the whole reason we are here. It will arrive early next week."

She motioned to a small circle of chairs around a makeshift plywood table. "We can talk here." A shield of heavy glass partitions surrounded the table. Around the group, workmen busied themselves in what was then only a partially completed office area.

Walker turned to Olga. "Would you please see that our bags

get to wherever we will be sleeping and then get my two technical teams with some of your folks and get them started on their tasks?"

Walker turned just as Chet Williams handed May a box of Krispy Kreme donuts that he'd picked up on the way to meet the Gulfstream at Boeing Field. "I think I remembered your favorites, Dr. Washington. I figured that they are a little hard to come by a thousand miles out in the Aleutian Islands."

"I accept them as a token of your remorse in hauling all of these fine folks out here to interrupt my work," Dr. Williams said.

"Don't blame Chet or Markus for our trip," replied Walker. "Just over a month ago I was sitting on the dock of my home on a beautiful lake in Montana when some ass buzzed me in a helicopter and then landed in the horse pasture next to the house. "My name's Thadius Walker, and at one time I worked for the Agency." He turned to Gritt. "This young man is the cause of all of us being together this evening. Lieutenant Gritt, you are on."

Gritt had traded his small laptop for one with a larger screen – one of the IT staff working for Team Walker pulling all of the files off from his old one and loading them on the larger computer before destroying the old one. He motioned for May, Markus and Chet to slide their chairs around to see the screen. He waited while May slid her chair as close as she could.

"A few months ago, I was analyzing several unusual findings at facilities that support the Navy. All were near the water, and all had been compromised in some way. What popped out at me was that every instance had probably been staged from the water and that every compromise appeared to somehow involve the Chinese PLA." He tabbed through several slides before stopping. "I will go back to the specific incidents later, if you need proof, but the reason we are here today is that we believe that there is no riper target for compromise in the world than the installation you are all building. As you know, the PLA Navy is already running spy ships close enough to monitor communications and are flying recon aircraft close enough to use sensors to try to figure out this base." He turned to Markus. "The design of the facilities and the way you are surging one piece of construction at a time before starting the next phase has given them little to read with their efforts so far." He nodded to Walker.

"The insight that fifty years in intelligence has given me says that the PLA are coming to this island and they are coming pretty damned soon," Walker said. "One more thing, this base makes it very difficult to attack the homeland by air. But what if we can't defense a stealth submarine drone packed with a nuclear device? You will see why that is important as we complete the briefing."

"Are you here to test our defenses?" asked May.

"Your defenses are not up to stopping whatever the Chinese are using to get their people to the sites that they have already targeted," said Gritt. "We are here to help position some additional defenses, but our mission also is to learn enough about what we believe is a virtually undetectable Chinese submarine and use what we find to protect all of our installations around the world."

Walker picked up the conversation. "We have only reviewed a sanitized version of the plans for, and operations of the Kiska site. We know that it is supposed to be part of a laser shield that can detect and shoot down all three types of missiles that good old Uncle Sam believe the Russians or Chinese target the U.S. with. It's clear that our government has invested billions in this project. It is also clear that the Chinese are desperate to find some way to neutralize this facility and..." He paused while he flipped through the pad that he never put down. "...and the other components that are planned. Now that last part is only speculation by my team, but multiple locations seems to be the only way to build a full shield."

"Just out of curiosity," started Markus, "why are the Chinese desperate right now?"

"Since the U.S. began moving much of their manufacturing to other southeast nations and back onto American territory the

Chinese economy has stagnated. The development of manufacturing in Viet Nam, Indonesia, Taiwan and to a lesser extent the Philippines has allowed those nations to be less dependent on Chinese products and even positioned them as direct competitors on world markets. The Chinese economy is actually positioned to begin shrinking soon, unless the Chinese can use their muscle to subjugate their neighbors. They are already trying to implement a policy of dominating the nations around the South China Sea, and the U.S. is in the way."

"Sounds like a bunch of speculation to me," replied Markus. "I don't see much of a threat. You would think that the PLA or whatever you call the Chinese threat would use their extensive hacking and in-person intelligence operations to study this facility before they would risk an actual armed attack."

Walker and Gritt watched the color drain from Chet Williams face. He struggled from his chair and started toward a door with a blocky black man stenciled on a placard. "Excuse me for a minute," he mumbled as he raced toward the door.

"What was that all about?" asked Gritt.

"Young man," started May, "I'm almost sixty. For four decades I've been in the Air Force. They paid for two doctorates. I like to think that my superiors thought that I brought something to the Force that made that investment worthwhile. I'm married to the Air Force. It is my family and my legacy. With that said, the only thing that I have ever come up with that makes me a little unique is an overdeveloped sense of intuition and a willingness to use it." She leaned back in her chair and smiled at Markus. "I think your assessment of how the Chinese would approach this problem is spot on. I suspect that when Chet gets back, he will tell us all about some effort to get him to compromise this base." She turned back to Gritt and Walker. "And I suspect that your analysis is also spot on. Markus has done an excellent job of compartmentalizing this project. No one has a really clear picture except Markus, me and a few people so far up in the system that few will ever know their names. Chet would never intentionally compromise this project and even if he did, he could only disclose the small piece that he is familiar with."

Gritt shook his head. "From the briefing documents we've studied, we know that this laser technology may render the Chinese nuclear deterrent obsolete."

"You don't know shit," blurted Markus, "and I just don't see any imminent Chinese threat to this site."

May looked over at Markus, a puzzled look on her face. "Markus, why are you defensive about this?"

"Like you, I can read between the lines. What these folks want to do is use this base as bait to study this Chinese sub. If the Chinese do bite, they could compromise this project it in a way that we will never see it fully operational."

May placed one of her large boney hands on Markus' arm. "Just why are you here, Markus? This site isn't some pie in the sky research project. It is being built to shelter our country from potential enemies. What we heard today is that one of those potential enemies is already attacking us by stealing secrets created to keep us safe. Secrets that are important, just like this base."

For a moment, Walker thought that Markus was going to walk out. Instead, Markus leaned back in his chair, as Chet Walker headed back to the table, wiping his face with a wet paper towel.

"It may be nothing," Chet started, "but I have a girlfriend, the first one I have ever had. She is just drop-dead beautiful." He turned toward Markus. "Polly is beautiful like Olga is beautiful, and a lot of fun." He paused before continuing. "The thing is, she was introduced to me by the Chinese girlfriend of another Boeing engineer. Not Chinese American, but a pretty Chinese foreign student."

"We can discuss Polly on the way home," offered Walker. "In the couple of days we are here, we need to figure out how to protect the secrets of this facility while using it to learn how to defense this Chinese sub."

"You don't know shit," repeated Markus.

CHAPTER 32
BEIJING

GENERAL YANG WAS too wound-up to sit as the five people that he had summoned filed into the conference room next to his office. He had invited the country's best agent. He wanted Ma available with his firsthand knowledge of the American installation. Behind him was the Navy commander of the stealth EEL submarine and with him, this executive officer who had participated in every American penetration mission. The next two men were not even military. Rather they were the commander of the National Police counterintelligence group known as Snow Leopard Commando

SLC) and his best field commander.

"Gentlemen, I asked you all here because the President has tasked me with a mission that he considers critical to the future of China. Please take a seat. I will have tea brought in in just a minute, or coffee for those who prefer it. But before we are interrupted, I want you all to know that I am planning a mission to not only penetrate an American base, but to steal as much of the American technology from that base as we can carry."

"General Yang," started the commander of SLC, we are a

police unit, not military. We are trained for hostage rescue and counterintelligence, not military expeditions."

"You are Chin," offered Yang. "The President spoke very highly of you when he suggested that you could be helpful on this mission. He has authorized your groups transfer to the PLA Operations Unit for the duration of this effort. Am I clear?"

The two SLC officers looked at each other, neither smiling before the commander responded, "Yes, General you are very clear."

Yang handed the five men a four-page memo that he had written just that morning. "Please read this. I have only days to prepare a full plan for this mission, and from that date, we must be prepared to launch the mission within two weeks.

Ma thumbed through the first two pages, a smile on his face as he recognized several direct quotations from his reports. "I am happy that you and the PLA are going to take on fleshing in the bones of what my agents have given us," he said. Inside, his stomach rolled as he thought about how little the man commanding really knew about the Americans.

"And I am pleased that your commander has agreed to loan you to me for the duration of this mission," replied Yang. "Your knowledge of Americans and language skills will be critical to the success of this mission."

Yang could tell that Ma was shaken by the news, and almost gloated in his success to have this man reassigned to the effort. He watched as each of the men finished the short background and scoping document. "Are any of you claustrophobic?" he asked. "It will take about five days in the EEL just to reach the island noted in your briefing."

"If you do not give us a couple of days to do local recon on the target, we will be risking failure," offered the EEL's executive officer.

"That is the kind of feedback that we need to make this project a success, gentlemen. Now I will call for tea unless there are some coffee drinkers. From this moment forward, Team Yang will be our name, and to keep our correspondence secret from those who are unhappy about this mission, I have assigned each of you a code name."

He turned to the two men from Sea Leopard Commando. "Commander, you are now Leopard One and your executive Leopard Two." Turning to the submarine officers, he continued, "and you will simply be Captain and Exec." Finally he turned to the ashen Ma. "Since nobody knows you exist except for a handful of people in your division, for you we will stick with Ma."

CHAPTER 33
KISKA ISLAND

"ALLOW ME TO describe this facility," offered May. "A part of this huge room will be a small reception area for the few visitors that may visit the Marine or Historical Park each year. In the corner will be a cantina that will serve as a food service area for visitors and a cafeteria for our staff except when visitors are present. When a tourist boat arrives the security tunnel you drove through will be left open with one of Olga's people dressed as a Park Ranger guarding it."

"We're really short on time," offered Gritt. "Can we move on to the important stuff and leave the general background for later?"

May looked over at Walker who had a grin on his face. She popped out of her chair, the heels of her boots making a clicking sound as she walked to the windows overlooking the bay. "Ah, the impatience of youth."

Turning to a white board on the wall, she picked up a marker. "The facility is divided into two operating sections. Arctic Angel Operations function is the interception and destruction of air targets pointed at North America. Arctic Angel Defense function is the use of powerful laser's and other weaponry to defend this facility. In addition, we have offices to support those activities." She began listing the items on the white board.

"We have an office to monitor the reactor and another to manage the environment. There are five support divisions in all, including Olga's base security."

Gritt was taking notes as quickly as he could, his fingers flying over a keyboard.

"Every function is replicated in more than one location, including a very secure vault like structure that could probably not be penetrated by an enemy without the use of massive bombs. Our living quarters are all dormitory style except for the officers, and all are located below ground. They are very secure."

May swept her hand from wall to wall. This area where we are now building out operating offices is the only area at any risk at all. We remain functional even if it is compromised.

"Ma'am, we don't think that the Chinese are coming to destroy this place. They will just want to understand the risk," finished Gritt.

"In the case of an emergency," May said, "we do have an emergency exit from the secure vault structure to a hidden safe room near the dock area. The tunnel between the two structures is almost a half-mile long. That safe room is hidden in a collapsed Japanese bunker from World War Two."

May stopped, staring at Markus before continuing. "Every entrance to a secure area will be protected by fingerprint and retinal scan security, as well as standard key code pads used to move from place to place by even the non-security cleared staff."

"We are installing the control rooms this week. Next week, the actual weapons systems will be on site, and we will add the operations staff that are now in training somewhere in California. We should be operational five days after that."

Markus smiled at May. Obviously, she was trying her best to answer Team Walker's questions while keeping Markus happy.

"Like I said, you don't know shit," he added. The nuclear power plant is fully automated, and its building would take a week to penetrate. The radar and laser facilities at the top of the hill are also built like a bunker with the only weak point on top where the devices are located. The tops, though, are defended by a series of interlocking defensive weapons." He turned back to Walker. "Your idea of using this site as bait will never work. Any small force attempting to penetrate this site will need a week to get in. By that time, a rapid defense force from Anchorage will be on the ground."

Walker was growing weary of Markus' arrogance. "You may be right, but in four decades of clandestine work, I have seen small groups do things that seemed impossible. But that is irrelevant; what we need is to give the Chinese enough access so that they think they have the puzzle figured out without giving them the whole picture." Walker used his cane to push himself out of his chair. He turned to Markus, towering over the man. "I don't know just how the whole laser defense works, but from what I can see, the facility planning offers an amazing level of security. You know its strengths and its weaknesses. If you would, you could really help with the plan."

"Not a chance," replied Markus. "I remain against this whole insane idea. You have no idea how many really intelligent people have invested years on this project. Even if there is only a one percent chance of compromise, I'm not letting some dumbfuck spooks who want to play Cold War screw that up." Pushing past Walker, he headed over to where May stood at the white board and entered a code into a pad under a digital clock, and then pushed his head close to the pad. The white board slid to one side and a huge steel door began to swing open. In seconds, Markus stepped through the door, and the wall was back to normal.

"Colonel," started Gritt, "if you don't mind a direct question from a junior officer, I'd like to know what that S.O.B. is all about."

"Markus and I have been involved in the Arctic Angel project since its inception. He may be the smartest man that I have ever met, which can cause problems from time to time. He doesn't trust anyone who is less intelligent than he is, and he's never met anyone who is."

"Does that mean that you will help, ma'am?"

"My life has been dedicated to 'war from the sky,' and there isn't a facility in the world more secure against aerial assault than this one. But a nuclear weapon delivered undetected underwater was something we never considered. The threat you have described needs to be stopped."

Walker plopped his body back into the chair. "Colonel, we don't want any enemy to put this facility out of action. All we want is to give them a reason to come look, then show them just enough so they can go home and work on the problem. Hopefully, we learn enough about this invisible sub to stop it."

"I have some ideas on how we might do that," offered May. "But first, how about a little lunch? Given some time, maybe I can get Markus to help."

CHAPTER 34

NORTH PACIFIC/SEATTLE

THE GULFSTREAM'S AIRSPEED from Kiska Island to Seattle was anchored at 650 knots, and with the push of a huge spring Pacific storm in the Gulf of Alaska, a ground speed of over 750 knots.

The takeoff had pushed Markus, who was already refusing to talk to anyone including Chet, into an almost fetal state as the pilots rotated the sleek jet into a steep climb. Gritt held the water bottle that the steward had offered before takeoff in front of him, amazed by how the water tilted in the bottle compared to the floor of the plane. The calm of the previous day had been replaced by gusty winds, which at the surface topped thirty. The turbulence pounded and twisted the plane for a quarter hour before the crew leveled the plane at just over 35,000 feet, before continuing a slower climb up to 45,000 feet.

With stability, Chad, Thad and Carl Quinto huddled around a map spread out on the table in front of the couch. "The Americans and Canadians avoided the harbor at Kiska when they invaded in 1943. Landing on the other side of the island, they had to wait for calm weather. That made more sense than attacking into the mass of artillery and automatic weapons around the harbor," said

Quinto. "Landing from a surface ship would have made an attack through the harbor suicide, and they had the entire month of August to launch the attack."

"My grandfather was part of the intelligence group that planned the invasion," said Gritt. "As it turned out, the invasion cost 300 lives for nothing. Family lore says that one of grandfather's colleagues talked the Japanese into withdrawing under the cover of a storm only a couple of nights before the landing began. Still, avoiding the heavy guns rusting away around the harbor was good planning."

The others stared at the young man, wondering about his history.

Quinto noted four sites on the side opposite the harbor with a felt tip marker. "A raiding party could easily come ashore at any of those places. From the closest it would be a full hour slog to reach the compound and from the furthest, a little over three hours. Phillips and I both believe that the Chinese will try to mount their raid in the dark or at least twilight which in the next couple of months means between midnight and three in the morning. I don't think they will risk traveling even a couple of hours to and from the target. That would leave them exposed in daylight."

"You both believe that any approach will be from the harbor?" replied Walker.

"Maybe not directly through the harbor, around the new dock, but within a mile either direction. It is the only approach that can almost guarantee calm waters no matter the weather and offers access to the site in less than thirty minutes from the water-line." He pushed the ball cap with a big blue 4 on the front up onto the top of his forehead. "My guys could be in and out of that facility in ninety minutes. Any decent special operations team won't risk getting caught in daylight."

"So, you don't recommend that we place any of the special sensors and surveillance devices on the other side of the island?" asked Gritt.

"If you have enough to blanket the harbor area and place some on the other side, they should go into the waters around the sites I just noted, but I'd give you four to one odds that they will come ashore where they can assault the compound within a few minutes of landing."

"Will they use their equivalent of you Seals to swim ashore?" questioned Walker. "That would keep them hidden until they start up from the beach."

"Unless it's the best hidden secret in the PLA, the Chinese do not have anything like a seal team. They will have to use something like their Marines with a couple of weeks of intense training. We think that they will use rafts. That means the sub will have to surface where there is little chance of it being picked up by shore sensors. The rafts will be ultra-low profile and probably powered by silent electric motors. The attackers will be dressed in waterproof clothing from their neck to their boots and will have the latest heat sensing and night vision equipment in their arsenal. I wouldn't venture a guess on how they will be armed."

"We have some intelligence that they will try to avoid lethal force, but that's just an educated guess," offered Gritt.

Quinto sucked down a Coke that the steward had just handed him. Turning to Walker he continued, "boss, what do you want us to do?"

Walker deferred to Gritt. "We are planning for two different contingencies. In the first we do just what we discussed with Col. Washington and her people, we allow the raid to take place and gather data, including underwater pictures of the sub. The second will depend on how the raid progresses. If things just happen to work perfectly, we will seize that sub."

"And Seal Team 4's role will be?" Quinto stopped staring at the empty Coke can. "Hold it, you just said seize the sub."

"Yup. I want half of your team to continue looking for places where we have already been compromised," said Walker. "I'd like you to gather the other half of your team and mobilize with the weapons you need to take over that Chinese submarine. Plan to do it without lethal force, but don't lose any men trying to meet that directive. The entire CIA science and technology group is available to you. The facility has a small underground room that is well hidden near the harbor. Once you are on the island you will remain hidden there until you are relieved or receive the order to take the sub. You will need to be self-sufficient, perhaps for a month of sitting on your butts. Chad here will fill you in on the details. Any questions, comments?"

"Well, for starters we will lose our edge if we are cooped up in a tiny room for weeks on end. I'll work out an alternative and run it past you two, okay?"

"Discuss it with Gritt," answered Walker as he used his cane to extricate himself from the deep cushions of the couch.

Walker slid into a seat next to Markus and Chet. "We need to talk."

The strain on Chet's face showed as he turned toward Walker. "I have been thinking about Polly and our conversations. Other than telling her that I had been in the Aleutians on a business trip and in my little time off had done a little diving, the only thing that I might have said was something about working on targeting projects for the company. We never discussed anything really technical." He paused for a moment. "Although for a travel consultant she seemed really interested in my work. I thought that she was just a good listener."

Walker handed Chet his smartphone. "Read the message. A guy is going to meet us at Boeing Field, and you are going to tell him just what you told me. He will do a little digging, but for now, there's been no damage done. If I were young again, and a girl like you described had taken an interest in me, I'd just enjoy it. But just in case, you can't discuss this trip or any of these conversations. Got it?"

"One of the advantages of being quiet," replied Chet, "is that I have developed really good listening skills. I get it. Have fun but remember that loose lips sink ships."

Walker couldn't help but like the tall gangly engineer who had spent the previous evening teaching him about how targeting for a project like Arctic Angel was really all about getting the computers that control the various part of the puzzle to work with each other.

"And, Markus," continued Walker, "I just want to make sure that we are on the same page, finally. You need to understand that Chet's loose lips sink ships also applies to you."

"I still think this whole fucking scenario is some big scam to either take over this project or scuttle it. I'm not through fighting this bullshit plan."

"That didn't address the issue at hand, Markus. I need you to look me in the eye and promise that you will not discuss any part of this trip or anything you have overheard or even any suspicions with anyone unless I personally approve it."

"Who in the hell do you think you are?" blurted Markus.

"I'm the guy who will make sure that you don't get off this plane in Seattle. You will end up in isolation somewhere in the D.C. area until the mission is complete. I'm also the guy who can let you go home, but if I ever learn that you breathed a word about this effort, I'll make sure that you spend the rest of your life in an isolation cell, counting cockroaches, in a federal penitentiary after the best minds in the Justice Department convict you of espionage."

The overhead speakers announced that the plane had begun its decent into the Seattle area. Walker glared into Markus' eyes. "You're a really smart guy, Markus, and you have done some really good things for your country. Don't fuck it up now."

Somehow Markus managed to open his clenched lips, the muscles in his beet red face barely moving as he said, "I will not disclose anything about your bullshit plan or this trip to anyone."

"That's good enough for me," replied Walker.

He checked his phone again and turned back to Chet. "That man we are meeting has just cleared the waiting room in the corporate aircraft servicing firm at Boeing Field. You and I will spend a few minutes with him while we refuel."

The FBI agent met the men at the door to the lounge. Chet offered a short version of his concern about Polly, actually producing a photograph of the two of them in diving gear.

"I'll let the two of you continue this conversation after we leave," offered Walker, handing the agent a card with just his first name and phone number. "You keep me posted, but for now, it is really critical that no action be taken that scares off anyone involved in this possible problem or that even hints of any investigation. I personally think that Chet deserves a girl like that, especially one that loves the same things that he does." He extended his hand to the agent. "Are we clear?"

CHAPTER 35

SOUTH CHINA SEA

THE *USS PINE Ridge,* had departed the base in Diego Garcia with specific orders to electronically sweep what only a few months before had been a sandy barren atoll in the South China Sea. Mischief Reef had been on the maritime charts since the 1700s with little interest from any of the three nations that could have claimed ownership. In 2010 that changed, as part of China's claim to all of the waters and islands of the area.

Diego Garcia was one of America's most critical foreign military bases. It was primarily an Air Force facility, but also a rally point for Naval operations in the Indian Ocean and Southeast Asia. American ships and aircraft from bases in Japan and Taiwan challenged China's claims of sovereignty from the north just as the destroyer *Pine Ridge* was doing from the south.

The freedoms of navigation had become the primary flash point in the area, with China now asserting ownership of vast areas of ocean and islands that by international law didn't belong to them.

The *Pine Ridge* had been trailed by a Chinese frigate since its transit of the Straits of Malacca. Now, only a hundred miles away from the manmade island, a Navy surveillance aircraft advised the Pine Ridge that two Chinese destroyers were closing from the north. The aircraft sent video of the island, now covered by buildings, radar like domes, hangers and a runway that could accommodate every type of aircraft the Chinese owned. The aircraft's fuel restraints allowed the Chinese to shut down all but one radar site every time American planes approached. They knew that the snooper planes would be gone in less than a half-hour.

The *Pine Ridge's* assignment was to slowly circle the island within visual range for three days. They would record every electronic transmission emitted from the island. It made sense that a Chinese PLA base would have aviation radar and marine radar, but there were seven radar domes on the island, and the United States wanted to know what they were.

That had become more important a week before when the Chinese had actually intercepted a Philippine Navy recon aircraft with fighters from Mischief Reef. The Chinese always treated the local nations more harshly than the Americans, but this time they had actually opened fire in front of the scout plane forcing it to turn away.

From the bridge of the American ship, Captain Frost discussed the welcoming party with the pilot of the American plane. "So, they did their normal warn off?" he asked.

"Yes Captain, as usual they warned us that any conflict or misunderstanding would be our fault. They ordered us away from the island, and as normal, we thanked them for their concerns."

"Anything out of the ordinary?" asked the ship's captain.

"Just a lot of new construction. We counted twenty heavy trucks on an island that is only a half-mile long. There were four freighters in the harbor and another at the docks. I'll send you the video."

"But you definitely saw two Chin destroyers?"

"Yes sir, two and they were hauling ass to get between you and that island. There is definitely something going on that they don't want you to know about."

"Thanks for the update. We will proceed with our mission. Consider us warned. Have a nice flight home. *Pine Ridge* clear."

Over the next two hours, the *Pine Ridge* closed to less than thirty miles from Mischief Reef.

"Captain, radar reports two targets emerging from the clutter of the island itself."

"Get a drone in the air. We need to keep an eye on those ships."

"American ship *Pine Ridge*, this is Mischief Reef," crackled over the international hailing frequency. "You are ordered to turn away from this base immediately. If you fail to turn, the two ships that were sent here to enforce the Chinese government's sovereignty will force you to turn away."

"Give me transmit on that frequency," ordered the captain.

"Mischief Reef, this is the *U.S.S. Pine Ridge* operating in international waters. We will continue our transit and intend to stay in the area for several days."

"*Pine Ridge*, that cannot happen. Our two destroyers and the frigate in trail of your ship have been ordered to keep you away from this base. If you move out to fifty miles, you will be free to continue your passage. If you do not alter your course away from this base, you will be responsible for the consequences."

The captain shook his head, thinking of the same warning to the aircraft only hours before. "Maintain this course and speed." He keyed the microphone in his hand. "Mischief Reef and Chinese naval craft in the vicinity of Mischief Reef, my ship is operating in accordance with maritime law in international waters. We will continue on our planned course. If you would like, we would be happy to anchor up and send a boat ashore for a cup of tea with you gentlemen." He turned to his executive officer. "How far out are those Chinese destroyers?"

"Eleven miles and making almost thirty knots, sir. Closing speed is over fifty miles an hour."

He keyed the microphone again. "Mischief Reef and Chinese vessels closing on my ship, be aware that the maneuvers of your ships are dangerous and provocative. We will defend ourselves. Battle stations. Get me Seventh Fleet command on the phone." Turning to the XO, he asked. "Distance to those two destroyers?"

"Eight miles and closing. Sir, the surveillance drone we launched is showing one of those ships swinging its gun in our direction. They have uncovered their missile tubes."

"American destroyer, this is your last warning. Move away from this base at once."

"Captain," said a seaman, "Command is on the secure com." The man handed the captain a handset just as the guns of both Chinese ships fired. Only seconds later, the water in front of the *Pine Ridge* erupted from landing shells. A shell exploded just off the bow, sending shrapnel clanging against the hull.

"Sir, the Chinese ships are firing. They are firing in front of us, but they have opened their missile launch tubes," the captain said to the admiral on the other end of the phone. "These bastards are not kidding this time." He hung up the phone. "New Orders. Turn thirty degrees to the left. We will back off. We are to retreat to the fifty-mile line and await further instructions."

CHAPTER 36

BEIJING

"GENERAL LING," STARTED Director Quing, "your team has managed to fit just enough pieces of this puzzle together to elevate this Kiska Island facility from worrisome to your country's top security concern. What they did not do was offer enough data on the facility to help us defend against it."

"Sir, that may take months. Still, it would be better than sending that child, General Yang, out on one of his insane efforts of self-importance. This may be enough to really bring the might of American military power down on our country. Our leaders know that any country that invades China will lose that war. But, sir, in every other way, in the air, at sea, and in long-range strike capabilities, we do not even come close to matching the Americans."

"General, that is a calculation beyond our pay grade. The President has deemed this mission critical to our national interests. General Yang will fulfill his orders. You will assist him in every way including sending your man, Ma on that mission."

"Sir," pleaded Ling, "Ma is critical to our small intelligence network on America's West Coast. He is a spy that we have groomed since he was in his teens, not a soldier. Yang has others with language skills; he does not need Ma. He requests him only to rub my nose in his ability to influence you and the President."

"Ling, allow me to end this conversation in a manner that leaves no doubt about the subject. I have already fought the battle you are fighting. That battle is over. If the EEL departs Huludao without Ma aboard, I am confident that you will be replaced the same day. The only thing that is in question is whether the President will arrange for you to disappear the next day."

CHAPTER 37

HULUDAO

THE EEL CAPTAIN was confident in the ability of his boat to creep within a couple of hundred yards of the coast at Kiska. His name was sewn into the patch on his cotton pullover shirt, but everyone simply referred to him as Captain. Many in the PLA Navy had forgotten that he had any other name. What he was unhappy with, was the decision to use his boat to transport a full assault team. He realized that it had originally been designed for this type of mission, but it had never been used that way.

Only the four crewmen he had personally recruited from the PLA Navy's fledgling special missions' group were trained in the use of underwater equipment. All of those men were part of his own crew and all but his executive officer were already training for a mission to plant surveillance devices at a base that the Americans shared with Australia. The Kiska plan proposed by General Yang required the EEL to transport twelve Snow Leopard Commandos in addition to his own four operators and the guy that Yang referred to as Ma, who was probably Army and worthless as hell for this type of mission. It required the EEL to surface enough to launch rafts and then remain on station while they assaulted the new American base.

Yang himself would be in Huludao in the morning to coordinate the final planning session. Leopard One, the commander of the SLC group and his second in command were already there, and the EEL's commander had assigned his exec to familiarize them with the low-profile rubber rafts and the waterproof suits that each would be wearing. The new low-profile rafts were really nothing but a wedge-shaped inflatable with a slightly raised transom powered by a newly developed silent electric motor. Instead of a propeller driven by a shaft and gears, the propulsion was developed by spinning an electric charge around a shroud surrounding a free-floating propeller. Electric current would drag the propeller around the shroud at the same speed as the charge rotated. The propeller was made from some alloy that allowed it to be magnetically driven; however, it contained no detectable steel or iron. It was the same technology that drove the EEL in the open sea and was almost silent.

A maximum of six men would strap their weapons onto each raft and then lie flat on the raft, the water flowing around them. Nothing on the loaded raft would extend more than fifty millimeters above the surface of the water.

At night, especially if it was raining, the rafts would be almost impossible to see, and with any wave activity at all, they couldn't even be detected by surface radar or thermo scanners. What the EEL planners had recognized in the fifteen prior successful missions was that the Americans relied on underwater sensors to protect their maritime installations with only the eyes of a handful of poorly deployed security people to watch the water's surface. Still, this would be the first mission where more than two operators would deploy. His trained crew had always exited and entered the submarine through a cleverly designed cavity in the bottom of the sub that didn't require air or water to be pumped to facilitate the divers. Captain was not happy about actually surfacing his boat even at this remote site. But no one cared if he was happy, only that the mission succeeds.

Once the commandos were away, he would submerge the boat and wait for one of his trained crew to signal it to surface again. With some training, the entire egress and ingress would take less than three minutes each. Still, they were vulnerable in comparison with every other mission where the EEL never surfaced.

Captain had ordered his three swimmers back from training on a small island just south of the city of Shanghai. They would be in one of the two meeting rooms next to his office, housed in what looked like a decrepit warehouse on the waterfront inside the Huludao shipyard. The commando team would join his three men.

As the six people tasked with planning the mission, joined by experts from Air and Navy recon, Captain and Leopard One had agreed to test every step of the plan by challenging their teams to find flaws.

The EEL was technically part of the PLA Navy, but in reality, every mission not originated by Yang's staff still required his sign-off. While Yang had a reputation for being a bit brazen and abusive, he had always been both rational and concerned about his favorite intelligence weapon and its crew. Yet when both the head of SLC and the EEL's commander had approached him after the Beijing meeting, they found him unwilling to even listen to their concerns. "You and I will figure out how to overcome any obstacles," he snapped. "This mission has been ordered by the President, and we will not fail him."

Captain brushed aside an instant chill. Yang had always been a lifeline and champion of the EEL. Today, Captain felt like a gladiator sent into a battle that he had not trained for.

The urgency became clear the day after the Beijing meeting when two Chinese destroyers fired in front of an intruding American ship after it refused to change course. The Americans then lodged a formal protest with the Chinese government and requested an urgent meeting of the UN Security Council. The Chinese vetoed the UN resolution lodged by the Americans. The Americans countered by directing six more ships to join those of China's neighbors opposing their expansion plans. Now the navies of Vietnam, the Philippines and Malaysia were challenging China's domination in the South China Sea. Even worse was America's push back on peaceful surveillance of Kiska itself.

Just the day before, a C-919 recon aircraft, flying twenty-five miles off from Kiska Island, had been attacked by the Americans. The Americans had used their laser to sever the cable of the towed sensor array, spilling a million dollars' worth of sensors into the North Pacific. The ability to hit a moving target so precisely that they could cut a half-inch cable from miles away ran up red flags in every department of the PLA.

President Xi's leadership was now openly being questioned. Captain couldn't ignore rumors of riots in some of the nation's interior cities, locations where the collapse of Chinese-American trade had idled hundreds of factories. Perhaps General Yang knew if the rumors were true, but the rest of China, even its military, suffered under a complete news blackout of the region. Captain knew that nothing scared the ruling party more than domestic unrest.

He dropped down the ladder into the bowels of the EEL floating in a massive tank underneath the disguised building. The tank included huge doors that closed under the EEL as it surfaced, allowing the seawater in the tank to slowly be replaced with a special nutrient solution, a solution that allowed the unique silent propulsion of the EEL to survive.

There was no obvious access under the building, no doors or openings. There was no need for any as the operating strategies for the sub required that it stay submerged from the time it departed on a mission until it returned. The only exception was a mission like the one to Kiska.

For missions in the Atlantic, or where the sub would need to be at sea more than two weeks, it could ride in the special cavity in the bottom of a huge container ship built just for that purpose. Captain was happy that Kiska was only a few days away. Riding in the container ship required the crew to hide in a row of specially modified shipping containers surrounding the water filled cavity that held the EEL while bombarded by the roar of massive engines that drove the ship. With no major port anywhere near, a massive container ship sailing anywhere close to Kiska would draw attention.

With no other crew aboard, he walked he full eighteen-meter length of the boat. He checked on the fold-down bunks for the landing party, bunks that had never before been used. The shape of the sub, more an oval than a circle, was possible because the boat was engineered for a maximum submerged depth of fifty meters. The small nuclear reactor that provided power sat in the center of the craft, surrounded by a lead shield. The revolutionary reactor could be started or stopped in just minutes. The reactor generated enough electrical power to drive the craft at twenty knots under water using primary ducted propeller pods that would be retracted when the sub needed to make a silent approach to a target. The pods resembled oversized tubes about the size of a fuel drum which could be extended from the rear of the EEL using unique arms of engineered composite metal that actually bent to position the pods giving off no mechanical sounds when deployed. Near the reactor a second small plant desalinated drinking water from the sea and stripped oxygen from the water.

Most of the sub's missions were relatively short. All of the food was prepackaged requiring no galley except for a small cabin where tea was always available. A row of batteries low in the hull provided power for silent operations. Every function in the sub that could be detected was shut down when close to a target. There wasn't a single piece of identifiable steel or iron in the boat, nothing that would register on a magnetometer.

The Captain made a note to discuss the food, sleeping and human functions design early in the planning session the next day. It was critical that everyone understood the limits of the craft. They would get used to the high energy, low volume food that was part of the design. He'd found that he got over being hungry within a couple of days of deployment.

Making his way from the boat, he smiled. This mission would test him and his crew like never before. He was confident and nervous at the same time. He wasn't comfortable with surfacing for several minutes within rifle range of an American base, but he would insist on two days of intense training before the mission. Getting the raiders on and off quickly and silently was the EEL's best defense.

The Captain offered both tea and coffee to the nine men assembled in a small training room. Yang took Captain's normal chair at the head of the table, Captain to his right, and Leopard One on his left. Each had their executive officers seated next to them. At the other end of the table, Ma's chair screeched as he slid it across the wooden floor. To his side sat a briefer from Air Recon and another from Sea recon, and in the back of the room, a weather briefer fumbled with a small stack of charts. The briefers had not been allowed to download any of their materials directly to the raider's computers.

"The President wants this mission moved up as far as possible," started Yang. "Our own scientists have identified only three areas that are keeping China from its own laser defense system. If the Americans have mastered those three things, their system will provide a blueprint for our own. Our missile planners have no obvious solution to the Kiska site. Until that happens, our deterrent to American intrusion in our backyard is compromised or even possibly worthless."

An aide clicked a button of his computer, displaying a photograph of the Kiska site on the huge monitor on the back wall. "This was taken only a few days ago by a satellite." Yang used a tiny laser pointer to highlight an aircraft on the runway in Kiska. "The Americans are flying VIPs to the site in one of their luxurious Grumman jets. In America that means they are about to go operational and they are showing off their new technology to congressional backers. The time to strike is right now. The site is probably operational but not tested."

"What exactly are you saying?" asked Captain.

"I want you on that island in the next ten days. Our scientists have added a request, and the President agreed to it – not only will you photograph everything you see and take every manual you find, but somewhere in that main building you will find a computer network that controls the system. Our scientists believe that it will be four or five relatively small devices. You will disconnect them and take them with you."

For the next six hours, the group hashed out how the raid would take place. As each component was decided, the plan was walked into the meeting of crew next door where they were given a half hour to brainstorm weaknesses. In the end, only the transport of the computer equipment was blocking the final plan. "I need a solution," said Yang, growing frustrated with every idea presented being blocked as unworkable by Captain.

Ma, who had been silent throughout the meeting, stood and walked over to a marker board. "Why don't we go ahead and use the idea of wrapping the devices in inflatable envelopes as one of the SLC commandoes recommended?" He sketched out a box with a large balloon around it. "The bag will be waterproof, and even if the device slides off from the raft, it will float. We can tow it to the submarine."

"As I noted earlier," replied Captain, "There are two problems." The color in his face showed anger. "We only have room for three rafts and transporting the crew and all that computer gear will require four or five, or we will have to remain on the surface long enough to make multiple trips to shore. Second, the hatch on the top of the EEL is small. We couldn't get those big balloons into the hull."

"So instead of loading the devices on the raft, we tie the balloons to a raft and tow them. We now only need the three rafts already planned. We move them to the hatch and rip the end off from the balloon and load only the computers. You might as well leave the rafts. If you aren't going to kill all of the Americans, they are going to know you were there anyway."

"I said in the beginning that I do not want lethal force used," added Yang.

The sub's executive officer nodded to Yang. "Years ago, PLA weapons designers developed a weapon with the range of about a hundred meters. It fires a dart molded of gelatin that contains the venom of tropical Bullet Ants. It is the most powerful non-lethal poison in the world. The dart penetrates the skin only a fraction of an inch and explodes. The pain is severe. It incapacitates anyone it hits instantly. The pain will continue for hours unless those wounded are treated with a neutralizer. But it is not lethal. We've only had to use it once. It is shocking how well it worked."

"We will leave all of the Americans alive," said Ma. "The Americans will know we were there. Trying to recover the rafts will just take time we don't have. Taking only the equipment and discarding the balloons solves the problem, doesn't it?"

"Okay, that will do," replied Captain finally. "We need a week to provision. It will take that long for our armorers to build another sixteen dart weapons and make the venom darts. From the time the venom is collected, it only has an effective use as a weapon of thirty days. Someone will have to design and build the balloons. We should use the time to practice launching the rafts and recovering the troops. I do not want to be on the surface more than three minutes."

Ma smiled and leaned on the table. "These things seem simple compared to operating a spy ring on American soil. I'm happy that I could help with your mission."

Yang glared at the man. "It is *our* mission, Ma. You had better hope that it all goes well since you will be part of the raiding team."

Ma had agreed to help plan the mission. General Ling had assured him that he had refused Yang's request that Ma accompany the mission. Two hours later, as they broke for dinner, he dialed Ling's private cell phone.

"This is Ling. I will be unavailable for the next five days," came the answer.

Ma turned to see Yang watching him, a huge smile on his face.

CHAPTER 38

MARYLAND

QUINTO'S EIGHT MEN would be on a cargo jet headed toward Alaska's Elmendorf Air Force Base in Anchorage. There they would spend a few days hitting the bars and loafing until Quinto ordered them onto the island. He reasoned that it would be easier for them to maintain their edge if they limited the time quarantined in the small isolation room near the harbor.

When Quinto called, they would load the small mountain of equipment and provisions they had borrowed from a seal team in San Diego onto a C-130 cargo plane from the Alaska Air National Guard for the final leg to Kiska. He didn't want his men spending any more time on Kiska than necessary. In case the op went all to hell, his men would not know enough to compromise Arctic Angel even if someone was captured.

In Maryland, the final operational meeting wrapped up a little before seven on Monday morning.

"I want to wish all of you a very successful mission," concluded Walker. "With my bum leg I'll just be a burden on your operational efficiency. Besides, the Chinese and I have a history, one that we compromised on years ago. Let me wrap up by asking that whether this thing goes like clockwork or lands in the sewer, you forget that I was part of this mission. I don't want to explain the bodies of a couple of Chinese hit men to the local Montana sheriff. He's a buddy of mine."

"You aren't going with us?" asked Gritt, his face showing his feelings.

"Nope. You're all more than capable of executing your part in this." Walker turned to the scientist, Dr. Davis, from Woods Hole. "Macey, you and Dr. Levitt here are part of this because you are our leading experts on research submarines and on underwater sensing and photography. When this starts, hopefully, you will have eyes on the Chinese sub and can gather all of the information we need to understand and defense it. You helped design the sensor array and selected the cameras. You will be at the consoles recording every reading."

"Commander Quinto, you and your team will standby for the opportunity to seize that sub. If it happens, that would be great, and if it doesn't, your team has been critical to understanding how it is being used. The new data on the sub's capabilities will help understand other locations where it may have been used. When we are done on Kiska, you and your men will continue to chase down those sites."

Walker pointed at Col. Phillips. "Bob, you will help Olga's troops get the sensors planted. Use Davis and Levitt if you need more hands. The sensors are designed to plug and play. You did the survey and the plan; it shouldn't take that long. The devices are already on the jet. Once you're done, lend a hand to Macey and Levitt." He shook Phillips' hand, as he had each of the others that he addressed. "Lisa, you will be the liaison to this office, and Director Chang and the extra set of hands that are needed on most missions. You are probably the only one available who speaks Chinese. Keep us posted and feel free to scream for help if you need it. If the assault gets bloody, make sure that Olga and May recognize that unwanted casualties are part of the game. He extended his hand to Lisa.

"Chad, you are the on-scene commander for this mission. Your initial job will be to add additional bait to the trap if needed. Your idea to strip the Chinese snooper plane of its sensors certainly had to get their attention. Whether they take the bait or not, it will be your call on the attempt the takeover of the sub. If you need to improvise to get data on the sub, do it. I have complete confidence in you and the rest of this team." He shook Gritt's hand.

"And sir," started Gritt, "where will you be if we need to discuss anything with you?"

"The minute you lift off, I'm taking Winchester back to Montana. If you think something is so critical that you need to reach me, think again."

"Just curious, Thad," interrupted Lisa Johnson, "why you don't want to be there on the finish with us? I'm a bit shocked."

"You don't need my help with this. I'm retired, remember? And..." He pushed out of his chair. "...I wasn't kidding about a decades-old compromise with the Chinese. I agreed to never personally participate in any operation where Americans and Chinese could end up killing each other." Walker watched the faces of those in the room. "That is all you will ever know about a mission where everything went to hell and still ended up successful.

"I'll be keeping track of your progress from the comfort of my lakeside house. Gritt has my cell number, but like I said, I really don't want to hear from you."

CHAPTER 39

KISKA ISLAND

THE GULFSTREAM WITH only Lisa Johnson, Bob Phillips, Macey Davis, Oliver Levitt, Carl Quinto and Chad Gritt touched down on the runway at nine that same night. The bright evening sun reflected on the flat calm waters of the bay as a forklift pulled up to the side of the jet. While the others headed to the van driven by Olga, Gritt inventoried the twenty boxes packed by Pete Wilson's CIA technology team, making sure each left the plane. He slipped the four packages marked with a star into a separate duffel bag. The rest went on to a pallet and was swung by the forklift onto a waiting truck.

May Washington waited at the bottom of the air stairs. "We finished the final installations of our systems a couple of days ago. I asked the contractor to keep his technology people for a few more days to help with the installation of your equipment."

"Did they agree?" asked Gritt. He shouldered the duffel and his own pack and started down the stairs.

"The contractor bills the government $200 an hour for his people. Giving us eight men for a couple of days was an easy decision. The guys themselves signed off on it when I promised them a ride back to Anchorage on the Gulfstream. I hope that is okay with the Navy and the pilots."

"The plane and crew are ours for as long as we need them," replied Gritt. "On the way here, we calculated that we can finish the grunt work in about two days. Only team Walker is cleared to do the final testing on any of the equipment. We should be able to get them out of here on Thursday evening."

"How can my people help?" asked May, as Olga's van pulled away, followed by a truck with the equipment.

Gritt handed the graying colonel three copied sheets outlining what needed to be done then referred to a display on his phone. "I'd like to send the techs out about four in the afternoon on Thursday. That would allow a Chinese surveillance satellite to get pictures of the departure. Quinto is going to bring his people in that night. The Chinese have retasked two of their satellites to watch this place since our last trip. They now have eyes on you about every three hours."

"That matches the briefing that the Air Force sent me a couple of days ago. They have also been doing aircraft flybys twice a day for the last couple of days. We thought that they might back off after we messed with their flight, but instead they doubled down."

"You are sure that your laser actually destroyed the sensor system that the Chinese plane was trailing?" asked Gritt.

"Your team asked for the strike, and as it turned out, it was an excellent test of our system. With no damage to the plane or crew, the Chinese had nothing to complain about. I have video of the actual strike and the sensors tumbling into the ocean," offered May. "We cut the half-inch cable holding the trailing sensors with a single pulse from twenty-five miles away."

"Wow, you actually have pictures. That is amazing," added Chad. "If they didn't have enough bait before, that should do the trick." He studied the satellite schedule on his phone. "The Air Guard would rather land here in daylight, but we don't want the bad guys to see any shooters arrive. They need to believe that everything is normal. Our weather guys predict that the cyclone that smashed the Philippines will rotate into the western Aleutians sometime Friday afternoon. Walker and Quinto think the Chinese will use that storm or the next one to launch their strike."

May turned toward the Jeep Cherokee with Park Service stickers on the side. "I guess I'm your ride, Mr. Gritt. By the way, most of the gear we agreed to is already being installed.

Gritt smiled. "Just in case the Chinese have some operatives in Anchorage, we had the Park Service publish an emergency request for all of that, to be delivered to their new facility here. It was amazing how fast they got that out, once their D.C. offices offered to pay for it out of just discovered funds." He carefully slipped the duffel into the back of the Cherokee and closed the hatch. "Are the computers here?

May nodded.

By the time May and Gritt arrived in the great hall of the main building, May's staff was already working with the newcomers to start work. The sensor installations would have to be worked one area at a time to avoid giving the Chinese pictures of unusual activity on the waters around the island. Everything else could be done under cover.

CHAPTER 40

HULUDAO

THE EEL'S CREW finished the provisioning, followed by filling what the designers called the *nutrient tank* next to the reactor. At eleven, the Snow Leopard team and Yang himself arrived and Captain began the launch procedures. The underwater trip from Huludao to Kiska Island was just over two-thousand-four hundred miles. With two scheduled stops every twenty-four hours it would take six days. Captain was anxious to get underway, especially as he watched the discomfort of the commando team trying to settle into a metal tube for days of travel.

The EEL could have departed early, except for Ma who finally arrived only minutes before noon after failing in a last-minute effort to escape the trip. "I assume that your appeal to General Ling did you no good," said Yang with a sneer. "I told you that my plan required your knowledge of Americans and your language skills, Ma. You didn't really think you could shirk your duty, did you?"

Ma said nothing. Ling had disappeared, refusing every attempt to reach him. He slipped the small backpack that everyone on the raiding party was allowed from his shoulder and handed it to a set of hands extended from the hatch before starting down the rubber-coated ladder. He was shocked that his knowledge of China's only intelligence group on America's West Coast wasn't enough to get him out of this trip.

"Open tank doors," ordered Captain.

He motioned for Yang to descend the stairs, and then motioned for one of the divers waiting at the side of the pool to open the huge doors beneath the sub. That same diver would unplug the outside communications cable from a dock receptacle as the sub descended and swim out to a waiting small coastal patrol craft at the dock next to the warehouse. There, the cable would be reconnected to one dangling over the side of the patrol boat offering the EEL outside communications for the first ten miles of their trip. A series of systems tests would be repeated three times in that distance assuring the sub was seaworthy with all systems functioning. With the completion of the last test, the same diver would drop from the patrol boat and disconnect the cable from the EEL, leaving them without any communications with the outside world for the duration of the trip. Captain had heard rumors of a discreet secure communications system develop by an American company. Yang had sent a hastily recruited agent to check on the technology. The agent, who purchased foreign technology for the PLA, had failed to report any progress. In an emergency they could surface and run up a radio antenna, but other than testing the system, it had never been used.

Captain closed and dogged tight the overhead hatch. Stepping into the tiny control room, he gave the order to descend. Unlike a regular submarine that would add water to flood tanks to sink the craft, the EEL had already trimmed itself for a planned equilibrium ninety feet below the ocean's surface. The slightly negative buoyancy meant that the craft would stabilize at ninety feet, but once at sea it would take fifteen minutes to reach that depth. The craft sank slowly until the depth meter showed that they were clear of the tank. Until they were clear of the harbor and their escort, Captain would use power to hold the boat just below their escort.

"Deploy thrusters," ordered Captain. "Make revolutions for quarter speed reverse. Hold descent at thirty feet abeam our escort until the communications are restored."

A preprogrammed sequence of mechanical orders was activated by one of the crew sitting at a computer workstation to the captain's right. From the activation of the run program key, the sub took over all maneuvering, its progress tracked by the operator on two computer monitors.

Two minutes later, the speaker above Captain's head came back to life advising that the escort vessel was leaving the dock and beginning a well-rehearsed departure from the harbor.

Traveling at five knots, the escort remained above and to the right of the EEL for the next two hours as the system checks were completed. "EEL, your big brother is ready to release your tether," came a call over the speaker.

"On my command," replied Captain speaking toward the controller's console. "All stop, all stop."

Less than a minute later, the speaker came to life again. "EEL we will disconnect on the count of ten. Good hunting; one, two, three, four, five, six, seven, eight, nine, ten." A small bell sounded as the cable was disconnected. Captain waited until he heard the sound of the patrol crafts engines revving up before turning back to the control console.

"Make speed twenty knots, depth ninety feet and execute travel plan to target outer marker."

The man at the console called up a second program and tapped the run program key. Inside the sub you could feel the speed slowly accelerate and the deck tilt downward.

"Fascinating," offered Leopard One. "There is almost no sound, in fact, I can hear the engines of the boat moving away more clearly than anything inside your craft, Captain."

"The thrusters are electric, with no moving parts except for the impellers; no gears, no moving shafts, even in the arms that change the direction of thrust. Those are of a flexible alloy. We use electric current to bend them to control direction."

"Systems check," said the captain.

"All systems performing as programmed," came a reply from the console operator. We will be at cruise speed of twenty knots and cruise depth of ninety feet in twenty minutes, Sir."

"Very well," replied Captain. "Advise me of any abnormality only."

He turned to his passenger. "The shape of the hull drives us down with thrust from the stern, and by changing he angle of the thrust, we climb. The sub is pre-balanced to stay at our cruise depth and the thrusters will adjust their angle to hold us there. When we get close to our target, we will set our environmental pod to strip excess oxygen from the water and slowly pump it into a balance tank to change the preset depth. That process happens so slowly that the expelled water leaves the ship with about the same sound as a handful of clams feeding on the ocean floor."

"The sub is virtually silent?" asked Leopard One.

"No, there is a tiny amount of cavitation from the movement of the water through the thrusters. We believe that the Americans have sensors around their critical facilities that can sense that cavitation. They can actually hear the tiny amount of sound from the environmental pod and maybe even normal voices. While we are close to the Kiska base, we will go completely silent except for whispered orders. That's why we practiced your departure from the sub. Once you launch the rafts, the surface noise will hide your approach."

"I will advise my men again on how critical it is that we use only our wrist keypads once you make the sub silent."

"Thank you, commander. Once we begin the final approach and activate the SILIA DRIVE, we will be so quiet that if you were isolated you could hear your own heart beating. That is critical to our mission. With luck, the only noise we will make is the sound of the hatch opening as you depart. Even that is a special brass alloy which makes about as much noise opening and closing as the zipper on a coat."

The commander of the police unit turned to leave, stopping only a few feet away. "Captain, you suggested that we each bring a tablet with movies and books. Still, for six days, those of us with nothing to do are going to get a little antsy. How do you deal with that?"

"My boat is fully automated. Even the captain has little to do while cruising. I rotate the two men on the console every six hours, and even their job is just to monitor. Two more of my crew are in engineering monitoring all of the operational systems. If you are into meditation, I suggest that you will never find a more perfect place than the EEL. For myself, my executive officer and I will play, perhaps, our six thousandth game of chess. We have other video games available that your men can access with their tablets. Our computer has a library of over 10,000 books. There is room in engineering for two men to work out. It is critical that your men stay busy even though they will spend ten hours a day seated and another ten hours in their bunks."

"I will keep an eye on my men, Captain. My exec and I will keep them busy."

"Again, thanks, and if you would, please keep an eye on Ma for me. He is the only one who desperately didn't want to be here. General Yang wants him on this trip, and he will keep an eye on him as well. But Yang has a hair-trigger temper. This is his first actual EEL mission as well. Both of them are more than a little stressed."

Leopard One turned and leaned close to Captain. "Just what the hell do you think is wrong with that young bastard, Ma?"

"I think that General Yang has it right. Ma is a spy who until today has seen his job as playing some kind of exciting game, one where countries never execute those they catch anymore. Even if they are caught, foreign spies are eventually traded for something their country wants. He didn't sign on for a mission like this." The man paused for a moment. "If I were to speak my mind, I would probably add a concern that Yang is in over his head. But of course, I would never speak my mind."

The stress testing that was part of the recruitment process for the SLC commandos had been a critical part of them being selected for the mission. Through the first three days all of them somehow managed to cope with being canned like sardines. Ma seemed lost as he sat hour after hour reading. Yang spent hours sitting with both the operational and engineering operators and reading their manuals.

During the second stop on the third day, Leopard One's curiosity finally forced a conversation he'd bottled up for days. "Why do we stop twice each day. Wouldn't we spend a half day less cooped up if we didn't?" he asked Captain.

"We stop to feed the grass," answered Captain.

"Feed the grass?"

"Until you return from your mission, that is all that I can tell you. It is the secret that makes the EEL completely unique."

CHAPTER 41

KISKA ISLAND

WHILE MAY TRAINED her own staff in the actual operation of Arctic Angel and Angel defense, the security people, contractors and Team Walker buried themselves in preparing the site for a Chinese raid. The sensors had all been installed and tested by noon on Thursday and at four that afternoon eight bone-tired contractors trudged up the air-stairs of the Gulfstream. Their luxurious three-hour trip on the private jet, now just offering a more comfortable place to sleep.

Gritt held the actual departure until he knew that the Chinese satellite would be directly overhead. He orchestrated four or five people out along the runway as the jet lifted into the air and headed northeast.

The jet gone, the group headed back to the headquarters to finish preparations and to test their technology. It was almost one in the morning when Quinto found Gritt leaning on a desk, using an electric screwdriver to reattach the back to a computer in the reception area on the main floor of the building. One of the small packages marked with a star lay empty on the floor.

"The C-130 just diverted to Dutch Harbor, Chad, some kind

of mechanical. The Air Guard is dispatching another from Anchorage to pick up my guys."

"Great, just fucking great." Chad finished closing up the last of four computers hard wired to the modular desks in the offices. He tugged his smartphone from his pocket and pulled up a display. He handed the phone to Quinto. "Those two windows are the only time before tomorrow that we can avoid surveillance. If May's folks detect a C-919 surveillance flyby, the plane may have to circle until the skies are clear. I don't want the bad guys to know that we are reinforcing."

"I'll get down to communications right away and make sure that everyone is on board with the timeline."

"Make sure that they are, we're cutting this really close now. That storm is supposed to be here late tomorrow."

The group took a few minutes for a light breakfast about six the next morning. They were ready, and the only thing on their agenda for the afternoon was setting up a schedule to monitor the instruments and get some sleep. May had returned the base staff to normal duty. Olga's security police went back to their normal routine.

Gritt's head had barely hit the pillow when Quinto tapped him on the shoulder. "My guys will be here about noon. They will be fighting bad headwinds in front of the coming storm. That gives us a couple of hours to get them settled and their plane out of the area before the next satellite pass."

"Good, now go away," answered Gritt. He sat up. "No, feel free to wake me if anything changes."

After two days with no sleep, it seemed like he had just dropped off when a hand shook his shoulder. "The C-130 is holding a hundred and fifty miles north of here. A second Chinese surveillance plane has just appeared on the radar. The last one circled about thirty miles out for over an hour. The pilot of the C-130 advises that even if he can get in by two this afternoon, he will be down to minimums on fuel for the trip back."

"Tell him to plan on stopping back in Dutch Harbor on his way home," answered Gritt.

"His estimates already include stopping in Dutch. The head-winds are really smoking up there, and they are picking up here," replied Quinto. "It's also starting to rain."

Gritt rolled over and sat up. He slid his feet into his favorite Keen walking shoes and forced his body to stand. "I'll take a minute to splash a little water on my face and then join you in our new offices."

"Did you get any sleep?" asked Gritt, as he approached Quinto, who stared out over Kiska harbor.

"I've managed a little over four hours in the last two days, Chad. Once I get my people on the ground and brief them, I've got nothing to do but sleep until the curtain goes up."

"Anything new on the C-130 or the Chinese plane?"

"The Chinese have just finished their fourth racetrack pattern. The last one flew six before leaving. If this guy does the same, he will pull out within a half hour of the next satellite pass. Our plane is still holding. The pilot grew up in Alaska, and he says it's about as rough as he's ever flown in before."

Gritt checked his watch. It was already 1:20. He opened his phone to the satellite schedule. "It's a little under 700 miles from here to Dutch. What does the weather forecast around five this afternoon?"

"Deteriorating, but still flyable according to the update from Anchorage. Probably not much worse than the day we came in."

"I'm inclined to order the C-130 back to Dutch right now for fuel. How long after each satellite pass before the surveillance plane shows up?"

"So far it's been less than an hour."

"If the C-130 gets here between 4:45 and 5:15, he should be able to get in and out without detection."

"I'll pass it on, Chad. I'd hate to think of a crew and my guys ditching up in the middle of a typhoon."

"I'll meet you in the canteen for coffee after you make the call," replied Gritt. "All of this surveillance tells me that the Chinese are getting really serious about this place. Our plane should be able to reach Dutch in an hour and a half. If you allow a half hour for refueling, he is on the runway here at five."

"I've spent a lot of time on C-130's," answered Quinto, as he started for the steel door in the back of the room. "They can handle almost anything as long as the pilots can see." He stopped and looked back at Gritt. "That's if the pilots are any good."

At 4:45, Gritt and Quinto were in the communications center as the C-130 pilot reported that he had begun his GPS approach to Kiska. Nine minutes later, he reported that he was executing a missed approach and was planning on circling out for a second attempt.

"I'm going up to take a look at the weather myself," said Gritt. "Keep me posted."

Climbing the stairs to the main offices, Gritt didn't need to cross over to the windows to see that the weather sucked. Rain lashed the windows, forcing him to find a corner of a window in the lee of the wind to stare down onto the runway and harbor area. It had disappeared. "Fuck, Fuck, Fuck," he mumbled as he started back to communications.

He arrived just as the co-pilot reported wind shear of plus and minus thirty knots only three miles from touchdown. Seconds later, he reported that the plane was down to fifty feet above the waves with less than a quarter mile of visibility. They had the island on radar, but no visibility less than a quarter mile out. Somehow, even over the noise of the wind, those inside the heavy concrete structure heard the roar as the pilot slammed on the power and banked toward what his GPS said was a gap in the mountains on the north side of the runway.

"No fucking way," crackled over the radio speaker, as the pilots headed back to Dutch. "We will wait it out in Dutch and try again as soon as the weather starts to break."

Gritt looked over at Quinto and laughed. "The good thing is that with the winds down on the harbor, nobody is going to launch any rafts tonight. Maybe this will blow through by tomorrow."

CHAPTER 42

LITTLE KISKA ISLAND

THE EEL COULDN'T get too close to the small island just to the south of Kiska. Captain's charts were Second World War vintage, and at a depth of ninety feet the boat was in danger of running into a reef or uncharted rock. Even at ninety feet, the slight rolling of the boat indicated that the storm forecast for that weekend had arrived a little early.

"Re-trim the boat for thirty feet," ordered Captain.

He turned to Leopard One and Ma waiting in the cramped con. "It will take about an hour to bring the boat up to thirty feet. We may already be close to the American sensors, even ten miles out. We will re-ballast in silent mode. I intend to leave the reactor up and environment systems operating for now. There is a storm above us. It will mask our sound."

Ma crossed his arms in front of his chest. "Is that wise, Captain. Why don't you switch to silent mode?"

In six days, Captain had not exchanged a word with Ma since he came aboard. To Captain's knowledge, Ma hadn't spoken to anyone in more than a day. His crew and the SLC team had all commented that the man seemed to be a powder keg about to explode. On a submarine, that could be catastrophic. Captain decided on flattery rather than telling the impudent ass to shut up.

"Good question. Ma, the compressors that pump the water from the ballast tanks make almost no sound. The tradeoff for silence is inefficient operation. They use a lot of power. That would drain the batteries quickly, and we may need battery power for more than a day, as we approach the target. We have done this more than a dozen times; do not be afraid."

"I am not afraid of this mission, Captain. I still don't know why I am even here, but I probably know more about this American base than anyone in the PLA. It must be either defeated or at least compromised. But if the Americans detect us this far out, we will fail and probably die in this tin can."

"Go find yourself a cup of tea, Ma. We are going to burn an hour changing depth and then creep into a bite on the outside of the small island off from the mouth of Kiska harbor. I hope to find calm in this storm. It will be dusk in five hours, but there is no way to launch rafts until the storm swings to the east calming the waters of the harbor. That means no mission for about thirty hours. In the interim, I am going to put two of my swimmers ashore to study the harbor for tomorrow night's raid."

"Is there any chance that I can accompany them, sir? I am scuba qualified."

"As I said, it is time for you to get a cup of tea, Ma. Let my experienced team do its job."

"I was just suggesting that my expertise might be--"

"Ma, if you do not depart the con at this instant, I will have you removed. Am I clear?" said Captain.

As Ma turned, Leopard One offered just loud enough to be heard, "I really worry about that young prick along on this mission."

"General Yang wants him along," was all that Captain said.

Three hours later, the EEL positioned itself only fifty feet from the shore of Little Kiska Island. Within minutes, two of the EEL's divers had slipped from the hatch into the cavity in the bottom of the boat. The cavity had been pumped full of air which allowed them to exit with no telltale bubbles.

They would be back within three hours, with infrared photographs and measurements of the harbor, at least the best they could manage in driving rain and winds that lifted rocks from the hillsides above the sub, dropping them into the bay. The occasional sound, as a rock sunk far enough to hit the hull, made sure that no one aboard got much sleep.

CHAPTER 43

KISKA ISLAND

THE FAILURE OF the Seal Team to reach the island needed to be remedied or any effort to seize the sub would be scrubbed. Gritt checked his watch as he had been doing for hours. The first two windows to bring the plane back without satellite surveillance had come and gone as the storm continued to rage outside. Gritt busied himself with familiarizing Lisa, Bob and Macey with the programs installed in the computer network set up in the newly finished glass cubicles. Two of Olga's security team were now part of the briefing.

One computer displayed telemetry information. Another displayed systems readiness and performance data. A third ran a program that displayed a series of videos from cameras hastily set up around the area, with a series of distance and detail data popping up at random. The fourth ran a targeting program while the fifth was a server to the other four. Rather than risk any of the highly trained operators, May's team would be operating from what she called the bunker. Even if the facility was compromised, none of the people in the office area knew enough to compromise the entire project.

Carl Quinto handed Gritt a cup of black coffee as both stood in front of the narrow windows overlooking the harbor. "Even if the Chinese could launch rafts in this weather, they would never make it to shore. But they would never attempt it in daylight anyway."

"The weather should break tonight," said Gritt. "Even if they are already out there somewhere, I think they will use tonight to reconnoiter which means we are at least thirty-six hours from a visit. We have a day to get your men here."

"Maybe," replied Quinto. "The optimum time to launch any operation is when the other side doesn't think you can. It troubles me that I am thinking exactly that right now." He turned back toward the glass-enclosed offices. "Once a Chinese team gets here, they will penetrate the perimeter in five minutes or less. It will only take a minute to blow an outside door to this building. We will have to leave the steel door to the dungeon open or our people will not have time to escape. The fake manuals next to the computers will be an easy target. The computers themselves are password and biologically protected. It would take days to crack them unless one of our people is captured. Even then it would be very difficult."

"Do you really think the Chinese attack will come tonight?" asked Gritt.

"Nope. But I think we better be ready just in case they are crazier than I am."

"The weather is supposed to lay down about four this afternoon," said Gritt. We may have to let the C-130 land even if that damned satellite is watching. We can hide your team in a truck or something until it's okay to get them into the tunnel."

"You know that the weather is moving east?" replied Quinto. "We both grew up in Alaska where only newcomers and idiots predict the weather, but even if it improves here, a storm like this will ground even an Air Guard plane in Dutch Harbor."

"The storm is supposed to cross the Aleutians and move up into Bristol Bay. Dutch is expected to get wet, but nothing like this," said Gritt as he walked over to help a young Air Force policeman trying to imitate a computer expert. "I'll personally call the head of the Alaska Air Guard and tell her that we need that plane here this afternoon. "I've known her for years. She went to school with my sister before joining the Air Force."

Quinto slapped a hand on Gritt's arm, turning him. "Is she the kind of officer that would go out on a limb to get that plane here?"

Gritt paused, running through several times he and the commander had crossed paths. "The answer is no; she will not order the pilot to do anything that could come back to haunt her."

"That's why I asked. Those of us in Special Ops have learned that most officers outside of our community live by different rules." Quinto headed toward the door. "If I had kept my head together, I would have never allowed the team to become separated. I am sorry. I overthought this whole fucking operation."

"Forget it, Commander. This entire mess is stretching each of us. But your question helps me right now. I'm not going to call the General. I don't want her ordering the aircraft commander not to fly. We will count on his pilot in command mind set. He proved himself last night. He gave everything he had trying to land. Let's get together about three and check on their departure."

Gritt's watch said 2:50 when he saw Quinto jog into the room. The look on his face was not that of a happy camper. "What's wrong?"

"The pilot of our plane just called. This storm is slamming Dutch. He was just about to load my guys for another try. A wind gust slammed a commercial freight plane. It landed hard and collapsed the landing gear. He's blocking the runway. Until they get all of the freight off and empty the fuel tanks, the airport manager refuses to move it."

"When will they get it cleared?"

"Our pilot says that he hopes to be off the ground sometime after midnight."

Gritt stared at the windows where rain still pounded against the glass. "I think we will be okay. Like I said, even if the bad guys are out there, I think they will use tonight to look around. Getting your guys here early tomorrow morning should work."

Gritt turned and headed to the small center in the back of the building, with a SECURITY sign on the door. He hadn't spent five minutes with Olga since arriving. That had been disappointing. He pushed the heavy door open to find her monitoring the six video screens on the wall of her office. "Got a minute, Major?" he asked.

He'd almost forgotten how stunning the woman was, but that evaporated instantly. The look on her face was all business. Her eyes locked on his and demanded all of his attention.

"Quinto's seals are stuck in Dutch Harbor," he started. "I'd like a minute to brief you on part of the plan that until now you didn't need to know about."

Olga pointed at a chair next to her heavy steel desk and turned toward a coffee pot on a cabinet. She filled two huge cups with coffee and slid one to Gritt as she dropped into her chair. "Okay Lieutenant, Shoot."

CHAPTER 44

KISKA SOUND

CAPTAIN'S TWO MEN tapped on the recessed hatch in the bottom of the hull a little after nine. While they were scouting, the boat remained in a slightly over pressurized state, allowing the hatch to be opened and the men to slip inside with no noise. Ten minutes later, the small galley had been cleared and Captain, his exec, Yang, Leopard one and Ma crowded around a small table with the two scouts.

"Show us what you have," whispered Captain, trying to exert control before Yang pushed ahead without adequate intelligence.

"The photos and scale model that we have been studying is almost perfect," offered the young lieutenant who commanded the reconnaissance. We were able to get laser measurements. The scale models used in planning are correct. There are no ships in the harbor. There are two passenger boats, about eight meters each at a small dock next to the main wharf. Both are powered by outboard motors. There is also a small barge and pusher boat. There are no people in the dock area. "

The scout took a minute to open a photograph on the small tablet that he carried and passed it around. "The facility itself is almost exactly like the model. A large fence encloses it with four guard stations at the corner. The weather broke for a few minutes a couple of times while we watched. They are open to the weather and there was a single guard in each. They did not appear very attentive, as the few minutes that we could study them, they were mostly worried about staying dry. I only have photos of the two towers at this end of the compound." He tapped the keyboard and pictures of each tower popped up.

"As we planned for, the towers in the rear of the compound are surrounded by higher hills. We have a clear shot at each of them within range of the dart weapon. The Americans have solved our dilemma of how to target the guards in the front two towers. There is construction equipment parked within fifty yards of each tower that will allow one of our people get high enough to slip a dart over the front of the guard box." He pointed to a small crane and an excavator in the picture before he called up another picture.

"This is a picture of one of the guards taken with our maximum telephoto setting and expanded again using the software of the computer." The picture was of a fairly tall black woman bundled into a foul weather suit that covered all but her eyes. She wore goggles. "The guards appear to have specially made rain gear, which makes sense in this environment. Even with the gear, this guard spent little time facing into the wind. You will note that there appear to be no bulges under the raincoat indicating that she is not wearing a bulletproof vest."

The next photo was of the concrete tunnel entrance to the compound. "As we suspected, there is a gate set just inside the tunnel and based on the length, probably a second in the rear, allowing security to allow access one vehicle at a time if necessary. We cannot tell you anything about the gates, but our planning assumes that they may be difficult to breach. It appears that the only weapons covering the wall are in the towers, so our plan to scale the walls of the tunnel to get in makes sense. Once in we will need to leave two of our people to blow the gates from the inside to allow a quick retreat."

"What about a location to go ashore?" asked Captain.

"The beach below the compound is still our best option. It is to the right of the airstrip. Our plan to use the ditch along the runway as cover for our approach, will not work. The ditch looks more like a river with all of the rain. We will have to use whatever cover we can find and move slowly to avoid being detected. With all of the weather here and continuing construction, our assumption that they are not using motion detectors is probably accurate. Our specially lined rain suits should hide us from the infrared detectors."

"I don't like those small boats," offered Ma. "They could be used to intercept us on the way back to the EEL, especially if we are towing the computers in balloons. We should disable them on the way in."

"We have exactly the number of men to accomplish this mission. We do not have the men or time to deal with a target almost two miles from where we land," said Chi.

"You continue to assume," countered Ma, "that the Americans are just sitting there dumb and happy. And while you are all looking at me like I'm the enemy, let me add that armed with only dart guns we could not stop reinforcements landing on that runway."

"Ma, your role tonight will be to quickly examine any documents we find and to check what we find on the computers before we haul them all the way to the sub. You will also be responsible for conversation with any people we capture," said Yang.

"I know my role," shot back Ma. "I understand that announcing that we have placed explosives on the runway should deter any landing while we are ashore is important. I'm just saying for the last time that that runway is a risk."

"Do your job, Ma, and the rest of us will do ours. The EEL team has more than fifteen successful missions."

"So, we are a go for tonight?" asked Captain.

Everyone but Ma nodded their heads.

"The launch site is eight miles from where we sit. The Silia Drive gives us a maximum of five knots of speed, but we will approach at three to minimize our water displacement. You will be ready to launch at 12:30, the darkest part of the night at this latitude."

"In and out in one hour," said Yang. "Just as we rehearsed.

CHAPTER 45

KISKA ISLAND

"ASSUMING THAT TONIGHT is quiet," said Olga, as she walked into the office commandeered for sensor monitoring, "the lot of you could really use showers."

"And I thought that you were taking a shine to me," answered Gritt.

"You're kind of cute, and you kind of stink. The showers in the old construction camp are only a few feet from your rooms. You have no excuse."

"I'm glad that we didn't have this conversation this afternoon," replied Gritt, "I would have taken it as an order from a senior officer, and it would have interrupted the three hours and twenty minutes of sleep that Quinto and I managed."

"Perhaps you will consider buying a fellow officer dinner some time when we aren't anticipating imminent death?" offered Olga. "I'll bet you clean up just fine. I get it about the sleep though. Anything on the sensors yet?"

Macey looked up at Gritt. "The young woman just asked you out. If I was you, I would accept before she changes her mind."

Gritt turned to Macey seated at the console. With his lack of sleep, the offer and Macey's comments went right over his head. "Well? Is there anything on the sensors?"

"Maybe," he replied bringing both Gritt and Olga around where they could see the screens. "And the pretty girl is right, you definitely need a shower."

"I just worked 44 straight hours, so let's get past what your nose is telling you and get to what the 20 million dollars' worth of junk you planted on the ocean floor is saying. Okay?"

The scientist pointed to a screen on his left. "This screen is monitoring underwater light. As long as the sun was up, it was worthless in shallow water, but with the dimming light it has indicated light disruption on two monitors set about a quarter mile apart. The problem is that it never gets completely dark. We may be seeing only odd refraction in the land of the midnight sun." The screen displayed two lines of data, each showing something detected for only a few seconds. He pointed to a screen to his right. "Just like the light sensors, the pressure sensors are set a quarter mile apart. Again, two sensors seem to indicate a tiny discrepancy from background density over a fifteen-minute period."

"With everything that you distributed out there, that's not much," replied Gritt.

Olga pointed to the two displays, one at a time. "Look at the timeline. Both types of sensor reflect disturbances at the exact same interval. If they are right, whatever they detected is moving at about three miles an hour."

"The beautiful officer has had more sleep than the stinky one," replied Macey. "That is exactly my calculation."

"How do we check?" answered Gritt.

"We watch for the next abnormality which will also give us direction. My guess is that we have company on the way, but maybe not tonight. Maybe they are just positioning."

Gritt stepped back smiling at Olga. "Good catch. I'm going to key an alert to the six people who need to know. Everything else has to look normal. By the way, the rest of Quinto's men should be here about two in the morning."

"I'm still not happy about leaving at least four of my people out there where they may be targeted," she replied. "If this actually turns into a shooting war, they are really vulnerable."

"If the sub that may or may not be out there was Iranian, I would never have set this up this way," lied Gritt. "They would have no concerns about killing everyone they could, but the Chinese have taken great care not to cause casualties so far. Anyway, I'm hoping that these are just sensor bugs and that we have another day. I'd like to get the rest of Seal Team 4 on the ground."

Macey looked back at Gritt. "I know you well enough by now to know you're a smart guy. You realize that the other side doesn't give a shit what you would like. I think you need to brief the folks up in your control room on just how fast they need to get inside that blast-proof door and get it closed. If it is still open when a raiding team blasts their way into the building, this facility could be compromised."

"Use your wrist communicator if anything solid comes up," said Gritt. He turned to Olga. "You should pull the SECURITY plate off from the door to your office. Neutralizing base security would be my number one objective if I was raiding this place. I'm sorry you have to stay in there alone, but you have the only cameras inside the compound. Timing on this is everything. The moment we document raiders inside the wall, Macey here begins a full scan of that sub."

"Thanks. If I see anything, I'll transmit the code to those with wrist-com devices and head straight for the dungeon. I can replicate much of my video feed from there." She watched Gritt jog for the stairs. "Stay alive, Lieutenant." She turned to Macey. "How is it that the youngest person on Team Walker is running the show?"

"Annapolis grad at twenty. Law degree while on active duty, in less than four years. Eighth generation of military officers and whip smart but humble. Thad Walker knew what he was doing. The rest of us are too far into our own little worlds to run this show."

Olga actually giggled, which shocked Macey. "Anything I can get you Dr. Davis?"

"I'd still like to see just what the base folks are getting on their consoles. It might help me define what I'm seeing."

"I agree that it is a bit ridiculous that you are only thirty feet away from those people, but not allowed to look over their shoulder; but only Lieutenant Gritt has full access and that is only because the Secretary of Defense overrode Air Force orders."

CHAPTER 46

KISKA HARBOR

CAPTAIN HAD BEEN right. With the silent drive engaged, you could hear people breathing in the next compartment and maybe your own heart beating. Yang felt a tiny tap on his arm and looked down onto the communicator strapped to his wrist. He'd wondered if he could sense the small pin that tapped his arm over his waterproof suit indicating that he had a call. He could, and he felt shocked as he stared at the message on the display. "We Are Here."

Captain held up one finger to the man on the control computer. The man moved the cursor to the SURFACE button and tapped execute. The boat had been creeping into the bay for two hours, all of the time pumping air into the ballast tanks. The EEL was only five feet below the still choppy surface when Captain stopped the approach. It would take ten more minutes to silently surface the craft, just enough time for the final check of equipment.

Six LED lights illuminated at the top of the ladder. Captain held up a second finger and a crewman climbed the short ladder and opened the hatch, pushing a rubber collar up through the water draining into the boat. The collar slid into a plastic clip, locking it in place and cutting off the water flooding into the boat.

Two men were up the ladder in seconds; a raft bundle passed into their hands the moment they cleared the hatch. Two more men and another raft followed them. Moments later, a third duo was on the deck. Next, three more men climbed the ladder where they were each handed tiny electric outboard motors.

"That's nine of seventeen on the surface," flashed over two-dozen wrist communicators. "Next up are the three officers commanding each raft." Moments later, the EEL's executive officer and the two SLC officers were up the ladder. "Twelve of seventeen on the surface," flashed.

On the surface, the men responsible for the rafts pulled the cords on eight compressed air cartridges inflating individual compartment in the rafts. In seconds, the motorman had his twelve-pound motor clamped onto the tiny hard rubber transom. As each raft was made ready, the raft commander signaled, "ready on raft one," and then "ready on raft two, and finally, "ready on raft three."

Five more men raced up onto the surface. Everyone on the outside deck of the EEL found their footing slippery on what seemed to be water soaked long shag carpet. As the last man climbed the ladder, a crewman unlocked the spray collar and slipped it back into the boat and then closed and dogged the hatch. A minute later, someone outside tapped on the hatch four times.

The first raft, with only five men aboard slid off from the deck, the motorman tilting the outboard into run position. He watched as the other four men slipped their arms into loops in the synthetic material of the raft, each checking to make sure the waterproof packs next to them were secure. Twisting the handle of the tiller, the motorman headed toward the faint shoreline in the dim light of the stormy night. In seconds all three rafts were headed to shore."

"Make depth twenty feet and hold at this position," whispered Captain to the man at the console. "Good Luck," he tapped onto his wrist com while the boat was still near enough to the surface to allow transmission. He would wait at that spot to see whether or not the raiders had returned. If they were not back in two hours, he would dive the boat and move to another location pre-designated as an emergency pick up point.

If things went well, a sensor on the top of the deck would pick up a color-coded light signal from the first raft back to the pick-up site. With the raid over by then, he would use all of the remaining compressed air to shoot the sub back to the surface where the launch procedures would be reversed. The emergency blow was noisy, but by then Captain figured that silence was no longer important.

Each raft started the five-minute run to shore. The one-foot chop on the water washed over each raft, surrounding the men and equipment with cold North Pacific water. The riders lay with their faces to the side, grabbing breaths between each wave. Only the motorman sat high enough to see calm water near the shore, the surface turned coarse by huge drops of falling rain.

CHAPTER 47

KISKA ISLAND

MACEY WAS CALM as could be as he tapped out a message on his wrist communicator. "One more light and one more pressure intercept on the same line. Four metallic sounding intercepts on the sound sensors. Location, 200 yards off from the beach on the southwest end of the runway. The party is on."

Macey busied himself with making sure that all of the recordings from the device array in the harbor were recording. He started his own tiny silent submersible, that lay under the huge freight dock, toward where he thought the Chinese submarine waited. The trip would take thirty minutes to travel to where he estimated the submarine had surfaced.

The disguised submersible descended after receiving the location instructions from Macey. It began its preprogrammed silent approach to where it was directed. Upon reaching that spot, it would begin a search pattern to find the intruder, moving away a short distance after it did and surfacing to await instructions to steal its secrets.

In the control room, six people busied themselves at their decoy workstations protected by thick bullet-proof partitions from the doors at either end of the room. The heavy steel door to the dungeon sat only half open. One tap on the emergency close button in the secure hallway would slam the door in three seconds. Anyone caught in the doorway would be sliced in half as it closed.

In security, Olga began a series of deep breaths, trying to calm herself, as she waited for indications of a compound breach.

CHAPTER 48

KISKA ISLAND

THE EEL'S EXECUTIVE officer pulled the first raft up onto the beach and secured it with the quarter inch bowline as the other four men on the raft unstrapped the packs. One man carried the pack with the dart guns up onto the beach and stripped away the waterproof wraps. He slipped a clip of bullet ant venom darts into each weapon and checked to make sure that the spare clip was still in the compartment in the stock.

As each raider passed him, he handed them their weapon. The last person traded him his pack for a weapon and the five men started for the runway embankment only 200 yards from where they had landed. The four included both of the snipers from the Snow Leopard Commandos and the EEL's two most experienced shooters. Their job was to neutralize the guards in the towers.

The next raft slid up on the beach seconds later. This time six men scrambled from the raft, repeating the process. This group's job was to scale the front gate, leaving their ropes dangling as they moved toward the small block building behind the main structure. Four of those men would secure the construction camp while the other two would move directly to what their planners figured was the power plant.

The third raft carried Yang and Ma and four men. One of those men would remain with the rafts. "You are the only man armed with a lethal weapon," said Yang. "You are carrying a Russian AK74 and Russian ammunition. I doubt that the Americans would be deceived, but it is part of the plan. Do not use it unless one of the Americans threatens our ride home. Got it?"

He, like many others, was more afraid of the General than the Americans.

The other five would use the climbing ropes to follow the earlier team. Once inside, two of the raiders would plant explosives to clear the gates that blocked the tunnel while the other three started for the main building. After the main compound was secured, Yang would send some men up the mountain to the actual laser site.

Ma jogged behind Yang who himself was following one of the EEL's most experienced raiders. The winds had dropped to less than twenty knots, but rain and mist still occasionally blurred the image of the huge building on the hill above them. The route chosen took advantage of the terrain, first along the runway and then moving along depressions left from trenches built by the Japanese in 1942. Ten minutes from the beach they passed the first of six collapsed WWII bunkers and several rusting field guns left behind as the Japanese had slipped more than 3,000 men out of the bay in only an hour, somehow getting past American submarines sent to bottle up the harbor just before the invasion.

Below the front guard stations, two SLC sharpshooters scaled the construction equipment left in front of the walls; then waited for the signal that the two EEL shooters were in position above the rear towers. Both men twisted their bodies away from the wind. Even the specially coated optics on their rifle scopes could fill with splattered water, making it difficult to pick out targets only fifty yards away in the rotten weather and twilight. They waited less than five minutes before first the number one and then two flashed onto their communicators.

Both snipers slid their weapons into the open, each finding a guard huddled in the same green rain gear that the scouts had seen. They centered the tiny illuminated red dot of their scopes on a shoulder and fired.

At the rear of the compound, the two EEL shooters had moved onto the hillside slightly above the height of the towers. The distance to the target was more than seventy yards for each of them. Luckily, they found rocks to rest their weapons, but with the wind it was still a long shot. Each shooter precisely measured the distance using a range finder and then lifted a tiny wind meter into the wind. In seconds, they had adjusted a dial on their scope for the distance and then a second for the wind factor. Centering the dots in their scopes on the lower torso of the guards, they squeezed the trigger.

The guard in the Northeast tower turned from the wind, wiping his goggles with a silicone cloth to improve their ability to shed rain, when something hit his left thigh. His scream carried across the compound, so terrifying that the guard in the Northwest tower turned just as a dart hit him in the butt. The two screams were enough to turn both guards in the front towers more than a hundred yards away just as darts lanced into their back and shoulder. Both dropped, writhing in pain, their screams joining those of their friends.

The winds and rain had forced the guards to switch their microphone communications devices from voice actuated to press-to-talk. Inside the facility, Olga heard nothing. The scanning surveillance cameras she was watching only focused on the guard towers about every two minutes. For the fifth time in five minutes she checked the infrared sensor screen above her desk. It still showed nothing unusual.

Shooters outside of all four towers rushed to the walls, lofting ropes with grappling hooks onto the towers, scaling the walls in seconds, their packs and weapons over their shoulders. The first one over the wall was one of the SLC snipers. Launching himself into the guard tower, he landed on the body of a small woman, her body twisting and pounding in pain. He didn't wait to see if she was conscious. Kneeling on her back to slow her movement, he used his knife to slit the guard's rain gear where the exploding dart had ripped the material. From a pocket in his vest he produced a syringe like device with a dozen short needles. He pressed the quarter inch needles around the bruised area and pushed a plunger until it clicked.

The anti-venom slowly working into her bloodstream hunting down the product of bullet ants and neutralizing it. He waited a minute and then pushed the plunger again until it stopped moving. The second dose was a sedative that should keep the guard asleep for at least an hour. His message, 4 clear, on his transmitter said that the guard at post four was subdued. He watched as 3 clear, 1 clear, and 2 clear appeared on his screen. Now he would wait for the team coming over the tunnel wall.

"Go, go, go!" yelled the SLC deputy commander, as his com showed that all four guard towers were secure. Knotted ropes with hooks sailed into the air, hoping to find something solid on top of the horseshoe shaped tunnel. Both slid back to the ground. "All the way over the top," ordered the officer. He jogged to the other side just as the hook rattled down the other side. "Hook both hooks together, then work them back to the roof." He sped to the other side, repeating the order. "Now tie off the ends somewhere and get the hell up on that wall. Use the other four ropes to get down the other side."

Inside the building, one of the camera screens froze, and a border around the screen went red. There on the camera at the front gate was a man with an oddly shaped weapon over his shoulder.

"Son of a bitch," she murmured. She tilted her left wrist and began to type on the unfamiliar com device. YELLOW, she typed and then hit send.

Going back to the four cameras on the inside of the compound she tapped on the FAST SCAN button. In seconds, all four cameras had stopped panning and the screens were frozen with pictures of men leaving the towers and others racing up the walls on either side of the main building headed toward the construction camp. She released the camera screen pointed at the gate. The live feed showed more people dropping into the compound.

Re-targeting the camera overlooking the construction trailers she waited a few seconds for some of the attackers to appear to either side of the camp. She watched as they kicked in the doors of each trailer and lobbed either smoke or gas grenade into them while the two men who had come from the northern towers covered the back. "Thank God the only people staying in the camp was Team Walker," she mumbled. She tapped the word RED onto the com device, hit send, and launched herself for the inside door just as she heard someone slam something against the door to the outside.

Inside the main building, Gritt looked up from his wrist just in time to see a tiny drone pass slowly in front of the windows on the left and then swinging to the ones in front. Whoever was coming would have a clear picture of the inside of the building before breaching. Nobody had considered drones. Hopefully, it makes no difference he thought, just as Olga ran into the room. The drone stopped where it could watch her.

"Clear the room!" Gritt shouted from his place in front of one of the computer terminals. He watched as Olga raced to the back of the room and turned the dial of what he thought was a thermostat. A loud bell sounded inside the room.

CHAPTER 49

KISKA ISLAND

YANG, LEOPARD ONE and Ma huddled around the screen of a tablet computer below the main building. "It's just as we suspected. There is only a small staff right now. Look, with no threat there are even empty desks," offered Chi.

"I still think something is wrong," said Ma. You think you have surprised them. Their camera's must have detected our approach, but many are still at their desks."

"Order the breach of all three doors," said Yang, ignoring Ma.

The Leopard Commando leader typed the code for breach onto his wrist communicator. In seconds explosives set against the two main steel doors and the one in the security office detonated. The men watched fascinated as their raiders entered from the left and right.

"The men on the back door are in what they think is the security office. It is empty, but there is another steel door keeping them from entering the building," said Chi. The team had switched to the faster voice communications since the enemy already knew that they were there.

"Tell your men to go to the door on the west side of the building; it is open," said Yang.

The three men headed toward the closest open door, arriving just as the men who had secured the guard towers arrived.

Leopard One stopped the men, pointing to a small four-seat vehicle that looked like an oversized golf cart. "You four men will take that cart and breach the laser building at the top of the mountain. Use the explosives in this pack to blow the back compound gate to access the road and then use what you need to gain access to the laser building. Take as many pictures as you can in ten minutes, grab any diagrams or manuals you find and dismantle any control systems that you can carry away with you. I want you back here in thirty minutes."

"You go with them," ordered Yang. "Let me know of any problems."

Yang didn't wait for the men to leave before bolting into the well-lit operations room. Behind a glass wall, the Americans were shutting down their computers. The man who led the breach pointed frustratingly toward a heavy steel door in the rear of the building. "The Americans are locking themselves in some kind of safe room."

Yang turned angrily toward the man. "I made it clear that we wanted to capture as many of the operators as possible, even if you needed to stop them with the venom. We need their passwords."

"I am sorry, General, but the glass barriers are of a very heavy material. Our dart weapons will not penetrate the glass."

"You were all issued breaching explosives. Couldn't you blow one of the walls?"

The man pointed at a computer terminal at a desk on the other side of the glass. "We didn't want to destroy the computers you came to steal."

Yang held out his hand. The raider dropped one of his charges in the commander's palm. He watched quietly as Yang slipped a knife from his belt and calmly cut the charge in half, leaving the detonator intact. He placed the charge against a heavy glass door only a few feet away and tugged the cord on the detonator. "Move, move back out the door," he calmly ordered, following the last man. Moments later, a small explosion and the sound of shattering glass brought a small army of men back into the building.

In the dungeon, the surveillance cameras hidden in the control offered an eagle's eye view of what was going on thirty feet above the bunker. Olga and Gritt pushed their chairs closer to the large thirty-six-inch monitor, as the Chinese raiders flooded the room.

"Those guys are really good," commented the head of base security. She checked her watch. From the time I saw the first man outside the front gate, it has taken them seven minutes to gain access."

They watched in horror, as the door to the woman's bathroom door flew open and one of Olga's guards who'd been trapped in the room as the attack started, made a dash for the steel door. She was less than halfway to the door, ignoring screams to stop when one of the attackers lifted his oddly shaped weapon and fired. The woman grabbed at the back of her left thigh and crashed to the floor, only feet from where the steel door slammed shut. Her scream, picked up by microphones hidden with the cameras, infuriated both Gritt and Olga. The woman's body twisted and writhed until one of the attackers pressed some kind of device against her leg.

Yang turned to Ma. "Talk to the people in their hiding place. I am sure they are watching and listening."

Ma scanned the room, finally finding a tiny red light in the center of an EXIT sign where there was no exit. He pulled at the scarf that he had added to his face in a weak attempt to hide his identity. "We are using non-lethal ammunition. The pain probably rendered your guards unconscious for a short period. The anti-venom stops the effects of the wound in seconds. Those in the guard towers also received a dose of sedative to keep them unconscious for an hour."

Olga picked up a microphone next to the console. "I am Major Olga Tvorshik, United States Air Force; what do you want?"

"The Chinese government believes that this base is a nuclear attack facility designed to allow a first strike at China in violation of international nuclear non-proliferation treaties," responded Ma. "We are here only to gather evidence of that provocation, and then we will be on our way."

"There are no nuclear weapons anywhere in the Aleutian Islands," replied Olga as Gritt slid from his seat and headed toward the room where Macey was monitoring his sensors.

"You will understand," continued Ma, "if we do not take your word for that. We have men on the way to the nuclear power station that you built, and others on the way to the facility at the top of the mountain where we are sure they will find missile silos. Our men have been ordered to take no action to destroy any missiles or in any other way release any radiation. Again, we are only here to secure evidence of America's treaty violation."

"You are wrong about the purpose of this facility," continued Olga, as she watched four raiders methodically search every desk and bookcase, piling documents and binders on a desk near the door where her guard lay unmoving. "You will learn that is the truth." Olga paused, remembering Gritt's briefings. "Still, I have to thank you for not using lethal ammunition on my people."

"We are not heathens, Major," continued Ma. "When the woman on the floor recovers enough, we will interrogate her and then we will take all of the materials we find and be gone. You will hear from my government soon, when we lodge a formal protest to your subterfuge."

Yang turned to the six men crowded around him and Ma.

Olga leaned back to where she could see four more monitors, duplicates of those in her security office. "I don't know your name," she started, "but I note that the men you sent up on the hill have just penetrated the fence around that building. They will find the same thing there as at the power station. It is built of heavy reinforced concrete with ten-inch thick steel doors. Your men will not be able to penetrate the building. Even the doors at the top of the building are made of heavy steel with no hinges exposed to the outside. The doors have heavy lips around the edges resting on reinforced concrete. There is no place to set a charge to open them. If you send men to the top, they will have exactly thirty seconds to leave before a fully automated weapons system will sweep the building. Your men will die. It can only be overridden from inside this facility."

She watched, as the man behind the speaker held a communicator similar to that strapped to her arm close to his face and began talking.

At the top of the hill, the commander of the commandos listened as Yang passed on Olga's warning just as the men, he now commanded placed two heavy charges against the edge of the only door to the building. Seconds later, the camera set below a light on a post near the front gate showed a huge explosion and moments later, showed the massive steel door still standing.

"The door is still intact," the raider into his communicator. "We used half of our explosives and barely made a mark. I heard your warning, but we need to see if we can penetrate from the roof. There is a large radar dome behind the building but other than that, no indication of what is inside."

Moments later, his men had launched two climbing ropes twenty feet onto the rooftop and started clambering up the wall. The first man pulled himself onto the roof and jogged to three steel hatches set in a row in the concrete roof. He knelt to study the first one as a siren and a red light began flashing. He watched in horror as a small cabinet shaped device began to rise from the roof, a door in the front opening to reveal the barrel of some kind of weapon.

The second man began to pull himself up as the weapon turned toward the corner of the building to his right and began firing, sweeping a swath from just above the deck and up more than five feet. The gun fire sounded like a bee buzzing. Hundreds of rounds poured from the multi-barreled weapon. The second man ducked below the edge just as the weapon swept where his rope had hung on a rain channel on the roof.

The man already on the roof ran and then jumped, his body just starting to drop, as the weapon swept past him. Twenty bullets riddled the man before his body dropped out of the killing zone. His body crumpled to the ground, a mass of blood and fabric.

"I am sorry about the death of your man on the mountain," said Olga even before the EEL's officer could report what had happened. "I tried to warn you."

The men at the top of the hill retreated, staring at their fallen comrade. A bell on another screen drew her attention.

Olga watched, as the raiders tried to unplug the computers at the workstations, finding the coaxial cables attached with some kind of locked-in fitting instead of a normal screw on type. The men were obviously in a hurry. Instead of taking the time to figure out the fitting, they used heavy clippers to cut the cables. She didn't know why, but Gritt had insisted on the odd configuration.

Yang's face turned ashen as the report from the top of the hill reinforced what the woman's voice had just told him. He leaned toward Ma, whispering.

"We will kill the woman by the door if you do not give us access to the building on the mountain," said Ma.

"I cannot open any of the facilities from this temporary security desk in our secure room. It would have been possible from the workstation directly in front of you, but unfortunately your men have cut the cables. It would take hours for a technician to build a new cable." Olga prayed that the men in the control room would not call her bluff.

What was obviously an argument had broken out between the man talking and the slightly older man behind him.

She watched as one of the raiders motioned those men to the desk where the raiders were piling the materials they were gathering. The two men stopped talking as they began sorting through dozens of binders created by Team Walker's experts. The man who was speaking English opened one at a time and translated the title page for the older man.

"We have documents on the power source, the power control and the laser itself," Ma told Yang. "There are instructional manuals for the computers, but nothing on the computer programs."

CHAPTER 50
KISKA ISLAND

GRITT SLID A chair up next to Macey. "What do we have professor?"

"Not a hell of a lot," replied Macey. "There are virtually no magnetic or electronic signals emanating from that sub. I could track its movement by monitoring water pressure, but I have absolutely no idea how it could move precisely with no sound of turbulence or harmonics. The only sounds are background noises common in any shallow water. I have the drone waiting only a few yards away, but the underwater camera only shows what looks like a big sea cucumber, almost black." He called up an image on a screen. "I'm not kidding. If I thought it was possible, I would be telling you that the raiders arrived in a whale or huge shark or something." He paused and looked up at Gritt's face. "Do you want me to move the drone in closer to see if we can get a clearer picture?"

"No, Professor, not until we get a little further into this. Quinto, Walker and I hope to actually grab that sub if we get the chance."

"But Quinto's boys are stuck 700 miles from here."

"Not anymore. In fact, they should be here in the next half hour," replied Gritt.

Before he could explain the contingency plan a speaker system in the dungeon drowned out his voice. "Kiska Island, this is Air Guard. I have your Navy boys aboard. We are twenty minutes out, and I have begun a GPS approach to the Kiska Airport. I have your automated weather but wondered if I could get a visual update."

Gritt winced, as he realized that he'd personally ordered that the aviation radio be connected to the public speaker system in the dungeon and in the control room above.

He rushed to Olga's station just in time to hear the Chinese response to the announcement. "Be advised," came the voice from the control room, "that we placed explosive mines on the runway before we began our assault."

Quinto trotted from where he had been briefing four of Olga's air guards in the room at the end of the emergency escape tunnel. Lisa Johnson who'd been operating the doors was right behind him.

"Did I hear that my guys are here?" asked Quinto.

"They are only a few minutes out, but there is a problem," said Olga. "I don't know whether the Chinese are bluffing, but they claim to have mined the runway."

Quinto stopped behind Gritt who turned. "Do you think that is possible?"

"If I thought there was any possibility of reinforcements screwing up a raid, that is exactly what I would do," answered Quinto.

Gritt bolted toward the door in the back of the room marked COMMUNICATIONS. He tapped the technician at the desk on the shoulder. "I need to talk to that plane," he ordered.

The woman pointed at a microphone hanging on the side of a cabinet. "You are on frequency."

"Air Guard C-130, the base is under attack. The attackers claim to have mined the runway. Go around."

"Sounds like a load of crap to me," came the answer.

"We are in no position to check it. Commander Quinto believes the odds are that it is no bluff."

"If you are under attack, I have just the guys you need on board."

"Listen to me. You are ordered to go around and hold. Those guys you have on board will do us no good spread all over the runway."

"Going around. We will hold out twenty miles. We can hold for an hour before we have to head back to Dutch."

Gritt raced back to where Olga and Quinto were into a spirited discussion. Lisa Johanson was sitting in his chair.

"The C-130 will hold for an hour," said Gritt. "Anything new?"

"The commander here doesn't want to continue whatever you and he have cooked up with my people," said Olga. "But unless it will wait until we can check the runway, he doesn't have much choice."

"The major has done a good job with her guards," interjected Quinto, "but boarding and clearing a submarine is a different skill. If we don't accomplish the initial tasks in seconds, they could submerge and drown us all."

Olga turned to glare into Quinto's face. "I told your boss that I had his back on this. You lead and my people will follow. We are here and your Seals aren't."

The microphones in the control room picked up the sound of the C-130 clawing its way back into the sky.

"Will the three of you shut up for a minute?" snapped Lisa. "I want to listen in on the conversation up in the control room." The microphones were picking up a spirited conversation in Mandarin.

CHAPTER 51

KISKA ISLAND

"I TRIED TO warn you," said Ma. "This entire thing looked too perfect to me. The only reason that a plane load of reinforcements would be standing by is that his whole thing is a trap."

"It is a coincidence, only a coincidence," answered Yang. "The plane is leaving. We will continue this mission."

"You have everything you are going to get," replied Ma. The power building and the one at the top of the hill cannot be breached with the tools we brought. Take what you have and get out of here before this gets any worse."

"Ma, I know that you never wanted to be part of this mission, but your presence has helped immensely. Now don't blow it while we are so close to what we came for. Order the woman who is talking to open the building at the top of the mountain."

"And if she won't or she can't, then what?" asked Ma.

Yang started toward the guard lying in front of the door, sliding a pistol from his holster. "Give her until the count of ten to open the building or I will shoot her soldier in the leg. If she does not open it by the time you count to ten again, I will kill her." He lifted his wrist communicator and ordered Chi to hold outside the building, and to report when the door opened.

Ma looked up at the one camera that he had identified. "My commander demands that you open the building on the mountain. I am to count to ten, and if you have not opened the building, he will shoot your soldier." He pointed at Yang pointing his pistol at the woman guard. "He will shoot her in the leg first and then give you ten seconds more before killing her." Ma began counting quietly in English and louder in Mandarin, repeating each number in both languages.

Olga leaned toward the monitor, studying Yang's movements. "I won't open that building, it would be treason," she whispered to the people around the console. She keyed her headset microphone. "I cannot open that door from here."

Ma reached ten and the sound of a gunshot echoed into the hidden microphones. "My commander just shot your woman soldier in the leg. I am going to count to ten a second time. You know what will happen if you do not open the building."

Lisa pulled the headphone from Olga's head. "My name is General Lisa Johnson, and I am the commander of this base," she lied in Mandarin. "I have just relieved the major of her duties and from now on you will talk only with me. The major told you the truth, we cannot open the mountain building from here. Furthermore, we would not even if we could. Now get the hell off my base before I call your bluff and order the plane full of Navy Seals that just flew over the base to land and kill every one of you bastards."

Someone speaking his language shook Yang. He lifted his wrist and ordered the group at the top of the mountain to abort their effort to penetrate the building. "Destroy every vehicle you can find on you way back to the beach," he ordered. He took a moment to tie a tourniquet around the guard's bleeding leg before holstering his pistol. "Call all of our men still around this building," he ordered Ma, "have them pack up everything including the computers and head for the beach."

As Ma used his communicator to pass on the order, Yang walked into the middle of the room and turned toward the camera. "Now that I know you understand me, it is easier. We are leaving explosives inside this building and around the perimeter as we leave. They will have motion sensors that will deactivate in two hours. He held up a red colored block. If you try to come out of your hiding place to intercept any of my men, you will be committing suicide. Do not blame us if you are so foolish. He placed the red block just outside of the steel door. "If you try to land your plane on the runway, do not blame us for that foolishness either."

The people in the dungeon watched, as the Chinese raiders emptied the small packs that each carried, stacking a dozen of the red blocks on a desk. Each then tugged three belts that wrapped their packs, opening then into huge duffel type bags with shoulder straps. As they began loading the manuals, files, papers and the computers into their packs, Yang circled the room placing red blocks everyplace his men vacated.

He looked up at the camera as his men began filing out of the door. "I am placing charges against the garage doors below the main building. They will detonate if anyone tries to open them."

CHAPTER 52

KISKA ISLAND

GRITT TURNED IN the massive dungeon and then passed through the desks of the section labeled ARCTIC DEFENSE as he made his way back to the communications room. "Tell the Air Guard to continue holding as long as they can, but not to attempt a landing until we clear the runway."

Stepping into the next office where Macey continued monitoring his instruments he asked, "Anything more?"

Macey brought up a new picture of the strange craft. "I moved the drone in a little closer. It looks like they have coated the vessel with some kind of long fibers to insulate the noise from inside. That still doesn't explain the silent propulsion."

"That drone of yours is crucial to finishing our efforts here. Once the raiders begin loading their haul aboard the sub, I want you to call me. When they get at least three of the computers they just stole aboard, enter the code that I gave you and press run program. After that, run the drone right up to the sub and take all of the readings and pictures you can."

"Where are you going to be?" asked Macey.

"I'll be just across the room watching the bad guys all retreating to the beach. I'll call you when the first raft starts back to the sub. Colonel Washington tells me that she can use the Arctic Angel system to give us eyes on the entire surface of the bay."

"Are we a go for the takeover?" asked Quinto.

"Not yet, Carl," answered Gritt, as he leaned closer, amazed by the detail coming up on one of the overhead monitors. He watched as two trucks parked inside the compound exploded. He could literally see the ripples in the suits worn by the attackers as two of them ran to a garage a hundred yards outside the fence and lobbed red blocks through a side door. Moments later the entire building exploded.

"Are all of the vehicles from our surveillance counts accounted for?" asked Yang as he jogged down the runway, lobbing red blocks every few yards.

"All of the ones we can find," replied Leopard One as he led his small team behind the Polaris vehicle that he'd ridden up the mountain. In the bed was a plastic bag containing the torn body of the raid's lone casualty. "There are two more buildings near the large vessel dock where there may be more. It is more than a kilometer away. They are not a threat."

Yang looked over to the procession of men following the trail to the beach where the rafts waited. "I told you to leave your man."

"General, we may bury this man at sea, but I am not leaving him here."

"Fine," replied Yang. "I am sorry that he died. The damned Americans armored this facility more than our recon showed. Still, I think we got everything we came for."

Ma was already on the beach listening. He tugged the facemask that covered his nose and mouth, relieved to be able to take a deep breath again. He'd insisted on the mask realizing that the Americans would probably have cameras in the facility where they would record everything and everybody. Without the mask, and with modern facial recognition software, his career as a spy would be over. He leaned his head back allowing the light rain to wash the sweat from his face. He had just recovered his face when he and the rest of the raiders heard the sounds of a plane out over the water.

The Captain flying the C-130 had explained the situation to Quinto's second-in-command, who had immediately used his secure communicator to request permission to attempt a landing. His chain of command had quickly figured out that a lowly Navy lieutenant did not have the authority to order the plane not to land. Since the Seal's on-board officer hadn't been part of the need to know for the mission, he was unaware of the Presidential orders.

"The American's are calling my bluff," screamed Ma into his communicator. They have figured out that there are no mines on the runway."

"Shut the fuck up, Ma," ordered Yang. "Everyone, we will ignore the American plane and finish this mission just as planned."

In the cockpit of the C-130, the copilot trained a pair of precision binoculars on the runway, as the plane began its descent. The optics, loaned to him by one of the Seals, were better than anything he had ever used, like prime rib is better than hot dogs. "Were still too far out to see any detail," he said into the intercom. "But I see nothing obvious. With the paved runway, they couldn't bury any mines."

The first raft left the beach with six men aboard, including the EEL crewman who carried the infrared strobe that would signal the sub that it was time to surface. It was halfway to the precise coordinates programmed into the crewman's communicator when the C-130 roared over.

The copilot sat as far forward as he could, as he trained the optics on the runway, now less than a mile away. "Oh shit," he mumbled, and then he repeated it. "Abort," he screamed, "abort; there are little red things scattered all along the runway."

The second raft was just leaving, towing two of the specially made plastic balloons behind it as the plane raced over their heads, the engines at full power. Yang stood on the beach watching, and then he began to yell and shake his fist at the departing plane. He lifted his arm to his mouth. "I told you that the plane was no threat. Now get the last of the computers and materials into the bubbles and let's get off this beach before one of the Americans decides to test my explosives bluff."

In the bunker, Gritt watched as the last raft was loaded before retreating to where Macey wiped his face with a paper towel from a roll sitting at his feet. He raised his arm to transmit just as Gritt leaned over his shoulder. "I hear the sounds of compressed air just about where I estimate that sub has been waiting. He's surfacing."

"Go ahead and bring the drone in close enough to watch them loading," said Gritt. "I hope that the top of the drone looks enough like driftwood to fool the Chinese. I'll be back watching from above. It's amazing what the cameras at the top of the mountain and the software they use to manipulate the image are picking up." He grabbed Macey by the shoulder and squeezed. "Remember, when they get the third computer loaded, run the program."

"Got it. For now, I'm concentrating on recording everything we are sensing. I'll have a good view of the sub once it is on the surface."

CHAPTER 53
KISKA BAY

THE EEL SURFACED almost directly under the first raft. "We are at the surface," called the man at the control console. "I am extending the camera arm." From a few feet behind the hatch, a thin pipe rose above the surface. A moment later he reported, "surface is almost calm. The first raft is waiting."

"Bring her up far enough to facilitate loading. I want a couple of hundred millimeters of deck above the water to avoid taking on too much sea water." The sub rose again and then stopped. He turned to the man at the ladder. "Open the hatch, no sleeve."

The man scrambled up the ladder and opened the hatch, allowing it to clang open. He scrambled up the ladder, catching the line thrown from the first raft. He pulled the raft up to the edge of the deck where two men scrambled from the craft, each carrying a duffel bag over their shoulder. They slid their feet along the slippery surface of the sub and, one at a time they handed their bags to waiting hands inside the EEL. Next, they slid the body bag along the deck and passed it through the hatch. The first two men followed it down the ladder.

On the deck, another of the raiders carefully checked each of the dart weapons handed to him to make sure that there was no dart in the chamber. Once he'd checked all six weapons he moved to the hatch and handed them to those below, then followed. The fourth and fifth men carried the last two duffel bags to the hatch. Finally, the motorman twisted the throttle of the electric outboard wide open and used his foot to turn the raft out to sea. He waited with the EEL's crewman for the second raft.

"Five men from raft one are inside the sub," announced Macey. "None of the computers were on that raft. The last man is waiting on the deck to help unload the other rafts. They don't seem to be in any hurry."

Watching the video feed above Olga and Lisa, Gritt's view was probably even better than Macey's. Somehow, the software of Arctic Angel manipulated the camera shots from the mountain into a clear image that appeared to be streaming from directly above the raft and sub.

On the water, the second raft slid up to the side of the odd shaped craft. Two of the men scrambled aboard and disappeared down the ladder. The next man carried a rope onto the sub's deck and pulled two large plastic bubbles up the side of the sub. A second man from the raft used his knife to rip the ends off from the bubbles, carefully lowering one computer and then a second through the open hatch. Both men disappeared into the sub, as the fifth man carried another duffel to the hatch. The last man again, opened the throttle of the motor wide open before pushing the raft away from the sub.

Macey watched through the lens of the camera fitted into the drone that looked like a floating log with an extended branch. "Two computers inside the sub," he reported. "Two men still on deck."

On the deck of the EEL, the two crewmen watched as the raft circled the submarine and ran itself up on the deck on the opposite side, just as the third raft approached. "Before you unload, would you pull that other raft out a bit where it will run out to sea," called the EEL's crewman.

The motorman in the third raft didn't wait for Yang's response. He turned the raft to the other side of the EEL where one of the people riding pushed the raft away. Yang glared at the motorman. "The raft would have floated away on its own when the EEL submerged." He was just about to order the others to begin unloading when he noticed the tiny glass eye in the branch of a floating log only a few yards from the EEL.

His stomach wretched, as his throat went dry. Even if this wasn't a trap, as Ma had argued, they were being observed. "Hand me your gun," he snapped at the guard from the beach. Before Macey could do anything, Yang lifted the weapon and fired a full clip of thirty bullets into the branch and the log below it. Both sank in seconds. "Get the rest of this stuff into the sub and let's get the hell out of here!"

"We've lost the drone," yelled Macey, racing from his desk toward where Gritt, Lisa, and Olga sat stunned. "We've lost most of the data on that sub."

"Oh fuck," screamed Gritt launching himself from the chair. "Without hard data…and without the Seals to capture the sub, we've got nothing." He paused for a moment contemplating any recovery. One moment turned into minutes. He swallowed hard as he remembered ignoring an offer by Olga when she learned the seals were not going to arrive. They had invested millions of taxpayers' dollars for nothing. Gritt picked up his secure phone and started to enter Walker's phone number. He paused.

Figuring he was about to learn what crow tasted like, he offered, "Olga, we might be able to use your people. The crew would be disabled. but I can't detonate the gas canisters."

"What gas canisters?" shot back Lisa.

"There are gas canisters planted inside all of the computers taken from the control room. I was going to detonate them using a device on the drone when at least three of the computers were below. It will take that much gas to knock out the crew."

"We have some data on the sub," replied Macey. It may be enough for our own engineers to make an educated guess." He paused for a moment. "Maybe enough to figure out a defense."

"Maybe, isn't why we put this op together," replied Gritt, staring at his watch. A Chinese satellite was overhead at that very moment. "The bad guys are watching this in real time." He paused again, staring at his watch. Those around him watched as his face turned ashen.

"What?" snapped Lisa.

"The moment that the Chinese cut the cables to the computers; it triggered a backup timer on each canister. They will detonate ninety minutes from that moment. If they go off inside that sealed sub after it submerges, it will kill everyone aboard."

"I can live with that," said Olga as she launched herself from her chair. "One of those bastards shot one of my people. With the risk of booby-traps we can't reach her. She may bleed to death."

"Dozens of people have spent months planning this mission," said Lisa, standing to confront Olga. "They may lose this one sub, but they know how to make more, and we may not have enough data to defense it."

Olga glared at the senior officer; hands glued to her hips. Finally, she turned and started into the bay labeled ARCTIC ANGEL. "Colonel Washington," she called, striding across the room, "these folks need the kind of help that only your baby can provide."

May Washington motioned for Gritt, Lisa, and Macey to enter the one area of the dungeon that had always been off limits to them.

May sat at a desk almost touching a second, where a young technical sergeant slowly manipulated a joystick. The young woman had four tattoos on her neck and Gritt's gaze was drawn to her tiny hand on the controller. Every fingernail was painted a different color and what looked like a tattoo of chain mail circled her wrist. On the screen she stared at was the same visual image that Olga, Gritt, and Lisa had been watching at the security desk.

"I thought this was going just fine," said May.

"Right up to where the Chinese sunk the drone that everyone was counting on for detailed information," said Olga.

"That's just part of the problem," interrupted Gritt. "The computers they are loading are all booby-trapped with gas bombs. We were going to detonate them using a communications device on the drone. There is a backup timer on each bomb that will detonate ninety minutes after the computers were disconnected. If they are underwater, three canisters will probably kill all of those aboard. We were counting on fresh air circulation to diffuse the gas."

"Those bastards just attacked a United States military base," replied May.

"Colonel Washington," started Lisa, "we may not have enough data from the monitors to figure out how that sub works. If the hard data stored inside the drone was compromised when the Chinese sunk it, we may not have shit."

"How long until the devices detonate?" asked May, as Macey leaned over her shoulder studying the monitors.

Gritt checked his watch. "The timers just rolled past seventy minutes. They will detonate in less than twenty minutes. The sub will be gone in ten."

"You want to hold that sub on the surface?" asked May.

"If we could," replied Gritt.

"Watch the magic of Arctic Angel, all," said May. She pointed at the screens in front of her. On the center screen was the image of what looked like a large B-2 stealth bomber, but bigger and shaped more like a pure flying wing. Three lines of data were displayed below the image. May centered a cursor over a red button on that screen and typed *arm*. She turned to the young woman next to her.

"Julie get me a real close up of the deck of that boat again. I want to count the hairs on the crewman's arms."

The young woman continued manipulating the joystick with one hand, as she typed a few commands on a keyboard. The image of the sub began to enlarge until first the bay disappeared, and then the raft tied to the side of the boat, and then finally most of the boat. The image of the hatch on the monitor seemed as close as it would have been if you were standing on the deck. "Is that close enough, ma'am?"

"Perfect for now," replied May. "Standby for a tighter shot if we need it and keep the camera on the hatch for now. All right everyone, look for someway of sabotaging that craft in a way that doesn't sink it. We can't do it in a way that scares its captain into sinking her himself."

"The hatch opened by swinging it toward the bow," said Macey. "Can you get a closer look at the opening along where the hinges are anchored?"

"Julie, you heard the man," said May.

The image narrowed until only about four inches of the opening to the hatch showed. The picture showed hands busily passing bundles and weapons through the hatch.

"There along the seam of the hatch, there is a ribbon hinge," said Macey. "Since there are no ferrous metals in that sub, it has to be some kind of alloy, probably a brass alloy. If we can melt just a little of the hinge, they can't close the hatch."

"Okay if I try that," asked May, looking up at Gritt.

"Can you do that without blasting a hole right through the hull?" asked Gritt.

"My baby can do almost anything," replied May. "Does anyone know the melting point of brass?" She turned toward another airman who manned a research computer.

"It depends on the composition," said Macey. "This may be a very exotic alloy, but you can melt most brass at 920 degrees C."

A half-dozen stunned faces turned toward Macey when he added, "We build a lot of our own instrumentation at Woods Hole, and we use brass housings as often as possible because it is easy to cast."

May tapped a few more keys on her keyboard and a new screen filled the corner of the large monitor. Five small windows opened.

The first was labeled DISTANCE TO TARGET. It showed 77,672 feet. May tapped the OK button.

The second was labeled TARGET SIZE. May typed in 2 centimeters by ten centimeters.

"Will that do Mr. Davis?" she asked Macey.

"That should be perfect."

The third window was labeled TEMPERATURE ON TARGET. May overrode the MAXIMUM displayed in the window and typed in 920 C.M A link transferred local atmospheric information to the targeting computer.

The next window allowed her to set the time on target, and she entered five seconds. "That should be enough," she commented. "Julie, I need the crosshairs centered on the far left of that hinge. Let me know when there are no packages or arms blocking the target and then monitor the burn."

Ten seconds later, the young airman called out, "Fire, fire, fire."

A tiny wisp of smoke rose from the hinge, clearly visible on the screen, but so little that those loading the sub ignored it. They watched as the smoke moved from left to right.

"Now, Lieutenant," said Washington, "we wait. In an actual intercept we could watch the damage tear a plane or missile apart, but there is no way to tell if we have damaged that hinge enough to keep it from closing."

"Stay on target and crank up the power enough to blow a hole right through the hatch if they start to close it," said Gritt. As I recall that part of the bay is only about a hundred feet deep. Even if they sink, we can recover that boat. If it kills all of them, my conscience is clear."

"Macey, keep an eye on that boat. If the gas goes off, you should see a red vapor around the hatch. If you have to blast the hatch before that happens, we will try to save some of those men."

He turned as Olga tapped Quinto on the arm. "I know you and Lt. Gritt think we are just one step above rent-a-cops, but I know better. I stationed several of my best troops in that bunker your Seals were going to use. They are waiting for orders."

"Now it's time to reel in our fish," replied Gritt. He bolted for the door to the underground tunnel and the waiting Air Force guards. "Lisa, you have the doors again."

The raced through the two large bays of the dungeon, divided by a large planter box full of trees and vines and into an underground shelter complete with kitchen. At the other end of the shelter, a massive steel door began to open, revealing a long tunnel.

CHAPTER 54

KISKA BAY

RED NIGHT VISION LED lights illuminated the passage. The door to the bunker closed behind them. Chad, Olga and Carl reached the end and waited for a few seconds for Lisa to open the second blast door. Emerging into the well-lit room on the other side, the three rousted five of Olga's guards who, knowing nothing about what was going on outside, were resting in bunks. There had been no communications from the dungeon.

"Saddle up ladies and gentlemen," said Olga, "we're on."

The newcomers slipped packs from a rack near the door onto their backs and followed the others past a gun rack where each picked up a M-4 carbine. Each already carried a holstered Glock 9mm pistol. Gritt carried a small duffel bag as did Quinto. They pressed a button next to a third steel, soundproof, door and stepped into the 1940s Japanese bunker. Two extended Polaris ATV's waited inside the partially collapsed structure for the one-mile dash to the small boat dock.

Olga piled into the back seat of one, Gritt next to her, as Quinto started into the driver seat of the second. "Let the kids drive," suggested Olga, "they grew up using these." Seconds later they raced along an old Japanese era trench, a more direct route than the improved road.

At the harbor, the group trotted onto the dock. Two Hewescraft twenty-six-foot Sea Runners waited. The newcomers leaped into the boats followed by two guards, both women, who slid into the captain's seats, starting the twin 150 horsepower Yamaha motors. The remaining guards released the dock lines, somehow throwing themselves into the moving boats as the drivers slammed one motor into reverse while gunning the other. The boats pivoted almost like synchronized swimmers and started away from the dock.

Gritt tapped the driver of his boat on the shoulder. He used his communicator to send the same message to the second boat. "We are waiting for confirmation that the gas bombs have detonated."

"Chad, this is Macey," came from Gritt's wrist. "They just figured out that they can't close the hatch. Two men just muscled it most of the way shut, but it will not close. I think they just sent someone below for tools."

CHAPTER 55
KISKA SOUND

ABOARD THE EEL, Captain examined the hatch from below. "I don't see any major reason why the damned thing didn't close; there's something wrong with the hinge. It almost looks like it is melted. My men will remove the bolts holding the lower hinge to the hull and we will manually close the hatch and dog it."

Yang stood next to Captain. "Have you ever had this type of problem before?"

"Not this, but the EEL is a mechanical device. Something goes wrong on every trip." He looked over at the pile of packs and equipment stacked in the control room. "While my men fix the problem, distribute that equipment equally throughout the length of the boat. The EEL is pre-programmed to balance as we descend. That much weight forward will make us bow heavy. Distribute the men the same way."

Two EEL crewmen pushed past them and up the ladder, each carrying a tool bag.

Yang himself began grabbing packs and computers and handing them to men waiting nearby. "You heard the Captain. Just drop the packs along the hull from here to the stern and put the computers on top. Don't damage them. He turned to Chi. Position your men at their bunks. Stay in the stern in case we need you there." He grabbed the last pack and stashed it forward as Ma handed him the last computer.

"It's not perfect," he said, but we can fine-tune it later.

A loud bell began to sound.

"What in the hell is that?" asked Yang, as Captain rushed to the control console.

"Fire Alarm!" shouted Captain.

Behind the men, a loud *bang* sounded. The men in the control room turned to see a fine red smoke billowing from the computer.

"I warned–" started Ma just as his knees buckled. Behind him, Yang who was desperately trying to cover his nose and mouth, stared as Captain collapsed over the man at the control console. Moments later, the man at the top of the ladder collapsed, dropping onto Yang's head, knocking his hands from his face. His own scream was the last thing he heard.

At the top of the hatch, the last crewman working on the hatch hinge leaned down to see what had happened. The fine red mist billowed up the ladder engulfing his head and shoulders. He collapsed, his legs stretched out on the deck, his upper body inside the boat.

CHAPTER 56

KISKA ISLAND

INSIDE THE DUNGEON, May and Macey watched the man's collapse and then the telltale red haze that indicated the gas bombs had detonated.

"Chad, it appears that your bet is paying off. We have a red haze billowing out of the open hatch," Macey said into his communicator. He hoped the call reached Gritt's boat out on the bay. He stared at the communicator before transmitting again. There was no response. Thirty feet underground they had no communications with the boats.

"Damn," he shouted, launching himself toward his instrument console which controlled an outside antenna on the transmit frequency. A Bluetooth connection linked the communicators inside the dungeon with those outside. He'd forgotten to activate the link. He hadn't run that hard in thirty years. Between gasps he managed to get out, "Gas in the boat."

CHAPTER 57

KISKA SOUND

GRITT, OLGA, AND Quinto all heard the call through their transceivers. Gritt leaned over to the twenty-something woman running his boat. "Kick it in the ass."

He looked over at the second boat as it launched itself up onto step.

"Now what?" asked Olga.

"We put one of the people in our boat aboard that sub along with Quinto, and two men from his boat. Quinto has hundreds of Zip ties and four gas masks in his pack. Those four will drop into the boat taking only a pistol. Their job is to make sure that anyone who shakes off the gas can't interfere."

"And our job?" asked Olga.

Gritt reached into his pack and produced a quarter-inch super fiber rope. "We get this rope tied off to something on the bow or stern and begin towing that craft into shallow water." From the duffel he produced a small high velocity electric fan. "Once we have the sub underway, I'm going to clamp this on the open hatch and start driving as much fresh air as I can into that hull. Until we get inside and see how to get the unconscious Chinese out of the boat, this will hopefully keep them from dying."

"You want me and our driver to tow the boat? That rope looks damned puny."

"It is a synthetic winch cable, stronger than steel. Try to get the sub to shallow water and then tow it along the beach to the docks."

The two boats covered the three miles to where the EEL rested at the surface in less than four minutes. "My God, look at that thing," mumbled Gritt. "It is covered in a shag carpet with four to six-inch strands. It looks like some kind of living organism that eats people through a hole in the top." The strands were all moving as if they were sea worms trying to find something to eat in a moving current.

Gritt and Quinto were the first people onto the sub, as their boats slid their bows up on opposite sides of the craft. One of Olga's people followed Gritt, as three others followed Quinto. While Gritt made his way to the bow, the others pulled gas masks over their heads, Carl, leaving his mask on his forehead. He used one hand to lift the body of the man draped into the hatch, flopping him onto the deck. He grabbed three nylon ties from his small duffel and wrapped the man's wrists together behind his back, then his ankles, finally using a third to pull the two together. The entire process took less than a minute. He turned to Gritt. "Based on the size, I doubt that there are more than thirty people aboard, maybe less."

Turning back to the people around him he added, "that's what we want down below," he ordered as he pulled down his mask and followed the duffel through the hatch. Three burly air police followed him.

At the bow, Gritt crawled on his hands and knees, his hands searching through the odd feeling strands as he looked for somewhere to attach a rope. There was nothing. He had no illusions about running the sub from the inside. "Pull the boat around in front," he said to Olga. "Tell me what you see below the water line."

Moments later, her answer offered little help. "There is nothing."

"There has to be something we can tie to."

"The only thing I see are two small grates about two feet below the water, one on each side, maybe six feet apart. They are covered with crisscrossed rods. There is nothing to tie to."

Gritt slipped from his hands and knees, to resting on one knee as he slowly watched what he hoped would be an easy finish to the mission turn very complicated. He stared at the boat only five feet in front of him. The helmsman used the motors to keep the Hewescraft positioned. "Are those halibut rods?" asked Gritt, pointing at four fishing rods in holders attached to the roof of the boat cabin.

"They are," called the woman at the wheel. "We love to fish in our spare time."

"Here's what I want you to do for me," continued Gritt. "Find the two biggest halibut hooks you can and string as much steel leader as you can get through the eyes between them, then knot it off. Make sure that the finished rig leaves at least eight feet between the hooks. I need a couple of hundred pounds of pulling strength so get me as many strands as you can."

While Gritt waited, he worked his way across the slippery surface to the open hatch. Pulling the fan from his duffel, he snapped the heavy lithium battery into the back of the fan and clamped it to the partially opened hatch. All of the gas had dissipated as he turned the fan on high. Having no idea how the sub's environmental system worked, he had no idea if the fan would do any good.

Below deck, Quinto and the three air cops began working to bind all of the unconscious men. What had taken Quinto a minute on the deck, took three times that long in the cramped space. In several spots, they had to pull people from piles of bodies before starting. As they moved from compartment to compartment, Quinto would lead, his 9mm Glock in front of him.

With sixteen crewmen trussed and the air clearing, Quinto

took a deep breath and pulled his mask away. He pointed at two of the men working with him. "You two go all the way to the stern and start working back. If you find another hatch, open it." He pulled his mask back down and drew a deep breath.

In the stern, the two men found exactly what they had seen forward. Everyone on the boat was unconscious. They trussed up the four people they found in the rear control room. Near a back bulkhead, they found another ladder and above them another hatch. "I'll get it open," offered one of the men. "You move forward and keep tying up these men."

Even in the front of the boat, Quinto could tell the difference in the atmosphere as fresh air flooded into the boat from the second open hatch. He and the man working next to him pulled their masks from their faces, as they continued to secure the Chinese raiders.

"How many in the back?" he asked as he met one of the men working from the stern.

"We tied up seven more."

"We've secured another five ourselves," replied Quinto. "That makes twenty-nine. Did you get them all?"

"I think so. There is a small interior metal door right in the back that we couldn't get to open. We un-dogged it and got it open a crack, but it wouldn't open enough to see inside."

"All right, I want you to stay in the forward control room. I'll take a look at that rear hatch." He turned to the third man. "I want you to go topside to see if anyone up there needs any help."

"Lieutenant," called Olga, as the bow of the Hewescraft again pushed up against the sub. She held out the mishmash of steel leader and two shark hooks that her crewman had made. "Jen got eight loops of hundred-pound leader between the two hooks. A couple of my guys had no idea what they would be fishing for out here. They brought some really heavy gear."

Gritt stepped on one end of the contraption and held the

other in his teeth as he quickly tied a knot of his rope around the middle of the device. He tossed the other end of his rope to Olga. "There is a cleat on either side of the stern of the boat. After I get the hooks set, tie this rope across the cleats and form a yoke. Let it trail between the motors."

Both of the men who had been below with Quinto were approaching from the opened rear hatch. "Once I get this set, you two lend a hand getting me back out of the water," called Gritt.

Gritt didn't wait for an answer before sliding down the slick side of the sub and into the water. *That is just fucking cold,* he thought, as he took several deep breaths before dropping his head below the surface. The small grates were hard to find, and anywhere else on the boat would have been impossible in the long shag covering. On the bow, however, the strands were only a couple of inches long and positioned so none could be sucked into the ducts.

Gritt worked one of the huge hooks through the grate and then pushed to the surface for a gulp of air. Every orifice in his body was clamping as he dove a second time, repeating the process. "I think they are in securely," he managed as he surfaced again. He reached out to the four hands helping him back onto the subs deck.

His shivering was uncontrollable as he somehow motioned to Olga. "P, pull it up r-real slow. W-when it comes t-tight, start a s-s-slow pull to s-shallow water, t-then toward the d-dock." He watched as the super strength line came tight and the bow slowly turned, following the boat.

"You got it, sir," congratulated one of the airmen. "But you will die of pneumonia if you don't get out of those wet clothes and into something warm." He waved at the second boat just drifting along the sub.

"Meg, dig out a survival suit and toss it over to me," he called. He turned back to Gritt. "Sir, get all of those wet clothes off; we have a warm suit coming."

The sub was moving at a snail's pace, but it was moving, as Gritt fought his numb and trembling hands to strip off his clothes. God, I hope nobody has a camera on this, he thought, as he stood naked while one of the airmen unpacked a bundled marine neoprene survival suit. It came with a towel that Gritt used to wipe most of the moisture from his body.

Moments later, the same airman helped Gritt zip up the suit and wrap the straps around the wrists and neck. He was still bitterly cold, but it took only a minute or two for the inside of the suit to start warming up.

"Not bad, Lieutenant," called Olga from the boat only thirty feet away.

"S-shit, I d-didn't think a-about you watching," managed Gritt.

"Don't forget the view from the Angel," replied Olga. "By now every woman on the base will be watching you."

CHAPTER 58

KISKA HARBOR

INSIDE THE SUB, Quinto braced his feet against the bulkhead below the hatch at the stern. He guessed that it closed off the propulsion compartment in the stern. Slipping the fingers of both hands under the slightly opened hatch flange, he wrenched for a full minute. He stopped to rearrange his feet twice, trying to gain more leverage. Nothing happened.

He tried pushing the hatch completely shut and wiggled it up and down the fraction of an inch that it would move, and then tried opening it again with the same results. Giving up, he worked his way around and over the still unconscious crew. Back in the control room, he relieved the one guard still aboard and sent him to the deck, and then followed.

He found Gritt cinching the wrist communicator back on his wrist. "Chad," yelled Quinto, "call the dungeon and get someone out to clear that runway. Once we get the Chinese ashore, we will need more help since we have no place to lock them up."

Gritt's shaking had slowed just enough to relay the request to Macey.

"Already on it," called Macey. "One of Olga's people and two of ours are clearing the runway. The bad guys just tossed a bunch of explosive bricks out on the pavement. None of them are armed. I've already called the Air Guard. They are holding five minutes out for the all-clear. The pilot says he will have to manually check the fuel in the tanks before he tries the flight back to Dutch."

"Where are you?" asked Gritt. "We have the sub in tow and will be in shallow water in just a few minutes. You really need to get down here and see this thing."

"I've closed up shop. The guards clearing the explosives in the compound found the same thing as on the runway. None of them were armed. If you will send the extra boat back for me, I will grab the jeep in the garage."

Turning to Quinto, Gritt confirmed that he had monitored the entire conversation.

"I'll be the guy down in the tube," replied Quinto. "I want to keep an eye on the Chinese just in case one or two wake up and decide to cause trouble. Wait until you see the inside. The whole boat is barren with almost no wires or pipes, just the most compact computer consoles that I have ever seen. My eleven-year-old son could probably figure the controls out, but I am way over my head."

Gritt plunked his butt onto the odd surface of the deck after sending the second boat to pick up Macey. The rain had stopped, and the surface of the Harbor had turned a dark steel grey as the water calmed. He conjured up an image of his grandfather who had spent days hiding in the mountains of Attu Island hundreds of miles west in the Aleutians, the only other American soil occupied by Japan in the Second World War. He and two young Aleut men had spied on the Japanese army and relayed precise information to the American and Canadian forces that retook the island after months of occupation. Gritt couldn't imagine weeks sleeping in soggy sleeping bags with no protection but a tarp, all the time hunted by Japanese patrols. "Those guys were just tough," he said.

"What's that, sir?" responded one of the guards who'd remained standing to avoid soaking his pants.

Before Gritt could answer, Olga called from the towboat. "We've got about twenty feet of water under the keel. We're starting our turn for the dock. Speed's up to four knots, so less than an hour."

"Keep up the good work," replied Chad. He turned to the guard to explain what his grandfather had done when the rear hatch tipped from the open deck and started to close. "Hey, Quinto, are you closing the rear hatch?" he spat into the communicator.

"Nope, I'll check it out."

Inside the sub, Quinto raced toward the rear. The difficult hatch in the far rear stood wide open. He raised his Glock just as two feet appeared, descending the ladder. "Come down very slowly or you will die."

Instead, a body tumbled to the deck and rolled to Quinto's left, momentarily hidden by a partition. Quinto stepped to his right just as the man from the ladder rolled onto a knee, a pistol aimed right at Quinto's chest.

"Drop the weapon," ordered Quinto. "We have your submarine in tow, and all of the rest of your crew secured."

The man held his pistol steady, their eyes locked. "Who are you?" he uttered.

"Carl Quinto, Commander, United States Navy and the head of SEAL Team 4. And right now, I am in command of this vessel. Drop your weapon."

"And I Colonel Chi, Snow Leopard Commando, and you not welcome on EEL."

"Snow Leopards, I've heard of them. Top-notch outfit. You should be proud of the work your men did today. But now they are all prisoners until our two governments work out what to do about your attack on an American base."

"How you know we come?" asked Chi.

"Your government has been working on how to raid this base and steal the technology. We have been working on how to stop just such a raid. Now, Colonel, it is time for our diplomats to settle this matter. It would be an honor to buy you a drink when we reach shore." Quinto could see the frustration in Chi's face. "We are not enemies, just men who defend our countries. Now, drop the weapon."

Chi's eyes drifted toward the floor. "You not take Chinese ship," he blurted then fired.

Chi's first shot shattered the communicator on Quinto's arm before tumbling into the right side of his chest. A second shot slammed him against the bulkhead, just as he squeezed the trigger. He saw the bullet hit Chi, center mass, as Chi fired a third time smashing Quinto's Glock and his right hand. Quinto stumbled back, tripping over one of the Chinese crewmen. With a lung punctured, there was no way that he could rise even as Chi staggered forward, his pistol aimed at Quinto's face.

"I very sorry, Commander," managed Chi. "You not take the EEL. I sink."

Chi lowered the pistol and stepped past Quinto, heading toward the control room, his pistol sweeping from side to side as he moved. Years of meditation had given him a keen sense of his own body. He was bleeding inside. He was dying. Maybe he could remember enough about the controls to run the EEL into deeper water and then sink her. He had to try.

On the deck, Gritt stared at his communicator. The only answer to his call to Quinto had been four pops that had echoed from the hatch. He called again with no response.

Rolling onto his feet, he slid toward where his wet clothes were piled on top of his personal sidearm, a Ruger 9mm. Just as he un-holstered the pistol, a strange sweeping motion of the long strands on the deck started, rolling across the deck from front to rear like waves. Slowly, the waves changed direction. He could feel the submarine start to change course.

"Run the boat and sub up on the beach," he shouted at Olga, crawling toward the open hatch. He looked up as the second boat, with Macey aboard began to slow its approach.

He turned to one of the guards who had helped fish him out of the water. "Have that other boat get in behind the sub and push it. We need to beach this sub."

Gritt crawled to the open hatch, realizing that starting down the ladder feet first would make him a sitting duck for anyone with a weapon inside. The sub was now pulling against the towrope, but all it was doing was keeping Olga's boat from running ashore. Behind him, he could hear the guard screaming at the second boat.

Gritt jacked a shell into his Ruger and slid his hands and head down the hatch. As his shoulders cleared, he saw an older Chinese man at the console only fifteen feet from the ladder. Blood dripped onto the deck from where he sat, his hands flying over the console. The man threw up his hands and screamed what had to be a blistering list of profanity before dropping his hands to the keyboard and starting again.

Gritt steadied his body as much as possible hanging upside down and extended his arms, the Ruger held tightly in both hands. He paused for one second. If he missed and hit the console, many of the secrets of the sub might be lost. "Stop and stand up!" he yelled.

The man at the console stumbled to his feet, the front of his shirt soaked with blood. He picked up a pistol resting on a shelf and stood just as Gritt fired twice, rolling the man over the chair behind him. Gritt watched for any movement. There was none.

Gritt felt the change in the sub as the second boat slipped up to the stern and the driver opened up the throttles of the twin outboards. He pulled his upper body from the hatch, swung his legs around and dropped onto the ladder, just as the C-130 planted itself on the runway a half-mile away and then turned to taxi toward the water.

Inside the sub, he crossed to the helm and leaned down to check the pulse of the man he had just shot. "You died a brave death," he whispered. The man blinked his eyes a couple of times before they locked open. Gritt somehow navigated the length of the sub in the bulky survival suit.

"How badly are you wounded?" asked Gritt, as he leaned down to where Quinto sprawled against a bulkhead.

The man used his wounded left hand to touch his chest on the right and the left, unable to speak.

"I understand; stay quiet. Your guys just landed. I'll get help."

Gritt stumbled to the open hatch. A man with a pistol was standing at the top. "Help me out of here. Hurry."

"SEAL Team 4," he called, his communicator almost in his mouth to counter the noise of straining outboard motors. "This is Gritt. Commander Quinto is down with bullet wounds to his chest. We need a medic and oxygen."

"Read you, Lieutenant. On the way."

Gritt watched as the towboat tilted its outboards in shallow water, just before Olga threw the rope off from the rear cleats. Her driver spun the boat and swung around behind the sub, adding two more 150 horsepower engines to the push. Below Gritt's knees, the strange grass continued sweeping in waves, as he felt the sub bounce off from underwater rocks. The way that Olga had pulled the boat, the sweeping motion was now helping drive the sub ashore.

"Amazing, just fucking amazing," came a voice from behind him. Macey leaned down to where Gritt was clearing a live round from his pistol. He was stroking the long strands, finally plucking one from the mat. A milky solution ran down his hand and dripped onto the deck. "These things are alive," said Macey. "They must control them with ultra-weak electric current channeled along the hull. Whatever the inside hull is made from remains to be seen. The external hull is some composite that is porous enough to allow whatever this mat is to bury its roots. The sounds that it would give off would sound like the swaying of seaweed or kelp. We got what we came for."

Gritt slid the Ruger into a pocket of the survival suit. "It may have cost us Quinto," he answered, as he dropped back onto the ladder.

CHAPTER 59

KISKA HARBOR

"NOW COME AROUND and push on the sub's side," called Gritt. "We want to pin the sub here, not sink it. When we get her stabilized and whatever this propulsion system is shut down, we can continue the tow to the harbor."

Gritt looked back toward the beach as eight Navy Seals jogged to the water. Each carried heavy packs and weapons. "I'll send one of the boats to pick you up," called Gritt.

"Don't bother, we will swim," came the reply. Gritt was amazed at how fast the first two men reached the side of the sub, each carrying heavy packs above their heads. The Air Force guards lifted their burdens from their hands and then helped the two men to the deck. Both wore combat fatigues, not wet suits, and neither seemed to be the least bit cold.

"Quinto is below, in the stern," said Gritt. "I'll let you go first. I'm damned slow with this suit on."

"Any trouble below?" asked one of the seals.

"Nope, Quinto and the Air Force cops got them all trussed up."

"We're on our way," said the first SEAL as he dropped down the ladder. The second man handed down the packs and then hesitated. "Air Force cops, huh? When our next two guys get here, send them down to check their work."

"Macey," started Gritt, "follow me down and see if you can get this sweeping thing stopped. I'm going to see if I can help with Quinto."

Gritt helped pull Chi's body from under the console. Macey slid into the captain's chair in front of the screens. "In twenty-five years of service, this is the first combat fatality I've ever seen. My God, there is a lot of blood."

"Quinto shot that man dead center and he still made it to the console and tried to sink the sub. I shot him twice more to stop him." Gritt took a deep breath. "I've always loved target shooting but hoped that I would never have to shoot a man." He paused for a few seconds more. "I'm going to see how Quinto is doing. Have you got this?"

Macey turned to the screen and keyboard. "I have no clue, but with Lisa's help, I'll give it a shot."

Macey watched Chad shuffle over and past the Chinese crew. He turned back to the console just as two SEALs dropped down the ladder to begin checking how secure the crew was tied. One pointed to the man at Macey's feet. "He doesn't need any help," Macey said as he studied the screens. He shook his head. There were no obvious controls and he could not read the information on the screens. "Lisa, are you on the secure com system?"

"Right here where it's warm, drinking a nice cup of tea May Washington just handed me."

"I'm activating the camera feed on my communicator. I'm sending you the screens in front of me. I'm trying to shut down the silent drive on the sub. First is the one on the left."

Lisa took a few minutes to study the tiny display on her wrist, enlarging the code one line at a time. "That screen controls the attitude and pitch of the sub. If I am reading that correctly, the sub is supposed to be submerging to ten meters. That is not what we need it to do as we tow it." She paused for another minute. "Show me the keyboard."

Macey stood where the camera could take in the entire keyboard.

"Okay, Colonel, the cursor is probably controlled by the tiny joystick on the right."

Macey moved the small stick and watched a cursor move on the screen opposite the one he had displayed for Lisa. "Wrong screen," he said.

"Show me the screen where it moved," replied Lisa. Moments later, she continued. "We're good. This screen controls the drives and preprogramed routing." She studied the screen for a couple more minutes before adding, "At the bottom of the screen there are two round symbols, one dark colored and the other just an empty circle. Move the cursor over the bland one and click on the enter button on the keyboard. It's in the same place as enter on most laptops."

"I'm not quite sure," murmured Macey.

"Show me the keyboard again," said Lisa. "Okay, go to the second line of keys and depress the key at the far right just before the break, above and just left of the keys with the up-down, left-right arrows."

"Got it," said Macey.

"Depress that button once," directed Lisa.

The screen on the right went all red and at the end of four lines of code, four zeroes came up. The strange hissing sound inside the sub stopped.

"We're good," said Macey.

"Not yet Colonel," came the reply. "The descend program is running, and we have no idea how to turn it off. If we try to refloat the sub, it may just sink right under you all."

"Can't we just push a button to turn it off?" asked Macey. "No hold it, I get it now. We have no idea how far into the program the sub has progressed. It could just sink like a rock. We need to reverse the command; we need the sub to acknowledge that it is to surface."

"And that is why we have a submarine engineer aboard instead of me," replied Lisa. "I would have just hit the stop button again and we would have lost the damned thing."

"There is a small manual on the shelf above the console," said Macey. "It may be a tutorial or a trouble shooting guide. I'm going to take it with me. For now, we leave the sub right here on the rocks."

"Good idea. I'll head down to the dock. Send a boat for me."

Macey stuck the small binder inside his jacket and turned to the ladder. He was on the third rung when his bloody foot slipped from the ladder sending his head smashing into a step. He wiped the gush of blood from his forehead and continued up.

"What the hell," commented one of the Air Force guards.

"I just banged my head. I need to stop the bleeding and then send a boat for General Johnson at the dock. Until then, we have to leave the sub right where it sits. It is programmed to descend if we pull it off the rocks."

The man stepped over to where the two Hewescraft boats continued pushing on the side and repeated Macey's explanation. Olga stepped onto the bow and handed the man a first-aid kit. "Macey," she shouted, "I'll go pick up General Johnson, but you can't leave that sub just sitting there! We're just past low tide right now and the tide here will come up about fifteen feet in the next few hours. If we can't float that boat, it will sink anyway."

Before Olga could order her boat to the dock, the rear hatch on the sub popped open. One of the SEALs appeared at the top and he reached down as his partner and Gritt passed an unconscious Quinto to the deck.

"We need to get the commander out of here. He's bleeding into both lungs, and I don't think he will make it on a four-hour flight to Anchorage," he yelled to the people on the boats.

"We have a full infirmary with telemedicine feed in the main building," called back Olga. "Our medic can help you with the commander." She turned to the woman at the helm. "Turn the boat sideways. Let's get that wounded man aboard along with the Navy corpsman."

She picked up the radio above the front windscreen and dialed in the base emergency frequency. Moments later the boat began a full speed run back to the dock area. Olga leaned down to where the corpsman had hung a plasma bag above Quinto's pale white face. "I have what we use for an ambulance on the way to meet us. Our Medic will meet you at the dock." The corpsman didn't answer, instead he rocked Quinto up onto one side allowing a small tube in that side to drain a small stream of blood into the bilge.

As the boat began the run to the docks, four more SEALs clambered aboard the EEL.

CHAPTER 60
KISKA HARBOR

"WE ARE SO close," offered Gritt to Macey, as he taped a gauze pad on the man's forehead.

"We still have a few things to tidy-up," replied Macey. "I'm counting on Lisa helping us with the controls on the sub. I can't believe that she is the only person on this base who can read and speak Mandarin. Once we get it to the docks, we can jury-rig enough flotation to stabilize it until we get it all figured out." He pressed his palm against the bandage, it came away bloody.

"You said things, not thing," said Gritt, as he unrolled four feet of elastic bandage and cut it off with a knife from his wet clothes. He pressed a second pad over Macey's wound. "Hold this tightly while I use the bandage to keep pressure on the wound."

"Thanks," offered Macey. "Walker really wanted this sub, but he wanted it to be a secret." He waited for Gritt to secure the end of the bandage before continuing. "Have you checked your watch lately?"

"No."

"Isn't it about time for a pass from that Chinese satellite?"

Gritt checked the time marker on the wrist communicator.

"Directly overhead right now. Another was overhead while they were trying to load the computers. A C-130 at this end of the runway and two boats right in this area point an arrow right at where we are sitting. They couldn't miss the sub up on the beach. I've seen the feeds from a couple of Navy surveillance satellites. You can count the freckles on a sunbather's chest." He paused.

"So, now we find out just how good our diplomatic team is." Gritt closed the first aid kit. "From what I can see, there isn't a prayer of any attack by aircraft or missile on this base, but I don't know about ships. If they want this sub back badly enough, they might just try to take it…This could get really bad if they don't think the Angel is operational."

"Tomorrow's problem," replied Macey. "Today's is simply securing the boat and the crew." He turned to Gritt, wiping blood from his face. "Just how long will that gas keep the Chinese crew under?"

"I was told by the docs who cooked up this plan that it was good for between two and three hours. We have another hour or so. We hoped to grab the sub quickly and then get it to the docks. From there, we were going to turn the problem over to the SEALs and Olga's people."

He turned to a SEAL standing nearby. "Any ideas on how to get the men we captured off this boat and then, what we should do with them?" He studied the name patch on the man's neoprene suit, and then added, "Chief Robinson."

"Well sir, after a walk-through of the sub and a few minutes studying the outside, there are only two hatches. We're going to have to lift those men out by hand unless we can rig some kind of winch or something. Our original plan was to get them stabilized and then march them up the ramp of the C-130 and head for Anchorage. Someone a lot higher up the ladder than me is going to have to figure out what we do with the prisoners. I don't think they qualify as POW's; maybe we hold them as terrorists. Anyway, that was the plan, but it isn't going to go down that way." He had both Chad and Macey's attention. "The Major flying the C-130 told me that he doesn't have enough fuel to make it back to Dutch. We are all stuck here until someone flies in more fuel."

"Chief," said Gritt, "I need your help to come up with plan B. If we can't stabilize this boat, it is going to fill with seawater in the next three or four hours and we can't just let them drown."

He studied the man's face as the boat that had transferred Quinto to the dock ran up behind them. He watched as Olga managed to slip over the side and then Lisa Johnson. Lisa dropped an ice chest next to Macey and sat down. "These are my best fatigues, Colonel, and from what I could see from above, there's no place to sit without getting wet." Macey stared at her sweat and coffee stained wrinkled green suit. Lisa was a kick for a general.

Behind her, Olga was helping May Washington from the boat.

"I'm a bit surprised to see you out here, Colonel Washington," offered Gritt along with his hand.

"Camera's never lie," she replied. "You have the sub, but nothing after that appears to be working as you had planned. Between Olga and I, we know almost everything about this base. We came to help."

Gritt introduced them to Robinson and then repeated the conversation that he and the SEAL were having, along with what he and Macey had discovered. "First thing is to get the sub stabilized and somehow reverse the submerge order programmed into the controls. Then, we still need to get it to the docks and get the prisoners out of the hull. The SEALs planned on flying them out immediately, but the C-130 is short on fuel. We will need to find some place to hold them."

"General Johnson and I were talking while they got Commander Quinto into the ambulance," replied May. "She is fairly confident that she can help Macey get everything shut down, but not sure that she can reverse the buoyancy problem."

"Excuse me, ma'am," said Robinson, "but if I understand the problem correctly, the Chinese designed this sub to automatically stabilize at a pre-programmed depth. That is a function of filling ballast tanks, but it's also based on the loading of the sub. We've deployed from American subs several times, including a couple of secret mini-subs. In every case, the ship's captain wanted precise information on our weight and our gear. The way I understand it, is that every sub can manage almost any load if everything is working fine, but if there is a problem, they need to run weight and balance calculations just like an aircraft commander does."

"Okay, Chief, what do we do with that information to help solve our current dilemma?" replied Olga.

"Well ma'am," continued Robinson, "the sub was floating just fine when you ran it up on the beach. Maybe it will just float right off again."

"Let's just take this a little further. If the program has continued to run for the half-hour that the boat has been on the rocks, won't it continue sinking when we pull it off, even if the systems are shut down?"

"Macey," called Gritt, "I'm sorry to interrupt, but we have a question." He repeated the conversation between Robinson and Olga.

Macey turned. "You aren't interrupting. The General is going to need a little time with her nose in the manual. I'm just wasted meat right now. We've been debating the same question. The key will be what happens after the ballast tanks reach the point where they are programmed to stop. Maybe with two feet of deck showing they will not fill completely, so she will float just like she sits, just a little lower in the water."

"Sir," interrupted Robinson, "what if we make the sub a lot lighter before we pull it off?"

Macey turned, looking out over the grey ocean beyond the harbor. "This boat is built to be as quiet as possible. They probably allow the ballast tanks to fill naturally by slow bleeding the compressed air from the tanks rather than flooding them. The noise of water pumping or being blown into the tanks could be detected. My guess is that they use multiple flooding tanks so that they only need to fill a few to maneuver when silence is critical. I'll bet that they have several small tanks and that they only need to fill one or two unless they are running deep. Five hundred gallons would add about 4000 pounds, probably enough to give the boat negative buoyancy."

Gritt had spent weeks and weeks with the geniuses recruited for the mission, yet his impatience with the scientific discussion was wearing thin. You could already see the ocean level moving up the rocks on shore. He was just about to interrupt when Robinson did.

"Sir, there are twenty-eight live men and two corpses in that sub. If we get them all off, we can lighten the load by about five thousand pounds. If you are right about the sub reaching its programmed depth slowly, maybe the tanks are only partially full, but even if they are full, we can neutralize the loading by getting the men off the boat."

"But that will only work if we can keep the sub from continuing to descend," replied Gritt. "If the systems are still running, she still sinks."

Macey scowled. "The first thing that Lisa and I figured out was that there are three power settings in the controls. One activates the reactor and brings it up to power. That's a simple on or off. The second activates the lithium battery bank for silent operation, and that one is also a simple on or off and can only be activated if the reactor is shut down. The last is a secure-all setting, for when the sub is at the dock. It closes all vents and valves and then all power." He tapped Lisa on the shoulder. "The reactor has to be shut down, because they were in silent mode. Let's you and I go down and see if we can shut down the rest of the power."

She stood and headed toward the hatch.

"Hold it a second," called Macey. "There is a dead man directly next to the control console and a lot of blood."

Lisa turned to face him. "I was a junior officer the last couple of years that we were in Afghanistan. It's better if the blood isn't American." Seconds later, she disappeared down the ladder. Macey followed.

"Which gets us to, how do we get thirty men out of that boat before we get it to the dock?" said Gritt.

"That's why I came," said May. There is a small flexi-float barge tied up at the big ship dock. It was used as a platform to build the docks. You move it with a small pusher boat with three big outboards." She turned to Robinson. "If your guys can get the Chinese crew on the deck, we can use the flexi-barge to carry them back to shore. I just need someone to run the boat."

Gritt lifted his arm and called Levitt. "Oliver, we need someone familiar with boats and barges to bring the flex-float barge from the docks as quickly as possible. If there are a couple of Olga's people close who can spare us a little muscle, we also need some hands to help move the prisoners onto that barge."

Five hours later, the EEL floated high and dry at the dock. The Air Force crew had emptied the small warehouse at the docks where a combination of Air Force and Navy personnel traded off guarding the prisoners who all sat on mattresses taken from the construction camp. Cold rations taken from the EEL were stacked in the corner as four men at a time were released to eat and use the chemical toilet.

In the dungeon, the officers sat around a table, cups of fresh coffee welcome after the night's activities. "I have to hand it to you and team Walker," said May. "When you first approached us with this, I figured that we had nothing to lose because of how the base is built, but I gave your chance of really getting what you needed from that sub about a ten percent chance of success."

Things on Kiska were settling down. A second C-130 with fuel and a contingent of Military Police would be there in the morning. The Gulfstream with a surgical team aboard would arrive in the next five hours to evacuate Quinto, who was as stable as the corpsman and medic could get him. Inside the sub, Macey, Lisa, Bob Phillips and Oliver Levitt had begun unlocking the mysteries of the EEL.

Gritt's secure sat phone rang as he got up to refill his coffee. "You won't believe who you have in custody," offered Thad Walker. "Our folks working with the CIA and the FBI ran the photographs of the prisoners. I just got a memo on my home computer. One of the men is General Yang, commander of PLA-3, special operations. Another is a face that has popped up from surveillance on several trips to the U.S. The consensus is that he is the handler for the Chinese espionage team on the West Coast."

"No shit," responded Gritt. "That can't make the folks in Beijing very happy. We sent electronic copies of the ships log. General Johnson thinks it includes records of all of the sub's missions. Assuming we are giving the sub back, I locked the log into the captains safe we took it from. Maybe they won't know we have a copy. That was one of your main goals in seizing the sub. Now we need to document how to defense this type of threat in the future." He paused a moment, and then added, "It didn't go quite as planned here, but we improvised and somehow got it all calmed down."

"Maybe for now," said Walker. "But in D.C. the shit is hitting the fan. The Chinese are calling us pirates and are threatening an all-out invasion if we try to move the sub or the crew."

"So, what are our orders, sir?"

"I've given the green light for the medevac, but I canceled the second C-130 until we get a handle on the situation. Tell all, well done and try to get some sleep; I think you all may need it. I'll keep you posted… You know, news of the sub getting out is fucking up a celebratory fishing trip with Director Wang."

CHAPTER 61

KISKA ISLAND

ABOARD THE SUB, Macey found himself stunned by the simplicity of the design allowed by the complexity of some science that he had never considered. The people probing the sub wore lightweight plastic suits with facemasks and gloves as protection until any residue from the gas could be mitigated.

The most amazing thing was the boat's covering. The surface appeared to be one large organism growing on the alloy of the pressure hull. While they hadn't risked restarting the power, concerned about a possible self-destruct program, they had begun careful optical measurements of the inside using a 3-D camera. Most intriguing was a large tank only a few feet away from the tiny lead-lined reactor closet. There appeared to be no piping allowing the tank to be filled through the hull. At the bottom, two tiny sliding piston pumps driven by compressed air allowed whatever was in the tank to be pumped out. A gage on the side of the tank indicated that it was still 60% full.

"We need to take a sample of whatever is in the tank," offered Levitt. "It could be anything from some part of an environmental system to a chemical fuel." He drank the last of the water from a plastic bottle and opened a small dogged cover on the top of the tank. He filled the bottle, drying his hands and the bottle with a towel hanging above the tank. "We can use the small medical lab at the base to try to figure out what this stuff is."

"I don't know about the rest of you," said Macey, "but this has been a hell of a day. I for one haven't eaten in so long my stomach thinks my throats been cut. I haven't slept in about thirty hours. "I'm ready to call it a day."

While they had been working below, base maintenance had been busy rigging a rubber sheet covering for the damaged hatch. One at a time the investigators climbed from the hull, Levitt, pulling the sheet tight and securing it with a ratchet strap. "That should keep it dry inside, even if it rains," he commented as he headed to the makeshift gangway to the dock.

"Hold it, Oliver," said Macey. "I want to try something. Dig out the bottle of solution that you took from that tank and pour a little of it on the surface."

As Levitt dribbled the liquid onto the long strands, they twisted and then began to stand up. The strands followed the stream of solution, as he slowly moved the bottle across the surface. "Nice catch, Macey," said Levitt. "This stuff is what they feed the monster with. Now the question is, how often does it need to be fed and how do we do it? The best way to learn how to defense this beast is to operate it."

"Gritt and the base people are rigging up a secure closed-circuit television feed. They are going to start interrogating the prisoners early tomorrow morning using interpreters from the CIA Let's make that one of the early questions. Maybe we can find one of the crew who will help us save their pet," offered Lisa. "In the intelligence world, one tiny connection is often all that it takes to open the floodgates."

Gritt turned his secure satellite phone over to Bob Phillips, who had proven his ability to sleep anywhere and anytime. As Gritt and the others tumbled into assigned bunks, a new crew replaced the Angel crew that had been on duty for twenty hours.

CHAPTER 62

KISKA ISLAND

IN THE WAREHOUSE, Yang slowly moved from prisoner to prisoner, delivering the same message: "Assume that everything we say is being recorded." Captain had already addressed the group, assuring them that their government would do everything needed to free them. As he passed that message, he was just as sure that his career was over. In a nation that rewarded discipline and achievement, in a military built on duty, any man who allowed his ship to be taken would never be trusted again. For the time being, he busied himself with taking care of the men. He was convinced that Yang's arrogance was at least a major factor in their capture.

"You know that they will interrogate us," Ma whispered to Yang. "The Americans will know who you are; they will probably start with you."

"You are too smug, Ma," replied Yang. I give you credit. I don't think that it was a trap, but the Americans were ready for us. We succeeded in our mission. When we are released, we will have a great deal of knowledge of this place." He propped himself up on one elbow. "Who would have figured that the very computers that they used would be booby-trapped if they were removed?"

"We know almost nothing, General," said Ma. "I doubt that any part of what we saw is real. You may find some way to go home and spin this so that your career will continue. Once they run facial recognition, my career is over. They may just shoot me as the spy that I am."

"They are treating us well," replied Yang. "Tomorrow, they will interrogate us or just transport us to one of their bases to let us rot until someone gives them what they will not learn from examining the EEL. But the new game requires them to return both sub and crew. If it looks like this is going to compromise our country, we will simply overwhelm the guards. Even if a third of us die, it will be better than compromising our leaders. I hope it doesn't come to that. I hope the Americans play the game the way you think they will."

"They are very good at this game," said Ma. "Don't think even for a minute that the guards watching us would not shoot us all. But you are right, they will want to return you unharmed and then trade me for something they want. They will learn everything they can from us and from studying the EEL, and then give the world's television networks film of our raid, including your shooting of that helpless young woman, before giving you and the submarine back to China."

"Would they shoot me if I strangled you right where you sit?" asked Yang.

"No, probably not, but that might just be enough to convince some of our comrades that helping the Americans is less of a threat than your type of patriotism. While you contemplate that, General, spend some time thinking of how General Quing will deal with you ignoring his concerns. Our effort to learn America's greatest military secret has cost us one of China's." Ma tucked the jacket that he wore during the raid under his head. "I am going to get some sleep. If you decide to kill me during the night, please do it quickly."

CHAPTER 63
KISKA ISLAND

INTERROGATIONS BEGAN THE next morning. A camp trailer had been moved to just outside the warehouse where Gritt and Lisa were waiting with online interpreters from CIA headquarters. Gritt's interrogation was directed at learning as much as possible about the submarine. He and Macey had developed a line of questioning over a four A.M. breakfast. Lisa and Ted Leonard focused their interrogation plan on the PLA and on how the mission plan had been developed.

The camera feed from each interrogation room connected to the secure communications links to conference rooms in Maryland. In each room, one interpreter's translation was fed back to Kiska where Gritt and Lisa asked questions. The second interpreter translated the answers, with a verbal translation to the half-dozen experts and company officers in the room. He then sent a written translation to the interrogators' computers.

The decision to begin at six in the morning was based on the four-hour time change between D.C. and Kiska. No food or drink had been offered to the Chinese crew that morning.

Gritt decided to start with the youngest submarine crewman

and work up the chain of command. The young seaman in the seat across the table was unshackled as a guard led him into the trailer. The guard closed the door after an orderly placed a pot of tea and a pot of coffee along with two foam cups on the table. A plate of freshly baked rolls waited.

"I know that your officers have briefed you not to discuss anything that is considered a military secret," started Gritt. "But under international law, we are required to get your name and rank. My first question is, who are you young man?"

"I am Chief Second Class Li Jung."

"Do you go by Li or Jung?"

"I go by Jung while aboard the EEL."

"Jung, would you like some tea and some bread before we start?"

The man nodded. Gritt poured him a mug of tea and slid the plate and a stack of napkins toward the prisoner.

As Jung sipped his tea and started on a roll, Gritt filled his own coffee cup. "Jung, you and your submarine will be returned to China. Our two countries will negotiate the terms of that return. China sent your boat here to spy on my country, to steal its technology. What happened, was that the officers who planned the mission underestimated the security of this base. Ironically, my country finds itself in possession of your submarine. We are already studying the submarine. I believe you called your boat the EEL."

Gritt paused to work on his coffee as the comments side of his screen suggested some ideas for questions. Jung finished his roll.

"Please take another, Jung," said Gritt. "Now before I ask you any questions, do you have any questions for me?"

That surprised the young man. He stretched his arms over his already greying head, finally answering. "When will we be going home?"

"That will be up to your diplomats and mine. There is no reason why my country will want to hold you one day longer than necessary. Now my turn. The ship's roster we found on the EEL says that you are…" Gritt waited for an interpreter in Maryland to find Jung's name on the log and then send the information back to his computer. "…an engineer. Will running your boat up on the rocks to keep it from sinking hurt the organism that provides the slow speed maneuvering?" He paused while the question was translated, watching the man's body language. In Maryland, an expert was doing the same thing and sending Gritt updates. Gritt read the next suggestion that popped up on his computer. "We are going to return the submarine, but in the interim, we have no interest in damaging it. There is no reason why the creature, that is part of your submarine, should be injured any more than has already happened. There is no reason for it to die. Have we injured the organism and, if we have, how can we heal it?"

"The Sillia's parts that were hurt when the boat was on the rocks will heal themselves as long as nothing else rubs those wounds while it regenerates."

"Which gets me to my second question. We note the tank of solution on the submarine and we have figured out that it is used to feed what you call the Sillia. If we want to keep the organism alive, how often do we have to run the pumps to feed it?"

"We feed the Sillia twice each day. The submarine must be stationary for the solution to surround the hull. The pumps will secrete the food into the surrounding water. We feed it every twelve hours."

"Thank you, Jung. We may have more questions later," said Gritt, "but for now, that is all. Outside the trailer, there are boxes of rations taken from your boat. Please refill your tea and take whatever you want from the rations. You will be taken from here to a new facility that is more like a dormitory. You will want to leave the best rooms for your officers, I suspect, but since you were the first to be questioned, that is up to you."

Three hours later, Gritt and Lisa broke for lunch. While Gritt had interviewed five crewmen, Lisa had started with Yang, and then Captain, finishing with Ma.

"So far, I haven't gotten anything of use," said Lisa, as she and Gritt sat down to a bowl of chili and cornbread. "The only prisoner that I think could be useful is that guy that came up in the travel photographs. This Ma guy is aware that he could be shot as a spy, but he refused to talk about any travel to the U.S."

"I had a bit more success," said Gritt. "We now have a fair profile on the slow speed propulsion organism. May's maintenance people are going to rig up a pump to spray the organism above the surface and to pump some solution under the water around the sub to keep it alive."

Gritt continued with his lunch as Lisa described both the conversation with Captain and Yang.

"I suspect that we are going to have to open up the computer network in order to really understand how the sub operates," offered Gritt, as he gave Lisa a chance to eat something. "In the interim, Macey and Levitt are opening every hatch and door and taking pictures of what they find. If we can figure out the mechanics, then even if we can't crack the computers, we will understand what we are up against."

"Not quite as good as actually running the boat," replied Lisa. "Do you think it will be enough to figure out how to defense it?"

Before Gritt could answer, one of Olga's guards raced into the cafeteria. It took her a minute to catch her breath. "Mr. Phillips and Col. Washington need you two down in the dungeon right away."

"Now what?" mumbled Lisa.

CHAPTER 64

FLATHEAD LAKE, MONTANA

WALKER HAD JUST finished his row on a mirror calm Flathead Lake. While he was young, Winchester could almost tip the boat as he jumped to the dock. Now, a little past middle age, he climbed onto a seat and then calmly stepped out of the boat. The boat secure, Walker planted his cane in the gravel of the path and started toward the house, stopping three times for the obligatory ball toss and retrieve by the dog.

Slipping through the door off from the porch, Thad filled a cup from his coffee maker and wandered into his office. A picture of an eagle was plastered across the screen of his computer. "Now what?" he voiced to Winchester who curled up in his favorite corner for a nap. Entering a twelve-digit security code, lit a light on the tiny camera lens at the top of his computer. Thad leaned in to only three inches from the lens and tapped the enter button. His retina security added to the codes. A moment later the screen cleared, and a picture of a conference room appeared. A woman's voice followed. "Mr. Walker, the Director will be with you in a moment. He will be joined by two of the assistant directors as well as the deputy secretary of the Air Force and the assistant secretary of state for Asian affairs."

Thad watched as the room filled. Finally, Mat Chang smiled into the camera and started. "I'm sorry that my trip has been postponed, but under the circumstances, it's probably better that I am here in the D.C. area. First, Thad, how was your morning row?"

"Just about perfect. I got a full hour in, and the temperature here is still cool enough in the morning to make it pleasant. Now, that we have that over with let me guess what's going on. The Chinese have figured out that we not only are holding their sub, but that we have at least two critical operations people in custody. They are raising hell and threatening everything short of nuclear war to get them and the sub back. How'd I do?"

Walker could tell by the smiles around the table, that he had damned near nailed it. "The only thing you missed was that their ultimatum came with a timeline. If we do not agree to free the raiding party and send them on their way in the Chinese submarine EEL within twelve hours, they claim that they are going to send an entire airborne division to take the base."

The assistant Air Force secretary identified himself, tossing in his name as if it should mean something to Walker. "The entire Chinese Air Force could not take the Kiska facility in days. Arctic Angel can protect itself."

Chang pointed to a thin black man in an old-fashioned double-breasted pin stripe suit. "Thad, do you remember Colby Jenkins?"

"I do. How are you Colby? Long time-no-see; what has it been fifteen years? I watched your confirmation hearings, they went light on you, you old scoundrel."

"I'm fine, Thad. Not quite as smart or rich as you, but I'm still in there pitching." Colby smiled at the camera. "It appears that you have a finger or two in the soup." He threw a loose salute at the camera. "Here is the problem, Thad, if the Chinese do try to take the island by air, it will be a bloodbath. The satellite defenses can detect the planes launching from China and track them all the way to Kiska. Within three hundred miles, those planes can be targeted precisely, accurate enough to just damage them. We can knock out their radar or even an engine. If that gets them turned around, we win. But if they keep coming, we will knock them down. Three hundred plus Chinese dead will almost assuredly force the Chinese to try to retaliate. After labeling us pirates and spending the last twelve hours pumping up their propaganda machine, President Xi will have to save face. The folks on the China desk think he is dealing with some social unrest, as the Chinese economy shrinks.

"If the air invasion fails, he will send in either surface ships or subs. Your guy, Gritt, triggered a preplanned Navy response the same hour that they seized the sub. There are already four attack submarines within a day of Kiska and a Carrier Task Force only three days out. Again, we will win, but it might be costly. If that Chinese effort also fails, who knows what Xi will do?"

"We win today, and it could just lead to a major war tomorrow," replied Director Chang. He watched heads nod around the room. "Win small, lose big isn't very attractive, is it?"

"I talked to my people on Kiska last night," said Walker. "What they got on the instruments placed to study that sub doesn't amount to a hill of beans. They need at least three more days to interrogate the crew and study the technology. They sent their initial findings up the ladder yesterday. The Chinese have managed to merge a submarine and an actual living organism. Without more data, all of this effort was for not. We still cannot defense this thing. The initial finding from the ship's log indicates that we have been compromised in twice as many locations as we considered."

"So that just about defines the problem, all," said Chang. "Now what do we do about it?"

Walker sipped some coffee and waited for the people in the room to open a discussion. A full minute later, he sighed. "When the chips are down and the shit is hitting the fan, the political suits never risk their careers. It's always the street folks who have to pull our ass out of the flames."

"What did you just say?" snapped the Air Force manager.

"I think that was fairly clear," replied Walker. "There are a few people in that room who I would go into combat with. The politicians and lifers trying to get in their thirty years were why I retired. They know who they are. That gets us to the dilemma. Just what exactly was the Arctic Angel designed to do?"

"It is a completely unique system of satellite, radar, and multiple laser weapons," said the Air Force assistant secretary.

"You missed my question," continued Walker. "I have people that I recruited sitting out there. Your vague deflection does nothing to help them or your people. Exactly how does it work and just what do you hope to accomplish with it?"

The Air Force Assistant Secretary sat mute, glaring at the camera. "You are as insolent as your reputation. You do realize that the Secretary and I could be in the President's office in an hour."

"It appears, that you, sir, are building a reputation of your own," replied Walker. "You either don't do your homework or you don't believe what your staff is telling you. Chang and I were on a conference call with the President this morning." He shook his head. "Can anyone there help out, since this stuffed shirt is proving to be worthless?"

"It has dual purposes," replied Colby. "First and foremost, it is a deterrent to any attack from China, North Korea or Russia on the U.S. West Coast. Secondly, if they do try to attack using aircraft or any missile configuration, it is designed to be a complete barrier."

"Thanks Colby. Now do this assembled group of experts have a plan?"

There was silence for another minute as Walker watched the people look at each other.

"Okay, then, my people will start figuring out what to do,

beginning with the primary purpose of this Arctic Angel thing. When we have something solid, I will get back to the Director. The one thing that we cannot do is release that Chinese sub until we figure out how to defense it. Thirty of those highly automated and silent subs could render all of your high-tech air warfare technology obsolete. Instead of attacking by air, they slip undetected right into our harbors and go *boom*."

CHAPTER 65
KISKA ISLAND

JUNG'S ABSENCE WAS noted by those held in the warehouse. "We already have one turncoat," whispered Yang. He turned to Captain. "One of your men is betraying our homeland."

"Jung would never do that," replied Captain.

Ma smiled. "Perfect, just perfect. This has only been going on a few hours, and the Americans have already divided us and started us fighting amongst ourselves." He turned to Yang. "I told you that they were very good at this. I also told you that you know nothing about the American weapon we were sent to steal. This entire mission has been what the Americans call a cluster-fuck. Before you respond to that General, you need to know that when you decide to attack the guards, you will have to lead. Most of our people think that losing Chi and one other SLF fighter on a wasted mission is already a very high price."

Yang just glared.

"Maybe to the leadership of our country, losing a few men, when they already outnumber available women by 30% is acceptable. But to those on this mission, to waste those men like they were, isn't."

CHAPTER 66

KISKA ISLAND

GRITT HAD JUST wrapped up a conference call with Walker. Colonel Washington and General Johnson, along with Olga, sat quietly digesting the news of a pending invasion. It had already been five hours since the Chinese ambassador to the United States had delivered his ultimatum. Behind them Phillips, Macey and Levitt sat contemplating the specific order that they were not to release the sub until they knew enough to defense it.

"If it takes the Chinese three hours to fly from a forward base to Kiska, we have about four hours to learn enough about that sub or to come up with another way to defuse this," offered Washington.

"I suggest that we skip trying to learn how the PLA operates and concentrate the next few hours on interrogating the submarine crew," replied Lisa.

"The recordings from the warehouse indicate that the captives are already arguing amongst themselves. Maybe we can take advantage of that," said Olga.

"At least we can try," said Gritt. "Let's get back on this. If we can't nail down the sub this afternoon, we need to get back together." He checked his watch. "We meet here at three?"

He turned to the men in back, "Learn what you can by then."

"Why are you cutting us short by an hour?" asked Lisa.

"General Johnson, you outrank me by decades," replied Gritt, "but Walker put me in command of this effort. I have just the beginning of a fallback plan kicking around in my head, but that's all that I have. We may need the hour to flesh it in. Even then, we still have a couple of hours before the Chinese planes will get close. I was told to defend this base against any attack and finish the mission to understand that sub. We will do both."

"Lieutenant Gritt," interjected Washington, "I've spent years of my life preparing this facility as a deterrent, I sure as hell don't want it to start a war."

"Colonel, hold onto that thought until we get back together. Now, let's run as many of the sub's crew through interrogation as we can in the next three hours."

The next three hours proved to be an exercise in futility. The submarine's crew had gotten the message from Yang and Captain. Other than Ma, who freely admitted that their mission was to learn about the American laser weapon, nobody had offered anything more than name and rank. The only member of the crew who had volunteered anything sat in a small room in the old construction camp, watching American television. And the only thing he had volunteered, was that the Sillia needed to be fed every twelve hours.

"How are you guys doing? Do you understand that sub?" asked Gritt as Macey and the two men with him filed into the conference room.

"Mechanically the thing is a marvel," offered Macey. We finally got into the rear compartment and studied the high-speed propulsion pods. No gears, no shafts, but I would guess that in the open ocean they can run at twenty-knots or more. They have mastered using electricity to reshape metal arms and brackets on the fly. They appear to use that instead of the mechanical processes men have used for centuries. The arms that hold the propulsion pods are curled up like a snake. There isn't a single gear or hinge used except the hinges that open or shut the hatches and doors to the outside. I'd like to record the outside sounds, but we can probably use artificial intelligence to anticipate the sounds. It isn't as good as hard data, but we may be able to detect this craft in the open ocean. In close, when they go to their animal drive, we are still blind."

"We got almost nothing from the interviews," added Lisa. The men in that warehouse are either very disciplined or scared or both."

"We tell the folks back on the east coast that we do not have enough to release the sub and that we are spending the next couple of hours preparing to defend ourselves," said May.

"For now, that is what I am going to report," replied Gritt. "Maybe the diplomats can buy us some time."

"I'll begin briefing a fresh crew on the possible situation," added May. "After a career of more than three decades, for the first time, I will be preparing my people to fire a shot in anger."

Gritt and Walker spent more than an hour on the phone, interrupted by Walker's side conversations with CIA people and Gritt's updates from his own staff and Washington's.

Both men were interrupted at almost the same moment by a notice that five large transport planes were detected climbing from an airport in Northern China, all of them heading northeast.

"I'll be notifying Director Chang of your effort on plan A," offered Walker. "You have an hour. Keep me posted."

Fifteen minutes later, May Washington and Lisa Johnson joined Gritt in the large waiting area of the interrogation trailer. Moments after settling behind a desk, guards ushered Captain, Yang and Ma into the room. The three men were offered chairs and tea.

"What do you want now?" asked Yang. "You have realized by now that there is only one traitor on our crew, and he doesn't know enough to help you." Ma translated before Lisa could.

"We are here to advise you that your country is sending an assault force to capture this island," replied Gritt. Both Ma and Lisa translated. "We are going to show you some video of the power of the weapons that defend this island. We are doing it so that you can advise your countrymen to return to base before we are forced to destroy their aircraft."

"Your defenses are adequate to destroy a small raiding party," said Yang, "but a major force will have the weapons to open your buildings like a can opener. You should release the EEL and us at once. From just outside the harbor we can call off the troops headed here."

Chad nodded at May Washington.

"Gentlemen, I am Colonel Washington, commander of the base on Kiska Island." She opened a large screen laptop computer and turned it toward the three men. "These are film of how precise the weapons here on Kiska are on previous Chinese targets."

She hit play, and the image of a Chinese electronic intelligence aircraft flashed onto the screen. The film's odd angle made it look like the video was being taken from directly above the plane. The image narrowed until only the cable towing an electronic array showed and then a cross hair appeared on the cable as the image continued to narrow. For just a fraction of a second, there was a spot of smoke on the cable and then it parted. The video pulled away quickly to watch the towed instruments tumbling toward the ocean.

"I am sure, gentlemen," continued May, "that you were aware of this action before you started this mission. Our laser can attack with that precision out to more than 300 miles. If we have to use it on the incoming aircraft, we will, but we do not want to."

"Anyone can create such a video," replied Yang. "People who make movies have been doing that for decades."

"That is why we wanted to show you something more familiar," offered May. She tapped a couple more keys and a new image came up. It was the EEL, strangely from above. Again, the image narrowed until only a small portion of the open hatch was visible. Again, a cross hair appeared, and the image narrowed until only the hinge inside the hatch was visible. A man's arm slipped into the picture and then disappeared. Again, a short burst of smoke was seen and then the image panned back out. "I'm sure that all of you are familiar with the problem you had closing the hatch on your submarine. You now know why."

The faces on the other side of the table were blank, almost as if rehearsed. "You have had more than a day to study our ship," started Yang. "You are very clever to find the malfunctioning hatch and to manufacture this video. Even if it was real, your ability to stage what amounts to pin pricks certainly does not convince us that you have the power to defend against aircraft."

"We will give you a half hour alone to determine whether you want to save your countrymen's lives," said Gritt as the three Americans rose. If you choose the wrong way, we will be forced to defend this base."

CHAPTER 67

KISKA ISLAND

"THAT ISN'T THE response we had hoped for," offered May as the three Americans walked down to the dock where a team was pouring over the EEL. As Gritt picked up a flat rock and tried to skip it across the calm waters, May and Lisa stood quietly.

"I can't help it," offered Gritt, "it is something genetic in the male of the species."

"Those same pre-dispositions are why women are needed in the Military," said Lisa.

If Gritt heard her, he didn't show it. "What we showed them was two pinpoint strikes that we had minutes to prepare for," replied Gritt. "This Yang guy knows that any attempt on this Island will include multiple attacks from several directions. If the Chinese have really decided to take back the EEL, they have already accepted casualties."

May Washington stopped, as they watched two of Olga's guards stacking personal items and weapons taken from the sub. "We wait for their answer. If they are not willing to help, it is time for the Army and Navy to see what Arctic Angel is all about. It will probably cost me my career, but if it avoids a major war, I can live with that."

"How's that?" asked Lisa.

"This base is set up like the old nuclear silos were. Each one of my people is an expert in one phase of its operation. The overall capability is considered beyond top secret. I am the only one here who knows what it is truly capable of doing."

"Can it defend itself against a multi-pronged attack, all happening in minutes, or even seconds?" asked Lisa.

"Arctic Angel is capable of defending America even if this base is totally destroyed. That is its strength and a worry to many of us who are not yet comfortable with putting the lives of the American people in the hands of artificial intelligence." She checked her watch and then turned back toward the warehouse. "That's all I am going to say unless the PLA officers in that room force us into a terrible situation."

CHAPTER 68

KISKA ISLAND

YANG, CAPTAIN, AND Ma stood as the American's filed back into the room. "We will follow our orders," started Ma in English. "We will not compromise the EEL or make any effort to stop our countrymen from releasing us from your custody."

Gritt watched as May Washington's back stiffened. She turned to the guards in the back of the room. "Keep these three idiots here. Bind their hands behind their back and find something to blindfold them with. If I call you, I want you to deliver them to the large room in the main building. You will have five minutes to get them there, so get ready. Make sure that the commander of the Seals is with you. She turned to the three Chinese officers. "It's too bad you have so little respect for human lives."

Both Gritt's and her phone beeped at almost the same moment. One conversation with Washington D.C. and one from Montana delivered the same message. The Chinese had launched two-dozen cruise missiles, calculated to arrive at Kiska at almost the same time as the aircraft. Intelligence satellites had detected pre-launch activities at other sites believed to house China's new hypersonic missiles, capable of traveling the 1500 miles to Kiska in about fifteen minutes.

As May slipped behind the wheel of her truck, she and Gritt just shook their heads. "Okay you two, what in the hell is going on?" asked Lisa.

"They are coming," replied May.

"And they are going to come with multiple weapons systems in one massed attack," added Gritt.

By the time the three reached the door to the bunker, sirens were sounding across the Kiska base. The work on the EEL ended as the guards outside scrambled to get themselves, Macey, Levitt and Phillips to the main building. Even the guards in the guard posts were pulled back into the main building where non-technical personnel were filing into an underground room separated from the dungeon. The men guarding the prisoners were ordered to pull back and lock the doors, and then part vehicles in front of them. They too were to retreat into the main building, leaving the prisoners.

"You remember the charges you left all over our base, the ones that were not armed?" offered Chief Robinson to Ma, the only prisoner who spoke fluent English. They are now surrounding this building and this time they are armed." He turned to leave. "I hope your country's satellite surveillance has pinpointed where you are being held. One missile strike on this building and every one of you bastards will be just a pale pink vapor."

May slid into her chair next to the same young woman who had targeted the hinge on the EEL. Chad and Lisa stood at her side, while behind them, two new people took seats at two identical desks, with an ANGEL TWO sign above them.

"I figure that we have about 75 minutes until the missiles and the aircraft converge on us," said May. "Let me show you what Arctic Angel is really about."

Ten minutes later, the same people who had met three hours

before, sat staring at each other. "Are we far enough along to release the EEL?" asked Gritt.

"Not if we want to defense it in the next couple of years," replied Macey. "We can try to recreate most of it, and then test what we built, but it may not be enough. Levitt here, has scraped a two-foot square of the living organism from the hull. We doubt that it will live, since it was rooted right into the material that makes up the hull."

Gritt nodded. "Walker and Director Chang talked to the President this morning. We have his blessing to do whatever we need to do to defend this facility. He also is not willing to allow this EEL thing or its clones wander all over the world's oceans undetected. The President made it clear that we were to use this weapon for its primary purpose if possible. It was conceived and built as a deterrent."

Colonel Washington stood staring out the windows. "Ladies and gentlemen, I have heard nothing from my headquarters. My standing orders mirror what the President has ordered; we are primarily a deterrent. We will act accordingly." She turned to Olga. "I am ordering that the three Chinese officers be delivered here immediately. I want you and Chief Robinson to escort the blindfolded men to my desk in the operations center. Be prepared to shoot all three of them if they get out of line."

CHAPTER 69

KISKA ISLAND

"PULL THE MASKS from the faces of these fools," ordered Gritt, and he watched as each of them took in the surroundings in the Arctic Angel operations center. "Gentlemen, we offer you a trade. You help us understand the EEL – operate it with us while we study it, and in return we will give you what you came for. We will not only tell you what this facility is designed to do, but we will demonstrate it."

Sensing that the Chinese now had the upper hand, Yang was the first to speak. "We will make no trade with you. You must release us at once or this base will be destroyed." Ma translated and Lisa confirmed the conversation.

Gritt turned to Chief Robinson. "I am not going to let this arrogant prick start World War Three. Take him outside the building and shoot him in the head."

Robinson stood unmoving. "Chief, that is an order from a superior officer in front of witnesses. Now go."

Yang's eyes were the size of saucers as Robinson blindfolded him and then drug him from the room.

"Now you two," continued Gritt, before you make a hard commitment, we are going to show you just a bit more." He nodded to Washington, who tapped on two keys, bringing up a treat display.

"Your transport planes are about thirty minutes out. They were just passed by a barrage of cruise missiles, which themselves will be passed in the next three minutes by a number of your country's hypersonic missiles. Please watch."

The display offered three different symbols and then multiples of each, all moving toward Kiska at different speeds. At the bottom of the screen, each symbol was followed by speed and altitude information. May tapped a different key, and a red circle appeared around the hyper velocity missiles. Moments later, the screen panned out and each individual missile was surrounded by a red circle.

"Our system detected twelve high velocity attackers. They are supposed to impact this site five minutes before the cruise missiles and only fifteen minutes before your troops arrive."

She turned to a man standing near her holding a phone. "Do you have a connection to General Quing's headquarters?"

The man reached out the phone that had two buttons at the bottom. "Button one is his headquarters, and button two is his personal cell phone."

"Excellent," said May.

On the screen in front of her, the hypersonic attackers began to separate so that they could approach Kiska from different directions. As they did, individual data appeared next to each one, showing that they were also changing altitude. Ma translated for Captain as tension swept the room.

May turned to the young woman at the next desk. "Please confirm that all of the targets designated 'A' are locked up."

"That is confirmed," replied the woman after a line of code ran out across her screen."

"I want visuals on each as we fire," added May.

"We are programmed for visuals on each." The woman brought

up the image of the first missile and then used a roller at the side of the keyboard to refine the image. A crosshair began tracking the missiles aiming just aft of the center. A box that simply said ALL appeared, and the woman tapped in *yes, execute*.

The image of the missile was as clear as if it were flying just outside the windows. A large wisp of smoke appeared in the center of the crosshairs. One second later, the missile disintegrated as a tiny tear in its skin widened, ripping away a panel. The computer shifted from the missile designator 1A to 1B and a new image appeared. Seconds later, that missile disappeared, and a new image came up. As that one exploded, May ordered Olga to release the two men's hands then turned to the man with the phone. "Hand the phone to one of the gentlemen from China."

Turning to face the same men, she smiled. "You will either tell General Quing to call off this attack, or the planes following the cruise missiles will all be nothing but holes in the ocean in twelve minutes. Tell him what you just saw. While you talk, we will be targeting the cruise missiles."

"How do I use the phone?" asked Ma a little panic in his voice.

"Push A for his office or B for his cell. If you have a better number, use it; the country code for China is 86."

"Don't forget to discuss our offer," said Gritt. "We will share the details on this facility, beyond what you are seeing with your own eyes in return for full disclosure on the EEL."

Moments later, Ma was almost screaming into the phone. He put his hand over the mouthpiece. "The General says he cannot confirm the destruction of the first missiles. He wants to talk to General Yang."

As the group watched, the last of the high-speed missiles disintegrated. The screen in front of May switched targets to the cruise missiles, again displaying them fanning out with speed and altitude information displayed for each. The now familiar process displayed the first missile. This time the laser held position a bit longer, penetrating the skin, igniting the fuel reserve. Moments later it exploded, and the view shifted to a second missile.

"You are watching us shoot down thirty-six missiles in less than six minutes," said May. If we didn't need to show you the targets being destroyed, it would take about half of that time."

Gritt added, "A conversation with General Yang is no longer possible."

By this time, Ma was almost out of breath. He handed the phone to Captain. "I think I got through to General Quing," said Ma as the tenth of the cruise missiles exploded, and the screen shifted to another.

Captain turned to Ma just as the last of the cruise missiles disappeared. The screen in front of Colonel Washington shifted back to a broad screen with only the five Chinese troop transports still visible. May turned to the young woman at the next desk. "Get us a visual of the troop planes, please."

A large image from above and the front showed the aircraft and slowly panned in until you could actually see the pilot and co-pilot through the windscreen. "You could see the strain on Captain's face as he watched. His voice became more animated just before he handed to phone back to Ma.

"What do you want me to tell the General?" asked Ma.

"Have him turn the planes. Even if they just circle for the few minutes it takes for him to confirm that all of the missiles that were launched were destroyed, it will keep us from killing all those men," replied May.

Ma calmed as he made the request then looked up at May. "I also told him of your offer. He is considering it."

There was silence for a full minute after that was repeated. "The General says that he is turning the aircraft around. He also asked if your agent Thadius Walker is among you."

"I studied under Thadius Walker," replied Gritt, but he is not on Kiska Island or anywhere near our nation's capital. I believe that he is retired where he can hunt and fish."

The aircraft on the screen began a sweeping turn to the south. May tapped a couple of keys, and the image returned to simple symbols representing the five aircraft. All were completing a 180 degree turn back to China.

The event, which had taken less than ten minutes, was followed by a loud rushing noise as all of the people in the room began to breathe again.

Finally, Ma handed the phone to Lisa Johnson. "The General wants to talk to a general officer of the American military to thank them for their generous offer to share information on technologies that may be misunderstood."

Gritt picked up a pad and scribbled a note to Lisa. "Tell him we will call back tomorrow at this time."

While Lisa and Quing talked, Ma turned to Gritt. "Is General Yang really dead?"

"God, I hope so," answered Gritt.

Ma smiled, "Me too."

CHAPTER 70

KISKA ISLAND

MACEY, LISA AND the Chinese engineer, Jung, waited in the control room of the EEL. Chief Robinson plus two SEALs followed Captain, one quartermaster, and one engineer as they dropped into the hull. As Captain noticed Jung, he froze. Lisa translated as the officer ordered the seaman to attention and began screaming at him.

"Captain, if you will allow a fellow officer a moment," she began. "Your man Jung did nothing to betray your trust. He believed us when we told him that you and the ship would be released. He agreed to help feed the creature that cleverly propels this craft so that it would not die. That is all that we learned from this man."

Captain backed away, his face flushed. He asked Jung what he had talked to the Americans about, and hearing the same story extended his hand to his crewman.

"Captain, it is very unusual for a Chinese officer to offer his hand to an enlisted man, is it not?" asked Lisa.

"It is, but I realize that Jung was not the cause of our failure. It was that hothead, Yang, who your man shot."

Captain ordered the quartermaster to the controls and his engineer to the engineering desk. "Have your men on the surface release the lines." From the top of the ladder, he noticed that the small section of melted hinge had been ground away allowing him to close and seal the opening. Moments later, he ordered the man at the controls to program in a short ten-mile pattern that Macey had given him. "I will tell you nothing that you do not specifically ask," he said. "When you are ready, I will demonstrate my ship."

In the dungeon, Levitt and Phillips began recording everything that the instruments planted in and around the sub were sending. Over the next three hours, they would add reams of information as the sub made several passes over the instruments originally planted to track the EEL. Hidden aboard the ship were more than ten tiny cameras that would capture all of the mechanical operations and every keystroke. Cameras and sensors had been placed as the Americans poked through every hatch and opening over the previous two days. A tiny camera above the control consoles recorded every entry and image.

In the dungeon, the deputy commander of the Seal Leopard commandos flanked Ma and the EEL's second in command. May tapped on her keyboard bringing up a strange outline that looked vaguely like some marine skate or stingray without a tail. "That, gentlemen, is Arctic Angel One. It is not on this island at all. You see you could have never captured it or even learned much about it without our agreement."

May waited as the men talked amongst themselves and began writing furiously on the pads given to them. "What is that, exactly?" asked Ma.

That is the first atomic-powered operational aircraft. It is powered by a reactor modeled on the Russian Topaz reactor of the 1960s but with a half-century of improvement. The craft is a stealth design with electro-optic coating. If you were to look up at the sky, it would appear just as the background behind it appears;

from the top it would look just like the sea below. It operates at extreme altitudes."

The look on the men's faces told May and Gritt that what they were seeing shocked them. They would learn less than half of the capabilities of the system, but Gritt and May hoped that would be enough to deter the Chinese.

"How can it generate enough power to stay aloft and still have enough residual energy to power the laser?" asked the EEL's deputy, his experience with the submarines own small reactor triggering dozens of comparisons in his mind.

The agreement on both sides had been that once the basics were outlined, only direct questions would be answered. May wished that this one had never been asked, but a deal is a deal… up to a point.

"Once we give the Angel the order to destroy a target or targets, most of the power is diverted to the laser. The craft will begin a low powered glide until the fire mission is complete. Once it ends, the Angel will regain its loitering altitude."

"If it is required to fire continuously, will it eventually descend a long distance?" asked Ma.

"Gentlemen, our intelligence indicates that China has fewer than six hundred missiles capable of reaching the United States. If they were all crossing within the firing parameters of the Angel, this one drone could destroy all of them in less than an hour. Even after that mission, the craft would still be thousands of feet above the flight path of a modern civilian aircraft."

Gritt watched, amused as she set up the closing statement. "And then there is always the capability of Angel Two and by next year, Angel Three."

"And if this control base is destroyed, what would happen?" asked the SLC deputy.

"Once we designate targets, the drone is capable of complete self-operation. It can identify its own targets, track them, warn them if it deems that reasonable for targets it believes are human guided. It will destroy them if they do not turn away."

May rose to face the three men. "I am not a huge fan of what society now calls artificial intelligence. I worry that without this base, or one on a ship positioned near Midway Island, that the Angels will educate themselves in a crisis. It is remotely possible that they could follow the tracks of targets it has destroyed and begin punishing the attackers in their own airspace."

"It would be better that humans remain in control of such power," translated Ma, as the three men talked quietly amongst themselves. "Three of our men have died on this mission, including the one who dreamed it up. Let that be enough death for now."

"Your man Chi badly wounded the commander of the SEALs aboard your submarine. He will live, but his career is over," replied Gritt.

He turned back to May. "Colonel, that was a very precise explanation of Arctic Angel and a remarkable demonstration. I believe that it is adequate for now. Let me suggest that General Johnson and I take these gentlemen back to their troops."

"Mr. Gritt, since these men now know that it is impossible to penetrate this facility, and if they will promise not to make any attempt to attack it or any of my people, they will be more comfortable in the construction camp," suggested May.

"Let me discuss the offer with my comrades," said Ma. "It is a very generous offer, the kind of offer that should be made between people who are rivals but not enemies."

CHAPTER 71

KISKA ISLAND

THAT AFTERNOON, MACEY, Phillips and Levitt found themselves in the base laboratory, carefully recording the information from the instruments and cameras that had followed their trip on the EEL. "Have you got it?" asked Gritt as he walked into the room.

"Maybe," replied Phillips. "We will need months to fully digest all of the data, but the sub does seem to have a couple of what a poker player might call 'tells.' One thing seems clear, the organism is controlled by minute electric currents that pulse through an electric grid embedded in the hull. The pattern dictates the direction of the propulsion and the speed."

Macey looked up from a small tank of seawater. "We took three specimens from three different locations on the EEL. We have several ideas on detection, but it will take some serious research to nail them down. It is clear, however, that once we detect the sub, we can disrupt the control of the biologics by simply supplying external electrical current with more power."

"You guys would be okay with us opening the diplomatic channel to release the subs crew and the vessel?" Gritt waited until each of the three men finally nodded yes.

"We will need another day to remove all of our instruments," added Macey.

Within an hour, Gritt was on a secure face-to-face link with Walker. "I have a very interesting report from the FBI," added Thad, as the two wrapped up the conversation about the EEL. "I'm forwarding it to you. See what you can do with it. In the interim, I am told that the Chinese ambassador and the Secretary of State will be meeting in the morning. They will be negotiating the terms for release of the crew and vessel. Our side is also going to request a summit between the two countries' presidents once the men who understand Arctic Angel have a chance to brief the Chinese authorities. The President isn't sure that he can stop the Chinese bullying tactics in the South China Sea, but he is going to make it clear that America is entering into a formal alliance with China's neighbors to tip the scales."

CHAPTER 72

KISKA ISLAND

THE NEXT MORNING, the Chinese officers were invited to discuss the raid and the negotiations for their release. "Ma," offered Gritt, as the briefing broke up, "could I have a few minutes of your time since you are the only Chinese officer that I can talk to without the problems of an interpreter?"

Ma explained Gritt's request as he turned back into the base conference room. "What is it?"

"I just wanted to pass on a quick hello from a couple of your 'friends' in the States,' replied Gritt. "Molly Wang from Seattle and Dr. Lia Chen in San Diego send their best and their congratulations on not getting yourself shot by one side or the other."

Gritt watched the man freeze.

"Our side is insisting on sending you, the SLA team and most of the EEL's crew home by air. Captain will select no more than six men to return the EEL to China. Our side will trade all of you for one person held in a Chinese prison. I believe that you know a Lou Chen. Her sister would like to see her again, but not where you or any others from your department can threaten them."

"This Lou Chen is a criminal, being held for crimes against

China," replied Ma, relieved to hear that he was part of the group flying home.

"So, that could be just what you tell your superiors to get her released. My thought is it might go like this." Gritt pulled up some notes on his laptop. "The U.S. is arresting Lia Chen for defrauding an American university. She has pleaded that it was only to get enough money to free her sister from a Chinese prison. If her sister is released, she has agreed to plead guilty, saving the government an expensive trial. Lia will be convicted, and the two women will serve their sentences together in the U.S." Gritt paused as he watched Ma squirm. "That is just one scenario. If you have a better idea, I will need to hear it by tomorrow morning. My country is not going to charge you with espionage; in fact, we hope that you continue in a similar role to that you are now employed. You and I could become really effective back-door negotiators for problems between our two countries. Our counterintelligence folks like the idea of knowing who is running Chinese spy rings in the U.S."

He watched Ma's body language. It told him that the man seemed lost. "The two women we discussed did not betray you. They were identified by our FBI and questioned only after the EEL story broke in the news and after they were told that you were a prisoner. Both have agreed to quit talking to you or any other Chinese agents in the U.S. and both will be allowed to continue their education activities. What your government learns about them will be up to you."

Three days later, a China Southern Boeing 737 rolled to a stop on the Kiska runway. The only passenger to leave the plane was a frail woman wrapped in a wool blanket. A picture of her was transmitted to her sister in San Diego who confirmed her identity. A refueling truck made its way from a C-130 loaded with rubber bladders of jet fuel to the side of the plane and began topping off the Boeing's tanks.

As the tanker rolled away, a truck rolled to a stop at the cargo door where four PLA sailors loaded the frozen bodies of two men killed on the raid. A short line of men made their way up the air-stairs for their trip home. "It would have been easier for me to explain all of this, better for my credibility going forward, if Yang's body had not been dumped at sea by your SEALs," offered Ma as he stood next to Gritt.

"We have discussed that with Captain," replied Gritt. "He was the highest surviving officer." He turned to Ma. "I sincerely hope that you not only live through your homecoming but continue your career. I was serious about how valuable a non-official level of contact can be to resolve problems."

Ma extended his hand, which as the two had earlier agreed; Gritt refused.

As the jet taxied for takeoff, Captain watched five of his crewmen descend into the EEL. Lisa smiled at the man as he stepped from the dock after watching the lines securing his boat pulled away. "Captain, I am happy that you and your ship are heading home. Before you go, there are a couple of things you need to know."

Captain turned to face the lean American officer with fierce eyes. "Yes."

"First, all of the weapons that we confiscated are back aboard your ship except for two of the venom guns. We are keeping those. The other weapons are in a chest behind the reactor room."

Captain seemed completely disinterested.

"Secondly, if you will run your boat on the surface to the small peninsula on the little island that shields the harbor, what we call Little Kiska, you will find a hut left over from the great war. Your man Yang was dropped at that remote site, along with enough rations to last a week. You may pick him up on your way."

"I thought that General Yang was dead," Captain replied, his body stiffening.

"My side believes that a dead General Yang would be good for both China and the United States, but under our rules of engagement we could not just shoot the bastard."

"How will we pick him up?" asked Captain. "The EEL already had damage to the Sillia from when you ran it aground."

"There is a large rock right below the shelter. The water is deep enough for you to push the bow right up to where Yang was told to be waiting for your signal."

"And just what is that signal?"

"You will take the rifle I just told you about and shoot one time and then a minute later a second shot." She extended her hand. "Good luck, sir."

In the control room, Gritt, Lisa, Olga and May watched the departure of the EEL through the cameras of the Angel. They watched almost an hour as the boat made its way across the harbor. The outer ocean had a large rolling swell breaking from the north as the sub slid into the lee of the peninsula. The hatch opened, and Captain climbed up the ladder. A moment later, someone handed him a rifle. While they could not hear anything, they could see him aim the rifle out to sea and fire, and exactly one minute later he fired again.

From the small hut only fifty yards from the water, a man walked slowly toward the large rock below the cabin. He was waving his arms and gesturing wildly. He pointed toward where he wanted Captain to pick him up. It took three minutes for him to make his way to the rock. He stopped waving his arms as the sub approached.

The man and Captain were yelling at each other as the sub slowed only a few feet from the man. The group watched, fascinated, as Captain raised the rifle and calmly shot the man, knocking him to the ground. The man staggered to his feet only inches from the water. Captain fired a second time. The man pitched forward into the sea.

"I guess that means that it is time to go home," offered Gritt.

As the group walked away, Olga tapped Chad on the shoulder. "I've been called to Washington to discuss the security issues raised by the Chinese attack," she said. "I thought it might be a good time to take you up on that dinner offer, the one that you meant to make."

"Is that an order from a superior officer?" asked Chad. Without waiting for an answer, he added, "Sounds good to me."

ACKNOWLEDGEMENTS

THE EEL AND THE ANGEL

Encouraged by my wife, Carmen and family, I walked away from a successful business and political consulting career to follow my passion for writing. That decision led to research discussions with my friends and contacts, many warriors, scientists and politicians. Thanks all.

Perhaps three dozen different websites, numerous research periodicals and books form the foundation for THE EEL AND THE ANGEL. The exploration of nuclear power and laser technology from the 1960's to the present paints an amazing picture of the rapid refinement of both technologies, one that could easily lead to conflict; not because of what we know of the other side's technology, but rather because of what we don't know.

Those who follow author Dale Brown's aviation series realize how little time separates futuristic aviation technology from what will be soon available.

As early as 1941, American author Ernest Hemingway completed a spy mission into China. His orders were to report on what the Japanese were doing there and secondly, to study the beginning of the political divide in China that would lead to the rise of the Chinese Communist Party. That change led to the current U.S.-China rivalry.

U.S.-China relations have fundamentally shifted from being allies to rivals in three decades. Gordon Chang's THE GREAT U.S.-CHINA TECH WAR offers an excellent window into the Chinese obsession with catching and surpassing the U.S. technologically. Michael Fabey's CRASHBACK is a very good analysis of why the rivalry in the South China Sea is critical to both nations.

For writing help, I would like to thank Gabrielle Raffuse, PhD., who tore herself away from her passion for literary writing and historical Russian literature to help this storyteller refine his sparse, 'just the facts' writing style.

Bestselling author Marc Cameron's encouragement when I turned to writing fulltime helped me stick with the program. Bestselling author, Sheldon Siegel's coaching and mapping convinced me to pursue a faster and less restrictive path to my readers. Senior Editor Grace Doyle at Thomas and Mercer, who could never fit my stories onto her publishing list, but who tried, offered excellent counsel and advice.

Finally, with the greatest appreciation and admiration, I want to thank bestselling author and friend Bob Dugoni for his constant encouragement, plot and editorial coaching, and willingness to kick me when I was not listening.

The support of my editor, Rob Bignell, helped make the book more concise. The professionals at Damonza provided the cover and formatting that turned my manuscript into this book.

RODGER CARLYLE is a storyteller who draws on an enormous personal library of experiences. An adventurer, political strategist, and ghostwriter whose love of flying began in the Navy, his experiences stretch from New York to Los Angeles, from Amsterdam to Khabarovsk in the Russian Far East, and from Canada into Latin America.

Through his passion for research, he treasures finding those events that are ignored or covered up by the powerful when some strategy or plan goes completely to hell. From there, he creates a fictional adventure narrative that tells a more complete story.

Rodger is comfortable in black tie urban settings, but he is never happier than in the wilderness. He has faced down muggers in San Francisco, intimidation by the Russian Mafia, and charging grizzly bears. Most of his stories take his readers to places they will never visit. He likes to think that he is there with them.

Made in the USA
Coppell, TX
02 July 2021